Brenda Jackson is a *New York Times* bestselling author of more than one hundred romance titles. Brenda lives in Jacksonville, Florida, and divides her time between family, writing and travelling. Email Brenda at authorbrendajackson@gmail.com or visit her on her website at brendajackson.net

For a complete list of titles available from Brenda Jackson visit her website, www.brendajackson.net

Finding Home Again

Brenda Jackson

MILLS & BOON

Mills & Boon
An imprint of HarperCollins*Publishers* Ltd
1 London Bridge Street
London SE1 9GF

www.harpercollins.co.uk

HarperCollins*Publishers*
1st Floor, Watermarque Building, Ringsend Road
Dublin 4, Ireland

This paperback edition 2023

1
First published in Great Britain by Mills & Boon,
an imprint of HarperCollins*Publishers* Ltd 2019

Copyright © Brenda Streater Jackson 2019

Brenda Jackson asserts the moral right to be
identified as the author of this work.
A catalogue record for this book is
available from the British Library.

ISBN: 978-1-84845-861-1

MIX
Paper from
responsible sources
FSC
www.fsc.org **FSC™ C007454**

This book is produced from independently certified FSC™ paper
to ensure responsible forest management.

For more information visit: www.harpercollins.co.uk/green

Printed and Bound in the UK using 100% Renewable Electricity at
CPI Group (UK) Ltd, Croydon, CR0 4YY

To the man who will always and forever be the love of my life, Gerald Jackson Sr. My hero. My everything.

To my sons, Gerald Jr. and Brandon. You guys are the greatest and continue to make me and your dad proud.

'And over all these virtues put on love, which binds them all together in perfect unity.'

—Colossians 3:14

Finding Home
Again

PART 1

There are years that ask questions and years that answer.
                              —Zora Neale Hurston

CHAPTER ONE

Bryce Witherspoon moved around the party intent on enjoying herself, although the host was the last person she wanted to be around. However, she knew Kaegan Chambray felt the same way about her. Yet, as always whenever he hosted one of his acclaimed cookouts, he'd included her on the guest list. They both knew the reason why.

Since moving back to town, their childhood friend Vashti Alcindor-Grisham, forever the peacemaker, had let them know she was best friend to them both and wouldn't take sides. Nor would she allow either of them to pit her against the other. So whenever Vashti was invited to one of his cookouts, Kaegan sent Bryce an invitation, as well, to keep the peace. Vashti's motto was There Are Things That Happen In The Past That Are Best Left There.

Bryce figured she could make things easier on Kaegan by not coming, but then, why should she? He certainly didn't try making things easier for her by coming into her parents' café regularly. Kaegan would arrive every morning at the Witherspoon Café for blueberry muffins and coffee, knowing she would be there and, more likely than not, be the one to wait on him.

It wouldn't be so bad if she could forget what he once meant to her. It had been ten years since their breakup. She wasn't twenty-two anymore. Since then she'd dated, but what she'd shared with Kaegan had been special. At least she'd thought it had been. He'd been her first in a number of things and on so many levels. That was why the pain of their breakup still managed to linger even after all this time.

And it hadn't helped matters when he'd returned to the cove four years ago with a chip on his shoulder, still believing he was the one who'd been wronged. She'd decided to show him that he wasn't the only one who could carry around a chip, and at this stage of the game he could believe whatever he wanted about her. All those years ago she'd tried proving her innocence and he hadn't wanted to listen to what she had to say, so what he thought now didn't matter.

Coming to his parties let him know she could be in the same room with him and feel absolutely nothing. She figured he was determined to prove the same thing to her, which was probably why he frequented the café every day.

Okay, she knew there was another reason why he patronized the café. He might not like her, but he loved her parents and they loved him. He was good friends with her two older brothers. But they didn't know the whole story. She'd never told anyone what had happened between them to end things. In fact, she'd only just told Vashti last year.

One night when Vashti's husband, Sawyer, was out of town, Bryce had stopped by her best friend's home. Once Vashti had put her newborn son, Cutter, to bed, they'd opened a bottle of wine and put on a sappy movie, and Bryce had told Vashti everything.

She could recall her conversation from that night like it had been yesterday...

★ ★ ★

"Kaegan and I decided we wanted to be more than friends while you were gone to that home for unwed mothers to have your baby, Vash. That's when we became girlfriend and boyfriend."

Vashti nodded. "But he left here two years before we finished school and rarely came back. How did the two of you keep the relationship going?"

Bryce took a sip of her wine. "You recall my mom's youngest sister, Janice?"

"The one who moved from Canada to live in DC?"

"Yes. I would make the trip by catching the bus to see her and would spend time with Kaegan, as well, since he was stationed in Maryland."

Vashti seemed to mull over that admission. "I remember in our senior year how you would occasionally take the bus on the weekends to visit your aunt. I can't believe you never told me what you were doing and where you were going," Vashti said in an accusing tone.

"I wanted to tell you, Vash, but you were in your own little world during that time. You were still grieving after losing your baby. The last thing I wanted to do was overwhelm you with my happiness when you were so unhappy…"

That same night she'd also told Vashti the reason she and Kaegan had broken up. Instead of the sympathy Bryce had expected, Vashti claimed she could see both sides and felt they were letting their stubbornness get in the way of them sitting down and talking through their issues.

As far as Bryce was concerned, there was nothing to talk about. His lack of trust in her was unforgivable. Had he believed in her and known she could never betray him, none of this would have happened. A part of her wished the hurt he'd caused could somehow eradicate her attraction to him. It didn't. Whenever she saw him she had to put up with seeing a man who turned feminine heads wherever he went. Including hers.

Kaegan was part of the Pointe-au-Chien Native American tribe. He was ultrahandsome and the mass of silky black hair that flowed around his shoulders made him look wild, untamed and absolutely gorgeous. She recalled the times she would part his hair down the middle and braid it for him, making him look even more alluring.

Usually he wore it in a ponytail, but not tonight. Bryce recalled telling him just what seeing all that hair flowing around his face did to her. How hot it made her feel. How so turned-on she would get. That had been years ago, but she, of all people, knew Kaegan never forgot a thing. That made her wonder if he'd worn it down purposely to make her remember.

Over the years his features had matured. He no longer had the look of the cute boy she'd fallen in love with so many years ago. His eyes appeared to have darkened somewhat but were perfect for his brown skin tone. His high cheekbones had always been his most captivating asset. They still were. Even with that dimple in his chin that couldn't be ignored. The dimple became even more defined whenever he smiled, which was rare when he saw her. She had a tendency to elicit his frowns.

She would be the first to admit that a younger Kaegan Chambray had been a heartthrob, but the older version of that heartthrob was now just too breathtaking for words. Whether she liked him or not, she had to give him that. Deciding she'd both scowled at him and lusted after him long enough, she glanced around.

Two years ago, Kaegan had torn down the house he and his parents had lived in to build this one. She knew the painful memories within the walls of his childhood home. His father had been an alcoholic. Most of the time, he managed to stay sober during the week to run his business. But on the weekends he would drink himself into a stupor.

It was during those times Kaegan would use the small boat he kept hidden away in the underbrush of the bayou and escape through the swamps to a place he considered his hideaway, a deserted, uninhabitable island called Eagle Bend Inlet. Bryce had feared for his safety, worrying that one of those huge alligators was going to eat him alive.

She continued to study his home. She'd never been given a grand tour, like a number of others, but she liked the parts she'd seen. It was right on the bayou, on land that had been in the Chambray family for generations. She could imagine waking up here every morning to such a gorgeous view. According to Vashti, due to the risk of hurricanes, Kaegan had built a home that could withstand up to four-hundred-mile-an-hour winds. And the tilt of the foundation, which wasn't even noticeable, was a deterrence to flooding.

She thought the place was huge for just one man but he'd always said that one day he would grow up and build a mansion…for them. Well, he had certainly built a monstrosity of a house, but it hadn't been with her in mind. When he'd returned to town it had been quite obvious he hadn't wanted her in his life any more than she wanted him in hers.

"Here you are."

She turned to greet Vashti. "Yes, here I am on a Friday night. I could be somewhere else, you know, and would be if I thought for one minute that I wouldn't hear about it from you tomorrow. One day you're going to realize that no matter what you think, Vash, all Kaegan and I feel for each other now is contempt. Total dislike."

Vashti rolled her eyes. "If you say so. By the way, did you see Ashley? She looks great pregnant. Ray wasn't messing around. Who comes back from their honeymoon pregnant?"

Bryce took a sip of her wine knowing Vashti had deliberately changed the subject, but she was fine with her doing so. "A person who comes from their honeymoon pregnant is someone who'd intended to get pregnant. According to Ashley, they spent the entire time trying and it was all about a promise Ray had made her. They've been through a lot, and I'm happy for them."

A friend of theirs, Ray Sullivan, had married Ashley Ryan six months ago. Last month the couple shared the news they were having twins. A boy and a girl. They'd even selected the names. The boy would be named Devon and the girl Ryan.

A smile touched Vashti's lips. "I'm happy for them, as well. I love happy endings."

Bryce rolled her eyes. "You also love torturing your two best friends. Why do you put me and Kaegan through this every time he gives a party? I don't have to be here and we both know that he doesn't want me here. The only reason he invites me and the only reason I come is because neither of us want to hear you bitch about it."

"Hey, it's not my fault that my two best friends fell in love behind my back."

Bryce rolled her eyes again. "That's what you get for leaving us alone for those six months."

"Like I had a choice."

Bryce knew at the time her best friend hadn't had a choice. Vashti had gotten pregnant at sixteen. Her parents had sent her away. While she was gone Bryce and Kaegan had grown closer, and all the love Bryce had secretly felt for Kaegan suddenly blossomed.

She tried to recall a time when Kaegan hadn't been a part of Bryce's and Vashti's lives and couldn't. Neither could she recall a time she hadn't loved him. K-Gee was what everyone called him. The descendants of the Pointe-au-Chien tribe mostly made their home on the west side of the bayou. Kaegan's family's ties to the cove and the bayou went back generations, even before the first American settlers. A few of the simpleminded townsfolk of Catalina Cove had never recognized the tribe, except when it was time to pay city taxes.

Although Kaegan was two years older than her and Vashti, the three of them had hung together while growing up since Kaegan hadn't officially started school until he was almost nine. Dempsey Chambray felt his only son was more useful working in the family seafood business and for years had claimed Kaegan was being homeschooled. When the Catalina Cove school board discovered otherwise, they presented the Chambrays with a court order that stated Kaegan was to be put in public school immediately.

Kaegan was a supersmart and intelligent kid, and it didn't take him long to catch up with the rest of the class. However, he couldn't be put in his right grade because he began missing a lot of days from school to help his father on the boat. It was Mr. Chambray's way of showing the school board that although they may have ordered that his son attend school, Kaegan was entitled to sick days. Most people knew that the days Mr. Chambray claimed Kaegan couldn't come to school because he was ill, Kaegan was out on the water working in the family business. It was only when the school board threatened to file a lawsuit against Mr. Chambray's business that he allowed his son to attend school without any further interruptions.

When Vashti returned to town after her pregnancy, Kaegan had advanced enough in his studies to be placed in his correct grade, leaving them two grades behind. But he didn't forget them. Although his school day ended half an hour sooner than theirs, he would hang around just to walk Vashti and Bryce home every day.

It was one of the times he could be with her. He would reach Bryce's house first and then cut through the woods to get to Vashti's place. On some days before she got home, she and Kaegan would take the small boat he kept hidden over to Eagle Bend Inlet. It was there that Kaegan had taught her how to kiss and where they'd made love for the very first time.

"You've gotten quiet, Bryce. What are you thinking about?"

She glanced over at Vashti. Instead of answering, she asked a question of her own. "Where's your husband? Shouldn't you be with him instead of here pestering me?"

Vashti laughed. "I am not pestering you and you know it. But to answer your question, Sawyer got a call and had to leave, so I'm going to need a ride home."

Vashti was married to the town's sheriff. "No problem. Just let me know when you're ready to go."

"Hmm, there might be a problem."

Bryce lifted an eyebrow. "What?"

"After Kaegan's parties, Sawyer and I usually stay behind and help him put stuff away and clean up. So that means..."

Bryce frowned, having an idea where this conversation was going. "It means nothing. Kaegan can tidy up his own place. Besides, I'm sure that woman over there in the white top and jeans would be glad to stay back and help him. She's been keeping her eyes on him the entire night."

"You noticed, I see."

"How could I not notice?" Bryce refused to consider the tinge of resentment she was feeling had anything to do with jealousy. She dated and so did Kaegan. They meant nothing to each other anymore.

"I noticed you've been keeping your eyes on him a lot tonight, as well," Vashti pointed out. Deciding not to give Bryce time to say anything, since it was obvious that she was in one of those bash-Kaegan moods, she said, "Now back to the issue of helping Kaegan tidy up. With the three of us working together it won't take long to get his place back in order. You and I can pack up the food while Kaegan breaks down all the patio tables and tents."

"Why can't he do it by himself?" Bryce asked.

"Because we're his friends and should help him."

"Speak for yourself, Vash."

"No, I'm speaking for the both of us, Bryce. Stop being difficult."

"I'm not being difficult."

"Yes, you are."

Okay, maybe she was, but when it came to Kaegan Chambray, she felt she had every right to be difficult. She'd told Vashti some of what had happened, but she hadn't told her all of it. Bryce frowned at Vashti. "Honestly, Vash. There are times when you really do push the bounds of our friendship."

"I do not."

"Yes, you do."

"What's the big deal, since you claim you're over Kaegan?" Vashti quipped.

"I am over him."

"Then act like it and not like a woman still carrying a torch after ten years."

Bryce didn't say anything. Did she really act that way? That was the last impression she wanted to give anyone, especially Kaegan. "Fine, but I still plan to ignore him."

Vashti shook her head and smiled. "You always do."

Kaegan Chambray glanced around and saw that everyone had left. It had been another great party. The food was good and there had been plenty of it. The September weather had cooperated. Tents had been set up outside, and huge buckets of seafood—blue crabs, shrimp, crawfish and lobster—had been served, as well as ribs cooked on the grill.

When he had a cookout, it was for his employees, although he always included his friends. He liked rewarding his workers whenever they broke sales records or if the company got a big business deal. He felt it was a good incentive. He also believed in giving his employees bonuses. That pretty much assured he was able to retain workers who were dependable and loyal.

He turned to look out at the bayou, which was practically in his backyard. As far as he was concerned, there was no better place to live. Those who called the bayou their home had a culture all their own. The people were a mixture of influences, such as Spanish, French, German, African, Irish and, in his case, Native American. Those with predominantly French ancestry still spoke the language. Together all the various groups made up the foundation of the Cajun culture.

"If you need help with anything, Kaegan, I will be glad to stay behind and help."

Kaegan turned to find Sasha Johnson. He thought she'd left. Her brother, Farley, worked on one of his boats. Sasha had moved to the cove a few months ago after a bitter divorce to live with Farley. Kaegan had invited both siblings to the party, but Farley was battling a cold. Sasha had come alone. "Thanks for the offer, but I can manage."

"You sure?"

"Positive."

"It was a nice party, Kaegan."

"Thanks." Landing the Chappell account had given him a reason to celebrate. His representative had been courting the huge restaurant chain for years, as Kaegan wanted to get in as their seafood supplier. Then out of the clear blue sky he'd gotten a call this summer. The Chappell Group needed more fresh seafood than their present supplier could provide and wanted to know if Chambray Seafood Shipping Company could deliver. Kaegan had said that he could and he had.

It had taken a full week of long harvesting hours, but in the end he and his crew had delivered, and the Chappell Group had remembered. When their contract with the other supplier ended, they had come to him with an awesome deal.

A flash of pink moving around in his house made Kaegan frown when he recalled just who'd worn that particular color tonight. He glanced back at Sasha. "Tell Farley that I hope he starts feeling better. Good night." Without waiting for Sasha's response, he quickly walked off, heading inside his home.

He heard a noise coming from the kitchen. Moving quickly, he walked in to find Bryce Witherspoon on a ladder putting something in one of the cabinets. Anger, to a degree he hadn't felt in a long time, consumed him. Standing there in his kitchen on that ladder was the one and only woman he'd ever loved. The one woman he would risk his life for and recalled doing so once. She was the only woman who'd had his heart from the time they were in grade school. The only one he'd ever wanted to marry and have his babies. The only one who…

He realized he'd been standing recalling things he preferred not remembering. What he should be remembering was that she was the woman who'd broken his heart. "What the hell are you doing in here, Bryce?"

His loud, booming voice startled her. She jerked around, lost her balance and came tumbling off the ladder. He rushed over and caught her in his arms before she could hit the floor. His chest tightened, and his nerves, and another part of his anatomy, kicked in the moment his hands and arms touched the body he used to know as well as his own. A body he'd introduced to passion. A body he'd—

"Put me down, Kaegan Chambray!"

He started to drop her, just for the hell of it. She was such a damn ingrate. "Next time I'll just let you fall on your ass," he snapped, placing her on her feet and trying not to notice how beautiful she was. Her eyes were a mix of hazel and moss green, and were adorned by long eyelashes. She had high cheekbones and shoulder-length brown curly hair. Her skin was a gorgeous honey-brown and her lips, which were curved in a frown at the moment, had always been one of her most distinct traits.

"Let go of my hand, Kaegan!"

Her sharp tone made him realize he'd been standing there staring at her. He fought to regain his senses. "What are you doing, going through my cabinets?"

She rounded on him, tossing all that beautiful hair out of her face. "I was on that ladder putting your spices back in the cabinets."

He crossed his arms over his chest. "Why?"

"Because I was helping you tidy up after the party by putting things away."

She had to be kidding. "I don't need your help."

"Fine! I'll leave, then. You can take Vashti home."

Take Vashti home? What the hell is she talking about? He was about to ask when Vashti burst into the kitchen. "What in the world is going on? I heard the two of you yelling and screaming all the way in the bathroom."

Kaegan turned to Vashti. "What is she talking about, me taking you home? Where's Sawyer?"

"He got a call and had to leave. I asked Bryce to drop me off at home. I also asked her to assist me in helping you straighten up before we left."

"I don't need help."

Bryce rounded on him. "Why don't you tell her what you told me? Namely, that you don't need *my* help."

He had no problem doing that. Glancing back at Vashti, he said, "I don't need Bryce's help. Nor do I want it."

Bryce looked at Vashti. "I'm leaving. You either come with me now or he can take you home."

Vashti looked from one to the other and then threw up her

hands in frustration. "I'm leaving with you, Bryce. I'll be out to the car in a minute."

When Bryce walked out of the kitchen, Kaegan turned to Vashti. "You had no right asking her to stay here after the party to do anything, Vashti. I don't want her here. The only reason I even invite her is because of you."

Kaegan had seen fire in Vashti's eyes before, but it had never been directed at him. Now it was. She crossed the room, and he had a mind to take a step back, but he didn't. "I'm sick and tired of you acting like an ass where Bryce is concerned, Kaegan. When will you wake up and realize what you accused her of all those years ago is not true?"

He glared at her. "Oh? Is that what she told you? News flash—you weren't there, Vashti, and I know what I saw."

"Do you?"

"Yes. So you can believe the lie she's telling you all you want, but I know what I saw that night."

Vashti drew in a deep breath. "Do you? Or do you only know what you *think* you saw?"

Then without saying anything else, she turned and walked out of the kitchen.

CHAPTER TWO

Vashti slid into the car and snapped the seat belt in place. Before starting the ignition, Bryce said, "I cherish our friendship, Vash, and I know why it's important to you that me, you and Kaegan remain friends. After all, it was your idea that we do this," she said, holding up her finger that bore the scar of the nick the three of them had made years and years ago. They had been in the first grade together.

"But not even this matters to me anymore. I heard what he told you after I walked out of the kitchen. He deliberately said it loud enough for me to hear. It really wasn't anything I didn't know already. He does not want me to come to his parties, so let me go on record as saying that tonight will be my last time attending one of Kaegan's parties, Vash. So please don't ask me to ever come to one again."

Vashti didn't say anything, and Bryce didn't expect her to. Vashti knew her and knew when she'd reached her limit about anything. Tonight she had with Kaegan. There was no way she could stop him from coming into her parents' café each morning as a customer, but she could continue to ignore him. And she would.

"Okay, Bryce," Vashti finally said when Bryce started the engine. "I honestly thought that being around each other would make you and Kaegan realize how much the two of you mean to each other."

"It did. It made us realize just how much we dislike each other."

"But it doesn't have to be this way. You can tell him the truth about that night."

Bryce didn't say anything for a minute as she put the car in gear. "I did. Or at least, I tried to."

"What! When? You never told me that."

No, she hadn't, mainly because after telling Vashti what had caused her and Kaegan's breakup, she'd been too emotionally drained that night to tell her the other part. "What I didn't tell you was when I got that call from Kaegan letting me know why he was breaking up with me and that he intended to block my number, I used every penny I had in my savings account and caught the bus from college, all the way from Grambling. That meant crossing four states and enduring an eighteen-hour bus ride to reach North Carolina. And because he had blocked my number there was no way for me to let him know I was coming."

"What happened when you got there?"

"Well, for starters, I couldn't get on the military base. But the soldier at the gate checked his log and told me that Kaegan wasn't on base anyway. That he was on a two-day pass and chances were he would be at the Mud Hole that night."

"The Mud Hole?"

"Yes. It's a hangout for the marines and located close to base. I checked into a hotel, freshened up, and that night I went to the Mud Hole."

Bryce paused a moment and then said, "More than anything, now I wish I hadn't."

"Why? What happened?"

Bryce tightened her hands on the steering wheel as she remembered that night. "Kaegan was there that night and he'd been drinking."

"Kaegan? Drinking?"

Bryce knew why Vashti was surprised. Because his father had been an alcoholic, Kaegan had sworn never to touch the stuff because it turned fairly decent men into assholes.

"Yes, he was drinking and had a barely dressed woman sitting in his lap. I approached him, and when he saw me, the look in his eyes was one I'd never seen before. He proceeded to say some not-so-nice things to me in front of the woman and the friends he'd been with. I tried to get him to go outside with me so we could talk privately, but he refused to do that and said he didn't want to hear anything I had to say. He said his father had been right about me all along. He told me to leave and that he hoped to never see me again."

Bryce paused again, and then she said, "When I refused to leave, tried to make him listen to what I'd come all that way to say, he got mad and left...with her. That woman who all but had her hands inside his pants. He kissed her right in front of me and then they left together. I went back to my hotel room and cried the entire night."

"Oh, Bryce, I'm so sorry you went through that."

"I am, too. But even on the bus ride back to Grambling, I kept telling myself it wasn't the Kaegan that I knew who'd said those awful things to me. It had to have been the liquor talking. I even convinced myself that I could forgive him for sleeping with another woman if he'd done so that night." Bryce felt the knot in her throat when she said, "I loved him that much, Vash. I've always loved him. I told myself I could wait for him to come around. That he would regain his senses and would eventually call me. Days became weeks. Weeks turned into months. Months into years."

She was quiet for a moment, then continued. "I ran into

Mr. Chambray at one of the festivals a year later and he accused me of being the reason Kaegan refused to come back to Catalina Cove, even for a visit. He said that I had hurt his boy and that he was glad Kaegan found out what a slut I was."

Vashti drew in a sharp breath. "Mr. Chambray said that to you?"

"Yes."

"Oh, Bryce."

She could hear the trembling in Vashti's voice and didn't want her pity. "It's okay, Vash. That day I finally accepted that Mr. Chambray probably had the same opinion of me that Kaegan had."

She pulled the car into Vashti and Sawyer's driveway. When she brought the car to a stop, she turned to Vashti. It was then that Bryce felt her tears. She hadn't realized until that moment that she'd been crying. "I've gotten over him, Vash—honest, I have. But it still hurts knowing he had so little trust in me after all we'd been through together. I had loved him so much, but I promised myself years ago that I would never let Kaegan hurt me again. And that's a promise I intend to keep."

Kaegan moved away from the window when Bryce's car finally drove off. He rubbed a hand down his face, feeling frustrated. Hadn't he made a vow when he moved back to Catalina Cove that he would not let Bryce destroy him any more than she already had? Each and every time she came to his house—the place that should have been their home—it took another bite out of him.

Tonight had been the last straw when he'd walked into his kitchen and had seen her on that ladder. First off, he had been concerned for her safety. But then seeing her from behind had totally unnerved him. She'd always had one hell of a figure and she still did.

Angry with himself for admiring her ass, he had snapped

at her and then the confrontation had begun. Although he'd wished otherwise, Vashti had been caught in the middle. But then, she was the one who'd insisted he invite Bryce.

In the past, it had been pretty easy to ignore her. But not tonight. It might have been her outfit, a pink shorts set with white sandals, that had been to blame. He'd always liked her in pink because he'd thought she always looked ultrafeminine in that color.

He had tried not to notice her but he had. He knew every damn man who'd tried talking to her tonight, and each time one would approach her, his stomach would tighten in knots. It had been ten years, so why was he stressing over a woman who meant nothing to him? Absolutely nothing.

An hour later he'd finished breaking everything down, at least as much as he intended to do tonight. Tomorrow was Saturday and after sleeping late he would wake up and do the rest. He began stripping off his clothes for a shower and for some reason his gaze went to a certain framed portrait on the wall.

There was nothing special about the painting, but behind it was his safe, where his valuables were kept. He walked over to it and entered the combination, then opened the safe. He stared at the only thing inside. That damn little white box.

He reached inside and pulled it out, asking himself for the umpteenth time why he still had it. He should have gotten rid of it years ago, but had convinced himself he needed it as a reminder of the time in his life when he'd been young, naive and gullible, and had allowed a woman to make a fool of him.

He'd left Catalina Cove the day he'd graduated from high school. Together he and Bryce had mapped out a plan for their future. He would serve six years in the military. That would give her time to complete her last two years of high school and four years of college before they married. After she finished college they would marry. She'd been in her senior year of college and he'd come home over spring break. It had been a surprise visit with a purpose. He was going to officially ask her to marry him.

Opening the box, he gazed upon the engagement ring he had saved his paychecks for almost a year to afford. When he'd first seen it in a jewelry-store window he had immediately known it was the ring he wanted to give Bryce. That was before he'd seen her in the arms of another man.

He closed his eyes for a moment when memories of that night assailed him and ripped into him. That had been the night she'd shredded his heart. His father had been writing and telling him that he'd seen Bryce around town with Samuel Abbott whenever she came home from college. But Kaegan hadn't believed him because his parents had never approved of his relationship with Bryce. They'd wanted him to be with a girl from the tribe.

Kaegan had known Samuel from growing up in the cove. He was the son of wealthy parents who'd owned the only pharmacy in town for years. In high school Samuel had been a star athlete in practically every sport he competed in. He was what the girls had called a superjock and they would hang around him like lovesick puppies.

Regardless of what his father had been telling him in those letters, Kaegan had trusted Bryce. He'd believed the plans they'd made for their future were solid and that some guy like Samuel wasn't going to turn her head. He hadn't cared they were attending Grambling together, which gave them every opportunity to be close. Bryce was his girl and that was that.

Although it was close to two in the morning when he'd arrived in the cove that night, he'd immediately gone to Bryce's house to surprise her. He'd been anxious to ask her to marry him and to give her the ring. Since her brothers had married, she had taken over the garage apartment at the back of her parents' home.

He had walked toward the garage when suddenly the door to the apartment opened and a man came out. She was walking him to the door and the man was Samuel Abbott. Kaegan had stopped and stared at them. Neither had detected his presence since he'd been in the shadows. In total shock, he watched Bryce lean up on tiptoes and wrap her arms around Samuel's neck. Angry and hurt, Kaegan turned and walked away while pain had sliced through him. He left town that night without Bryce or his parents knowing he'd even been there.

It had taken a week before he'd called Bryce. He'd even refused to take her call, the one she made to him every Sunday. When he did call her, he didn't give her a chance to say anything. He told her of his surprise visit home the week before, although he didn't tell her why he'd specifically come home that night.

Kaegan told her about seeing her in Samuel's arms on her doorstep at two in the morning. He'd told her he hoped to never see her again and that he would be blocking her calls. When he ended the call, he figured that would be that. She'd cheated on him and had been caught. There had been no one he could talk to about the pain he felt. Not even Vashti. She'd left town years earlier, the week after she'd graduated from high school, saying she would never return to Catalina Cove again. She had her own issues with the town and the people in it. He was left to deal with the pain of Bryce's betrayal alone.

He certainly hadn't expected Bryce to show up in North Carolina a week later wanting to see him and tell him her side of things. There was nothing she could tell him. It hadn't been about what his father had told him but about what he'd seen with his own eyes. He doubted he would ever forget seeing her in Samuel's arms as they'd been about to kiss.

Coming back to Catalina Cove to live was the last thing he'd planned to do. When he had returned home after his father's death it was to find a seafood shipping company that was barely making ends meet. On top of that, the machinery and boats were in need of repair or replacement, and it had been weeks since the crew, shrimpers and oyster shuckers had been paid.

He had made the decision to close down the company, pay the workers out of money he had saved and move his mother with him to Maryland, where he'd settled after his military career ended. He had a pretty good job working for NASA as a program manager. The plans to return to Maryland changed the day he was approached by Reid LaCroix, the wealthiest man in the cove.

Reid had invited him to his home and had made Kaegan an offer that nobody in their right mind could refuse. Everyone knew Reid was a man who detested change. He believed family-owned businesses in the cove should stay in the family. As a result of that belief, he'd offered Kaegan a low-interest loan to do whatever was needed to bring the shipping company up to par, but only if Kaegan returned to the cove and ran things.

Sensing there had to be some catch, Kaegan had asked his attorney and friend Gregory Nelson, back in Maryland, to review the contract. Gregory indicated it was a damn good deal and he could only assume the reason Reid LaCroix had made him such an offer was the man's doggedness to keep the family-operated companies in the cove in business so there would not be a need to bring in any new ones. Gregory saw LaCroix's generosity as a really good strategy if LaCroix was as anti-progressive as Kaegan claimed.

Even with such a good offer, Kaegan had to decide if moving back to Catalina Cove was something he wanted to do. He'd weighed the pros and cons. Living in Maryland and working in DC meant dealing with congested traffic, which had begun wearing him down. Then there were the advantages of being his own boss, an idea that he liked.

Returning to the cove for his father's funeral had shown him how much the people in the town had changed for the better. The old sheriff, who'd thought he ruled the town, was gone, and there was a new man in charge, a man he'd liked immediately upon meeting him—Sawyer Grisham. For the first time since leaving he could see himself making Catalina Cove his home again. The only problem he saw impeding his return was Bryce. Since there was no way the two of them could ever get back together, he figured the best way to deal with her was to ignore her very existence.

After much consideration, Kaegan had accepted Reid's offer. With the injection of money, Kaegan was able to pay his workers their back pay, call back the men his father had laid off, buy four new boats and update every last piece of his machinery. Reid even gave Kaegan and his crew permission to farm for tilapia and catfish on a tract of land off the ocean that Reid LaCroix owned but never used. That turned out to be an added investment for them both.

With numerous restaurants in the area needing fresh seafood daily, Kaegan's business began booming immediately. It was still doing well and in two more years he would be able to pay off his loan to Reid. Kaegan had discovered that without his father making his life miserable, he actually loved being on the water with the men. And he felt he had a dynamic office staff.

The one thing he did make clear to the townspeople was that he didn't want to be called K-Gee any longer. He couldn't forget it had been Bryce who'd first begun calling him that in first grade when she couldn't pronounce his name.

Once he'd settled back in the cove, he'd done a pretty good job of keeping his distance from Bryce and vice versa. The only time they would run into each other was when he went into her parents' café, which he tried limiting. At least he did until he and Sheriff Sawyer Grisham became good friends.

They'd bonded because they'd had a lot in common. They'd both been marines who'd served multiple tours in Afghanistan. They'd even figured they'd been in the area about the same time, although their paths never crossed. They'd enjoyed sharing war stories over beer in the evenings at Collins Bar and Grill, or in the mornings over coffee and blueberry muffins at the Witherspoon Café.

A couple of years later Ray Sullivan relocated to the cove to work for Kaegan. Since he was new to town and hadn't known anyone, they extended their friendship to Ray, and the three of them would start their workday by meeting at the Witherspoon Café.

Bryce was a Realtor in town but often helped her parents out at the café with the breakfast and dinner crowd. Just like he didn't want to have anything to do with her, she had the same attitude toward him, which he found crazy because she was the one who'd been caught cheating. He'd also discovered that although most people in the cove knew they were no longer together, no one, not even her parents and brothers, knew the reason why. He figured she'd been too ashamed to admit to anyone that she'd betrayed him and people had known not to ask him about it, so the reason remained a mystery to everyone.

Even though he saw her more often because of his daily breakfast meetings with Ray and Sawyer at her parents' cafe, he'd made it a point to ignore her. He'd done a pretty damn good job of it until Vashti moved back to town. She was determined to reclaim her two best friends and couldn't understand why two people who'd once been so into each other could share so much animosity.

Sighing deeply, Kaegan put the box back in the safe and

drew in a deep breath. Seeing it was a reminder that long-term relationships weren't for him and he never intended to trust another woman with his heart again.

CHAPTER THREE

"Good morning, Sheriff. Good morning, Ray. The usual?" Bryce asked the two men when they sat down at one of the booths.

"Yes, I'll take the usual," Ray Sullivan said, smiling up at her.

"So will I," Sheriff Sawyer Grisham chimed in, smiling, as well.

Bryce walked off while thinking that Vashti and Ashley were two lucky women to have found two men who were such jewels. Maybe one day her luck would change. She recalled an article she'd read just last week in a popular women's magazine. It stated women outnumbered men four to one. With so few men, she needed to get motivated and find her Mr. Right. She'd once had high hopes for Marcel, a guy she'd met at a real-estate seminar in Atlanta. They'd dated for almost eight months. When his ex-wife had reentered the picture, he'd dropped her like a hot potato. That had been four years ago, and although she dated occasionally, she hadn't gotten seriously involved with anyone since then.

"You okay, honey?"

She glanced over at her mother and pasted on a smile.

"Sure, Mom, I'm okay. Just had a busy weekend. I showed five houses on Saturday and one after church yesterday."

"How did that go?"

"I think it went well. No buyers yet, but I think one of the couples are really interested in the Flemings' place."

"That's good. Hmm, I wonder where Kaegan is this morning," her mother said.

Bryce bit down on her lip, coming close to saying that she didn't know, nor did she give a royal damn. Of course, she wouldn't say that since the woman standing beside her was her mother, although she'd been mistaken for Bryce's older sister a number of times. Her mom looked just that good for her age and her father wasn't bad-looking for his age, either. Good genes.

Years ago when her father, Chester Witherspoon, had graduated from Catalina Cove High School, he had fled to Canada to avoid fighting in the Vietnam War. It wasn't that he'd been a coward or anything; he just didn't feel the country needed to go to war. A few years later after the war had ended he returned with a Canadian-born wife and baby in tow. It was then that he'd decided to do his patriotic duty and enlist in the military for six years. During those years Bryce's parents had another son, Duke. Four years after Duke they had their only daughter, Bryce. Both Ry and Duke lived in Catalina Cove and were partners with their parents in the family-owned café. Her brothers were happily married to wonderful women with two kids each.

Although no one ever said it, if anyone cared to do the math, it would be quite obvious that Debbie Witherspoon had gotten pregnant before she'd married Chester. That fact never bothered Bryce. Her mother had adopted the philosophy that if you lived in a glass house you shouldn't throw stones. That was the main reason why, unlike a lot of the other parents in town, the Witherspoons hadn't bashed Vashti when she'd gotten pregnant at sixteen and refused to reveal the identity of her child's father. The Witherspoons had stood up for Vashti and had been quite outspoken in saying it wasn't anyone's business what Vashti decided to do and whom she told or didn't tell.

"I think I'll go help your dad and brothers in the back. Time to put my pies in the oven for the lunch crowd," her mother said.

"Okay, Mom."

Moments later, while Bryce was placing their orders in front of Ray and Sawyer, she felt heat behind her and didn't have to look to know Kaegan had arrived.

When he sat down she glanced over at him. "Your usual, K-Gee?"

He glared at her and she wanted to smile but managed to keep a straight face. He hated that nickname and she'd only called him that to annoy the hell out of him.

"Yes, my usual, Brycie."

She momentarily went still, not expecting him to retaliate by calling her that. Brycie had been his special name for her whenever they made love. Not able to deal with the memories right now, instead of saying anything she nodded and walked off to the kitchen.

When she saw her mother busy mixing up her pies, she said, "Kaegan is here now, so you can stop fretting."

Her mother chuckled. "I wasn't fretting. I'd just noticed he hadn't arrived at the time he usually does."

It was no secret that Chester and Debbie Witherspoon always had a soft spot for Kaegan. In fact, very few people knew that it had been Bryce's mother who'd gone to the school board and pushed for Kaegan to attend regular school and not the fake homeschooling his father claimed he was getting.

It might bewilder some people as to how her parents could still be so fond of a man who'd obviously hurt their daughter. But she knew her parents. The one thing she could give them credit for was not getting involved in their children's business. They accepted the fact that Bryce and her brothers were adults and treated them that way. They got along with their daughters-in-law, and whenever disagreements would come up, they didn't take sides.

She understood her parents' feelings for Kaegan. He'd been a part of their lives just as long as he'd been a part of hers back in elementary school. They loved him like another son. Although her parents didn't know all the details of their breakup, they believed it was something she and Kaegan would eventually work out. And just like the situation with her brothers and their wives, when it came to her and Kaegan, they refused to take sides.

Her brothers weren't as easygoing as her parents. All they knew was that Kaegan had hurt her, and in the beginning that had been enough for them to take sides. But when she refused to tell them what Kaegan had done, they soon took the same position her parents had. Kaegan was like a part of their family. Ry and Duke figured whatever had pushed her and Kaegan apart, they would either work it out or they would not. Her brothers made the decision to let her handle her own business when it came to Kaegan and not get involved, and she appreciated that.

Placing hot blueberry muffins in the basket to take to Kaegan's table, she wondered if his tardiness had anything to do with the woman who hadn't been able to keep her eyes off him at the party. It appeared everyone had left the party Friday night, but that didn't necessarily mean she hadn't returned later for a weekend sleepover.

Reminding herself that what Kaegan did wasn't her business, she went to pour his coffee.

"You're not very talkative, Kaegan," Sawyer said, stirring his coffee.

Kaegan glanced up. "Not much to say this morning."

Ray chuckled. "Well, I have a lot to say, mainly about Friday night. That was a damn good party and the food was fantastic, as usual."

"Glad you enjoyed it." And because he considered these two men his closest friends, he figured he needed to give them a reason for his solemn mood, even if it wasn't the only reason. "I anticipate a busy week. I got another big order for the Chappell Group that needs to go out Thursday."

"I'll be able to help," Ray said, smiling. "Ashley's parents are coming for a short visit. When it comes to her mother, I have to take her in small doses, so trust me, you'll be doing me a favor."

Kaegan chuckled. "Was it that way before, when you were that Devon guy?" For a few years Ray had lost his memory.

"It was worse. I think at times she's trying to determine how much of 'Devon' is still in me. Her only saving grace is that I understand she's happy and excited that I finally got her daughter pregnant. She's always wanted grandchildren."

"And now you're giving her doubles," Sawyer said, grinning. "You're going to love being the father of twins."

"Says a man who should know," Kaegan said, also grinning. He was happy for these two. He recalled how just a few years ago the three of them had been single men, without a thought of a female in their lives. All of that had changed. At least for two of them things had.

"I saw Farley's sister at your party. She came without him?" Ray asked.

"Yes. He wasn't feeling well, and I guess she didn't want to miss a good party," Kaegan said, chuckling.

"She's a divorcée, right?" Sawyer asked.

"Yes, that's right."

"She's pretty," Ray said, looking at him over the rim of his coffee cup.

He glanced at Ray. "Is she? I hadn't really noticed."

In truth, he *had* noticed, but not enough to warrant his interest. She wasn't his type. Not that he believed everything he heard, but on more than one occasion he'd heard his men whispering that she was into kinky stuff and that threesomes were her specialty. Personally, he wasn't into sharing.

He glanced up when a cup of coffee and a basket of blueberries were placed in front of him. When his and Bryce's eyes met, something stirred deep within his gut and he immediately resented the feeling. He also resented that he was noticing how pretty she looked this morning. Could it be the hint of blush she'd added to her cheeks? Or that her lashes seemed a little longer than usual? In the past, Bryce only put on makeup when it suited her. Was there a reason she was wearing some now? Was there a man coming into the café that she wanted to impress?

"Will there be anything else?" she asked him.

He hated that his thoughts had been on a past that could never be rekindled. She was glaring at him and he automatically glared back. "From you? No."

He saw her bite down on her bottom lip, probably tempted to tell him where he could take the coffee and muffins and shove them. Instead she turned and walked off. He watched her leave and figured that even if he no longer cared one iota for her, he could still appreciate a good-looking ass in jeans. He kept his gaze glued to her backside until she disappeared behind the counter. He wished he didn't remember a time he considered that ass and every damn part of her body as his.

"Keep it up and one day you're going to get hot coffee thrown in your face, Kaegan," Sawyer said, breaking into his thoughts.

He looked over at Sawyer. "If that happens, I'm sure you'll be quick to arrest her."

Sawyer shrugged his shoulders. "Can't say that I will. I might figure you had it coming."

"I will have to agree with him," Ray added. "I don't know what happened between you and Bryce years ago, but I'd think the two of you should—"

"Continue to ignore each other," Kaegan interrupted.

"The two of you don't ignore each other," Sawyer said, after taking a sip of his coffee. "You antagonize each other. You do her and she does you."

Kaegan wished Sawyer hadn't said that. Why did memories of him and Bryce together suddenly flash through his mind? Her naked beneath him while they made love. He had been her first and she had been his.

He glanced at his watch. "I got to go. Marty called and one of his kids is sick, so he won't be coming in. I'll be helping with deliveries today."

Ray raised an eyebrow. "Where's John?"

"On vacation. He and his family left Saturday for Walt Disney World."

Ray nodded. "You know if you need me to pitch in I'm just a phone call away."

Kaegan knew that was true. When Ray had first arrived in town he had worked for him, first out on the boat and then in the office as a bookkeeper. The man had a way with numbers and in the end it was discovered why. He was a Harvard man with dual degrees in computer technology and finance. Even after Ray had started up his own company, Ray Tours, he would often volunteer and help out in any way he could, especially during audit time. Kaegan always welcomed the help. He still did, but knew Ray's business had grown by leaps and bounds. Instead of one touring boat, Ray now had five. When Ray had gotten his memory back, it was discovered he was a very wealthy man. But Kaegan still appreciated that he hadn't changed. He was still the laid-back man he considered a close friend.

"I'll keep that in mind," Kaegan said, standing and leaving enough money on the table to cover his bill and a tip. He glanced over to where Bryce was waiting on another table. Why his gaze had been drawn to her, he wasn't sure. He never was sure.

"You're still leaving, Kaegan?"

It was then that he realized he had been standing there staring at Bryce. He glanced at his friends. "Yes, I'm still leaving."

He then turned and walked out of the café.

Bryce was aware the moment Kaegan left because she no longer felt the heat of his gaze on her. Why did knowing he'd been watching her, was always watching her, fill her with a degree of satisfaction?

She had taken extra time with getting dressed today. Although she'd told herself it hadn't been *for* him, she knew it was *at* him. Maybe it was time for her to let him see what he used to have, but wouldn't ever have again. One day he would regret believing the worst about her.

"That will be all, Bryce."

She smiled at the Coopers, the couple whose order she'd just taken. Like Ray, Kaegan and Sawyer, the older couple were regulars. "I'll be back with your tea."

As she walked off, she felt the cell phone in the pocket of her jeans vibrate. When she got to the hallway that led to the kitchen, she pulled the phone out of her pocket and saw the caller was Vashti.

She clicked it on. "Good morning, Vash, and, no, I haven't forgotten," she said, before her best friend could tell her the reason for the call. Bryce had promised to cover for her at the inn for a couple of hours while Vashti took her son, Cutter, in for his regular checkup with the pediatrician.

"Glad you remembered. What time will you get here?"

"What time do you want me there?"

Two years ago, Vashti had inherited the inn that sat on the

gulf, Shelby by the Sea, from her aunt. She'd spent a year re-modeling the place, not only bringing it back to its once glo-rious splendor, but also adding additional perks that made the inn one of the most sought-out places for newlyweds, cou-ples celebrating anniversaries and writers needing a retreat to be inspired. Reservations were booked months in advance and Shelby by the Sea always had a full house. Most people checked in on Mondays and stayed until Sunday, and some stayed more than one week. Vashti was expecting at least six couples to check in today before noon, which was why she wanted to make sure Bryce covered for her.

Bryce loved Shelby by the Sea and remembered spending a lot of time there with Vashti while growing up. When Vashti had reopened the inn, Bryce had agreed to be the inn's as-sistant manager that first year to help Vashti while she got things off the ground. That meant she was familiar with how things operated at the inn and could step in and help out any time she was needed.

"My appointment is at ten thirty."

"Then I'll be there at ten. My first appointment isn't until three."

"Thanks, Bryce. You're a lifesaver."

"That's what friends are for. I'll see you in a few."

She clicked off the phone when a man walked in. Isaac El-loran. He'd graduated from school the same year as her brother Ry and had moved back to the cove last year. His wife—or ex-wife—had graduated with them, as well. According to Ry, the two had been high-school sweethearts who'd gotten married but had divorced a few years ago.

Bryce didn't know Isaac that well, but he seemed like a nice guy. And he'd moved back to Catalina Cove to start a new life for himself. She'd heard he was a technology expert who'd sold his business and was able to retire early. It was obvious the man was loaded, with that fancy hot sports car he drove around town and that huge house he'd purchased near the ocean.

He was also handsome and had caught the attention of a number of the single women in town. However, she noted he didn't date much, as if refusing to let any woman get too close. She'd also heard from Ry that he was still pining for his wife and the divorce had been her idea and not his.

She grabbed a menu and headed in his direction when he sat down at a table. Although she was on the lookout for a nice guy, she wouldn't put Isaac on her list. The last thing she needed in her life was another man who still loved his ex.

CHAPTER FOUR

Kaegan got into his company's delivery truck, glad to get out of the office for a while, mainly to breathe in some fresh air. For some reason he felt annoyed this morning and seeing Bryce hadn't helped. But then, he saw Bryce most mornings at the café, so what made today any different? It could be because of the tiff they'd had Friday night, and then to see her this morning looking just as good, even better than she had on Friday, had annoyed the hell out of him. At the moment he was too mad to ponder why.

Kaegan had time before his delivery to Shelby by the Sea, so he decided to take what he considered the scenic route, which went through the main section of town. He would be one of the first to admit that Catalina Cove was a beautiful place.

Kaegan recalled resenting having to leave the security of the bayou to come to this part of town to attend school. He hadn't liked it until he'd met Vashti and Bryce. Because he'd gotten little schooling before, they'd started him in first grade instead of third, where he belonged due to his age. The other kids ignored him but Vashti and Bryce hadn't. It wasn't long before they'd become his best buddies.

Forcing his mind from that period in his life, he studied his surroundings as he drove through the historical part of the cove. The land the cove sat on had been a gift from the United States government to the notorious pirate Jean Lafitte for his role in helping the States fight for independence from the British during the War of 1812. Some believed Lafitte wasn't buried at sea in the Gulf of Honduras like history claimed, but was buried somewhere in the waters surrounding Catalina Cove.

For years because of Lafitte, the cove had been a shipping town. It still was, which was evident by the number of fishing vessels that lined the pier on a daily basis. That accounted for the fact there were a large number of seafood restaurants in town. The Moulden River was full of trout, whiting, shrimp and oysters. Tourists came from miles around to sample the town's seafood, especially the oysters. The cove's lighthouse-turned-restaurant was one of the most popular destinations in town. You had to make reservations weeks in advance to get a table.

It wasn't long before he pulled onto Buccaneer Lane, where Shelby by the Sea was located. It was a beautiful tree-lined street that ended at the ocean. He noticed the number of vehicles parked in the long winding driveway of the large mansion with the beautiful manicured lawn that sat on the gulf. He recalled hanging out here as a kid with Vashti and Bryce whenever Vashti's aunt Shelby had something for them to do.

When he pulled into the yard he was glad none of the cars blocked the lane that went to the back of the inn, where deliveries were made. Some people might find it odd that the CEO of a company would do such a task as he was doing here today, but he wouldn't ask any of his employees to do something that he himself wouldn't do. He didn't spend all his time stuck behind the desk. Usually on Fridays he went out on the harvesting ships with his crew.

As he got out of the truck to begin unloading, he could truly say that although he and his company were now taking on bigger clients, he still appreciated the local business owners who contracted with his company to provide all the seafood they needed. Shelby by the Sea was one such client.

When he got everything loaded on the cart, he pulled it through the back and rang the doorbell. He expected Mrs. Livingston, the inn's chef, to be the one to open the door for the delivery. Instead when the door opened, it was Bryce.

Kaegan frowned. He'd seen her that morning. Once a day was all he could tolerate of her. "What are you doing here, Bryce? Where is Mrs. Livingston?"

Bryce moved aside. "She had a run to make to the store and told me to watch out for someone from your company. I expected Marty or John. I wasn't expecting you."

"Well, you got me." The minute he'd spoken the words, it flashed through his mind that, no, she didn't have him. Not in the ways that counted with him.

"Fine. Just drop it here and leave it."

"That's not how things work. You need to count the number of boxes before signing off on anything, and then I load them in the freezer for you."

She rolled her eyes. "I know how it's done, Kaegan. Need I remind you that I used to be the assistant manager here?"

Honestly, he didn't need her to remind him of anything. "Why are you here?"

Instead of answering him, she took her pretty little time scanning the invoice. All four pages. Then she glanced back at him. "Not that it's any of your business, but Vashti had to leave for a couple of hours to take Cutter in for his checkup and asked me to fill in while she was gone. Anything else you want to know?"

"Not if it's going to take you forever to answer."

She glared at him and he ignored it and wished he could

ignore her. She was wearing the same outfit she'd had on this morning. That same blouse. Those same jeans. Definitely a turn-a-guy-on sort of outfit. When she leaned over to read the labels on each box while checking the items off the invoice, he honestly wished she didn't tilt her curvy ass up like that while bending over.

He recalled the times he'd made love to her from behind and how much they'd enjoyed it. On weekends, when he could send for her to meet him halfway between her college and his military base, he would always arrive at the hotel first and they would spend an entire weekend together in bed.

Kaegan knew he should have suspected something was up when she began canceling some of their romantic weekends, saying she was getting behind in her studies. He'd believed her and had begun feeling guilty that he was interfering with her schoolwork. He'd never suspected the real reason was because she was betraying him with another guy.

"Everything's all here," she said, straightening up and signing the invoice.

"Fine." He took the paper from her, being careful not to touch her hand in the process. "Let Vashti know the delivery was made and on time."

He headed toward the freezer and began unloading the boxes. She didn't say anything, but he could feel her standing there and staring at him. The same way he'd stared at her. The heat of her gaze was all over him—he could feel it. He started to say something about her standing there and watching him when the doorbell sounded.

"That's probably the Braziers. They're the last couple Vashti expected to check in before noon."

He wondered why she was telling him that. Why was she still there at all? He didn't get a chance to ask her before the sound of her heels clicking on the tile floor told him she'd left.

With her departure, he drew in a deep breath, inhaling her lingering scent. He liked it, even though he wished he didn't.

Trying to put Bryce, her scent and how good she'd looked out of his mind, he continued to stock the boxes in the freezer. But he still thought about her and couldn't understand why he was doing so. He tried to remember the last time he'd taken a woman on a date.

A number of the women in the cove were aware he and Bryce had been sweethearts in high school and had even talked about marriage once she completed college. Many figured it would just be a matter of time before they got back together. Those women didn't know how wrong that assumption was, but he was willing to let them think whatever they liked. He dated when he got the urge, and usually when he did there was a woman to take off the edge.

As he was finishing up, he heard the voices belonging to Bryce and two others, and decided he wanted to be gone if Bryce returned. Seeing her twice in one day was enough for him. Nearly too much. He quickly finished what he was doing and left.

"Thanks for helping out today. Anything interesting happen?"

Bryce glanced at Vashti. Had her friend known Kaegan would be making those deliveries and hadn't told her? She would admit that Kaegan seemed as surprised to see her as she'd been at seeing him. "Anything interesting like what?"

"Anything. Mondays are always interesting here at Shelby. Last Monday we had that dog deliver puppies on the roof of the gazebo. Not sure yet how she got up there. Then the Monday before that we had that paddleboat wash up on shore with clothes but no people. Sawyer is still working with the Coast Guard trying to determine if a couple who possibly went swimming skinny-dipping in the ocean were reported missing. So far no one has filed a missing-person report."

Bryce nodded. "The only interesting thing that happened around here was that Kaegan dropped by."

Vashti lifted an eyebrow in surprise. "He did?"

So she hadn't known. "Yes."

"Did he say what he wanted?"

"He made the normal Monday deliveries," Bryce said.

Vashti nodded. "I know John is on vacation, since he mentioned as much a few weeks ago, but where was Marty?"

"He was out today, as well."

Vashti came over to Bryce and looked her over. Bryce gave her a pointed look. "What are you doing?"

"Checking for battle scars."

Bryce rolled her eyes. "You won't see any. We were pretty cordial to each other."

"That's a switch. Especially after Friday night."

"I'm trying, Vash. Of course, he was in his usual foul mood, but I've made the decision not to let Kaegan rattle me any longer."

"Good. And I hope he's made that same decision about you."

"What's that supposed to mean?"

"Nothing. Did you see Reid's wedding announcement in yesterday's paper?"

Bryce knew Vashti was deliberately changing the subject. "Yes, I saw it." Reid LaCroix, the wealthiest man in the cove, was getting married.

"I'm happy for Reid. Gloria is a beautiful soul and just what he needs. Of course, the girls are thrilled to death about it," Vashti said.

"And how are the girls doing?" Bryce asked Vashti about her daughters.

"They love college and Sawyer and I are glad they decided to attend the same one. I'm looking forward to seeing them over the holidays since Kia will be spending Thanksgiving this year with us. Knowing Gloria and Reid, they will plan their wedding when they know the girls will be here to attend."

Bryce nodded. "Speaking of weddings, don't forget that I'm attending a wedding this weekend. I'm flying out early Friday morning."

"I remember. You'll have to tell me all about it when you get back."

"I will." Bryce glanced at her watch. "Time for me to go. I have that closing at three and want to swing by the office to go over the paperwork before then."

A few moments later Bryce was on her way home, but she was still dwelling on her encounter with Kaegan at Shelby by the Sea. Same scent from that morning, when she'd gotten a whiff of him, and he still smelled good a few hours later. While watching him put those boxes in the freezer she had admired his broad shoulders and the way his backside fit his jeans.

Suddenly she heard a pop and her steering wheel began shaking. A flat tire. Damn. She pulled to the side of the road and tugged the cell phone from her purse to call for roadside service when an SUV pulled alongside of her.

"Car trouble, miss?"

She glanced over at the handsome man. She figured he was in his midthirties, possibly a little older. "I believe I have a flat and was about to call for roadside service."

"There's no need to call anyone. I can change it for you."

It was a little after the lunch hour and a steady stream of vehicles was on the road. Catalina Cove was a pretty safe town. Sawyer made sure of that. "I hate for you to bother."

"No bother."

When he pulled off the road to park his SUV in front of her vehicle, she noticed his license plate was for a rental vehicle. Was he visiting someone in the cove?

She watched him get out of his truck and walk back to her

car. In addition to being good-looking, he was tall and well
built, dressed in jeans and a Western shirt. When he reached
her car, he said, "You don't have to get out. If you'll just release the trunk, I can get out your spare and everything else
I need."

"All right."

"My name is Jeremy Skinner, by the way," he said. He
smiled and offered her his hand through the open window.

"Hello, Jeremy. I'm Bryce Witherspoon."

"Hello, Bryce."

"Are you from around here, Jeremy?"

He shook his head. "No, I'm from Shreveport. I love to
fish and heard this is the best place for it and rented a cabin
near the water for a few days."

It didn't take the man but a few minutes to change the tire.
"You have a leak and will need to get it repaired. I got the
spare on for now."

"Thanks, Jeremy."

"You're welcome."

"What do I owe you?"

"Not a thing. It was my pleasure to help such a beautiful
lady."

His flirty words made her smile, and since he didn't have
a ring on his finger, she figured she could do a little flirting,
as well. "I really would like to show my thanks. Here's my
business card. If you ever return to the area, please give me a
call. Maybe we can get together for coffee."

He glanced down at the business card and then back at her,
and a huge smile curved his lips. "Thanks, Bryce. I'll do that."

CHAPTER FIVE

"Morning, Kaegan."

Kaegan turned when Ray walked into the office. "Morning, Ray. What are you doing here so early? I take it your in-laws are still in town."

"Yes, they're still here."

He'd gotten a call from Ray last night offering to do the audit this morning. Claimed doing so kept his mind sharp. "When will they be leaving?"

"Not soon enough. At least my father-in-law is handling his wife better than I remember. But she's still a pain in the ass. She told us yesterday that she doesn't like the names we've chosen for the twins. Like we give a royal damn."

Kaegan chuckled and then headed toward his office.

"By the way, I heard Bryce left town today."

Kaegan paused and then turned around, wondering why Ray thought he would care. "Did she?"

"Yes."

"And how do you know that?"

"She wasn't at the café this morning."

Kaegan didn't say anything. He'd deliberately stayed away

from the café this week as much as he could. At least until he could figure out why he was hell-bent on lusting after the woman who'd betrayed him. "And?"

"And I asked Mrs. Witherspoon where she was, in case she was sick or something. She assured me Bryce was okay."

Kaegan nodded. "That's nice." And because he figured Ray would know, he asked, "So where did she go?"

"To California to attend a wedding. Some guy she went to college with who also grew up in this town. I understand his parents used to own a pharmacy here."

Kaegan almost choked on his coffee.

"Hey, man, you okay over there?" Ray asked with concern.

"Yes, I'm okay."

He placed the coffee cup down, not believing what Ray had said. Samuel Abbott, the guy she'd betrayed him with, was getting married and she'd gone to the wedding? He'd heard the Abbotts had moved to California. Bryce and Samuel must have remained pretty good friends after they split. He was suddenly filled with anger at the mere thought. "When is she coming back?"

Ray glanced over at him. He must have heard the anger in his voice. "Why do you want to know, Kaegan?"

Kaegan met his gaze. "So now you want to get quiet on me?"

Ray shook his head. "No, I want to know why you want to know when Bryce is coming back. Especially with the tone of your voice. And please choose your words carefully."

Kaegan rolled his eyes. "I guess the next thing you'll be saying is that you intend to beat the crap out of me if I don't."

Ray nodded. "That thought has crossed my mind a number of times, to do just that when I see how you handle Bryce, but Sawyer wouldn't let me."

"Whatever." Kaegan leaned against a desk. "So are you going to tell me or not?" This time he tried asking in a calmer voice.

"I guess I will. She's coming back Monday, sometime before noon."

Kaegan nodded as he took another sip of his coffee, satisfied he had the information he wanted. He intended to see
Bryce for himself on Monday. There was one question he had
to ask and then for him there would finally be closure with
her. He'd always wondered why she and Samuel Abbott broke
up all those years ago.

"Bryce is a wonderful woman. Not sure what problems the
two of you had to break up, but I hope they can get worked
out," Ray said, breaking into Kaegan's thoughts.

"Nothing can get worked out between me and Bryce. It
would take a miracle," Kaegan said. Then he tossed his empty
coffee cup into the trash can.

Ray shrugged. "Considering how close I came to death
that time and what has happened in my life the four years
since, I happen to believe in miracles, Kaegan. Maybe you
should, too."

Bryce saw Kaegan the minute he walked into her parents'
restaurant. Automatically, he zeroed in on the area where
she stood and their gazes connected. Why today, of all days,
did he have to come into the café for dinner? A late dinner
at that. She had arrived back in town earlier that day and had
told her parents she would pitch in this evening.

The restaurant would be closing in an hour, and since
things had gotten slow and she hadn't expected many more
customers, she had convinced her parents to go home and
that she and her brothers would close the restaurant. Since her
folks had been there since four that morning, they'd quickly
taken her up on her offer. Her brothers were in the back, and
since Kaegan was her only customer, that meant they were
virtually alone.

She hadn't seen him for a while. Not since that day he'd

made those deliveries to Shelby by the Sea. He had not come to the café and she'd refused to ask Sawyer or Ray about him.

Pasting a smile on her face, she said, "Evening, Kaegan. Any particular place you'd like to sit?"

"I'll grab that table by the window."

She nodded. That was where he normally sat whenever he came in alone. No need to remember even when they were in high school that he would sit there to wait for her to leave the restaurant so he could walk her home at night. "And what would you like to drink?" she asked, walking over to the table to put down a place mat and eating utensils.

"A cold beer would be nice."

"One cold beer coming up. Here's the menu," she said and made a move to walk off.

"I don't need a menu. I talked to your mom earlier when I dropped by for lunch. She promised to put aside some of her lobster stew and corn bread for me."

"My parents have gone for tonight, but I'll see if Mom mentioned anything about it to my brothers," she said before walking off.

Her mother had indeed told Duke and Ry about it. After getting Kaegan a beer, she went behind the counter to wait for Duke to get the meal together. As she wiped down the counter she could feel Kaegan's gaze on her, but refused to say anything to him or look his way.

Why did he have to look so darn good today? Of all days? Being at Samuel's wedding and seeing how happy he was had made her wonder if there was a man somewhere out there for her. She hoped so because she definitely wasn't getting any younger. She was thirty-two and never had a ring on her finger. And she did want kids one day. She loved her nieces and nephews but they were just that—her nieces and nephews. She wanted to have children of her own.

A pain settled in her chest when she recalled how she would

often lie in bed and visualize how her kids would look. They were kids she thought she'd have one day with Kaegan. They would take on more of his prominent features. Her son would be strikingly handsome and her daughter would be eye-catchingly gorgeous. They would have their father's long silky black hair and that hawkish nose that she used to love rubbing hers against. Her son would grow up with his father's rugged good looks, chiseled jaw and those dreamy dark eyes. She would have to work hard to keep the girls from him.

Duke rang the bell for her to pick up the food. She carried the dishes over to where Kaegan sat watching her with those dark eyes. Why did he still have to be, after all these years, the work of impossible male beauty? She knew then that she needed to meet someone and get involved real quick-like. She didn't do casual sex but her vibrator had seen its useful days. She hadn't shared a bed with anyone since Marcel and that was close to four years ago.

Kaegan didn't say anything when she placed the food in front of him on the table. She was about to walk off when he said, "You're usually not here on Monday nights, Bryce."

How would he know that? And why did he have to say her name in that deep, husky voice that could still send shivers of desire down her spine? "You're right—usually I'm not. I was away this weekend, so I thought I'd pitch in so the folks could leave early."

He nodded. "Today your mom mentioned that you'll be taking a six-week class at a university in New Orleans."

She wondered why he was holding a conversation with her when all those other times he'd come into the café he'd acted like he could barely tolerate her presence. "Yes, that's right. I'm taking the class so I can become a licensed Realtor in other states. Very few people are leaving the cove and selling their homes, so I need to expand my horizons if I want to continue to make money." She wondered why she'd told him all that. It wasn't like he was interested in knowing any of it. "I'll let you get to your meal now."

Bryce walked away, and like before, she could feel his gaze on her. She wondered if, like her, he was remembering how things used to be between them. Every time she saw him, she was reminded of how close they used to be. How incredibly close, both in and out of bed. Each time she looked into his face, studied his lips, she couldn't help but remember how he'd taught her to kiss that first time and all the times after that, and just how much she enjoyed doing so. Kaegan had taught her a lot of things that she'd rather not think about now.

Bryce decided to wipe down the counter and restock supplies so her parents would have less to do in the morning. Anything to keep her concentration elsewhere and not on Kaegan. She moved from table to table, filling up the napkin dispensers and straw holders. Afterward, she wiped off the laminated menus and placed them back in the rack. When she saw Kaegan's beer had gotten low, she asked, "Would you like a refill?"

He glanced over at her, as if considering her words. Instead of giving her an answer, he asked one of his own. "Why did you and Samuel Abbott break up, Bryce?"

His question was like a blow to her stomach. She actually felt the sharp pain, which was why her hand suddenly covered the lower part of her abdomen. Honestly, she wasn't ready for this. In a flash, anger replaced the pain and she had a mind to go get that pitcher of beer off the counter and pour it on his head. But why waste good beer over a brutal hard head? The one still filled with untruths about her.

She crossed the room and stood beside his table with her hands on her hips. "I'm going to tell you the same thing I tried telling you ten years ago," she said, trying to hold back her anger and failing miserably. "There was never anything going on between me and Samuel Abbott. It was lies your father made up. Lies you chose to believe."

His jaw tightened and his dark eyes flared. "I saw the two of you together, Bryce. He was leaving your house at two in the morning. The two of you were hugging on your front porch. Do you deny that?"

She tossed her hair back from her face. "No, I don't deny it. It was a friendly hug that you tried making into something dirty."

"I tried making into something dirty?" he said, as if incensed with what she'd said. "Don't you dare blame me for what you did to us."

Bracing her hands on the table, she leaned in closer, almost right in his face. If he wanted a good fight, she would give him one. "I am blaming you, Kaegan, for not believing in me when you should have. For your lack of trust in me. I'm also blaming you for sleeping with another woman to spite me when you thought I had wronged you."

She drew in a deep breath and backed away from him, trying to get her anger under control, but she couldn't. "And as far as Samuel is concerned, he's living in California and I went to his wedding this weekend."

"So I heard."

Had her mother told him that, too? Was that the reason he'd asked why she and Samuel had broken up? "It was a beautiful wedding."

"Must have been pretty damn awful for you to be at the wedding. Seeing the man you once loved marry someone else," he sneered.

She lifted her chin. "No, it wasn't awful at all. In fact, I am very happy for him. Samuel deserves to be happy and I believe *Matthew* will make him extremely happy."

"Matthew?" he asked, as if to make sure he'd heard her right.

"Yes, *Matthew*. The reason Samuel and I spent so much

time together is because he needed a friend. He was having a hard time coming to terms with his sexuality. Since we both attended Grambling, whenever he came home he would offer me a ride back here. And he was in a number of my study groups on campus. That's when we became close and he would confide in me."

Kaegan glared at her. "You should have told me."

"And you should have trusted me," she snapped, glaring back. "That night when you thought you saw us in some kind of passionate embrace, I was giving Samuel a hug of encouragement because he'd made the decision to tell his parents the truth. He was tired of living the lie he had lived all his life and wanted to come out. And before you say I should have told you that, too, I tried telling you after I got that call from you, ending things between us. Just think of how different things would have been had you listened to me. Instead, you hung up on me and then blocked my number so I couldn't call you back."

She drew in a deep breath, remembering that day like it was yesterday. "But I didn't let that stop me, Kaegan. I was determined that you knew the truth. I used every penny I had to buy a bus ticket, and I rode that bus for eighteen hours all the way from college to see you. And what did you do? Instead of listening to what I had to say, you treated me like shit in front of some brazen hussy."

"Bryce, I—I'm sorry—"

Without saying anything else, she crossed the room and headed straight for the kitchen, ignoring Kaegan calling out to her. Duke and Ry looked up when she walked into the kitchen and snatched off her apron.

"Kaegan's still here but that's it for me tonight," she said, refusing to let her tears fall. "I'm done here and going home." She grabbed her purse out of one of the cabinets, walked out the back door, got in her car and drove off.

★ ★ ★

Kaegan sat stunned at Bryce's words. And then, like he'd been stung by something, he bolted out of the booth and charged into the kitchen. He looked at Bryce's brothers, who both stared at him. "Where's Bryce?" he asked them.

Ry answered in an angry voice, "She just got in her car and left, obviously upset, Kaegan. What's going on? What the hell did you do to her?"

Kaegan wanted to go after her but knew that wouldn't be a good idea. Not tonight, anyway. He had a lot to think about. A lot to take in. What she'd just told him had shocked the hell out of him. It had been like an enormous kick in his gut. How could he have been so stupid? So fucking stupid? How could he have been so wrong about her? For ten fucking years he had believed the worst about her and he'd been wrong. So damn wrong, and she was right. He only had himself to blame. He'd been more than stupid, more than a moron, worse than an ass...

"Kaegan? Dammit, what did you do to Bryce?" Duke asked, raising an angry voice.

Bryce's brothers had every right to be angry, but this was between him and their sister. "Bryce and I had an argument." And that was all he intended to tell them about it.

"I left the money for my dinner and beer on the table." Then he turned and walked out of the kitchen and left the café, feeling at the lowest point he'd ever felt in his entire life. He felt sick. His guts felt twisted with remorse. He had a feeling Bryce would never forgive him for what he did, and at that moment he doubted if he would ever forgive himself.

CHAPTER SIX

"Hey, Bryce. What's up?"

Bryce adjusted her cell phone in her hand as she sat down at her kitchen table. She was still trembling, inside and out. "It's about Kaegan, Vash."

"Kaegan? What about Kaegan?"

Bryce sighed deeply. "He knows the truth about Samuel."

"How did he find out?"

Bryce closed her eyes and fought back more tears. Why was she still crying? Why was she crying at all? Hadn't she sworn years ago she wouldn't shed any more tears for Kaegan Chambray? That he didn't deserve them? "Kaegan came into the café for dinner and I waited on his table. When he asked why Samuel and I had broken up, in anger I blurted about Samuel and Matthew and their wedding this weekend before I could stop myself."

She heard Vashti's sharp intake of breath. "So now the entire town knows about Samuel, as well as knowing why you and Kaegan broke up?"

"No, Kaegan and I were the only ones in the restaurant. It

was late, near closing time. My brothers were in the kitchen, but they didn't hear anything, either."

"I bet he feels bad about how he's been treating you all these years. Did he apologize?"

"Good, let him feel bad. All he had to do was listen to me ten years ago. I tried telling him about Samuel then, but he refused to listen. Instead he wanted to lash out at me. Break my heart with another woman to my face. He succeeded, Vash. And as far as apologizing, I didn't want to hear his apology."

Bryce paused a moment and then added, "As my friend, I'm going to ask that you don't try to change my mind about how I feel about him. I respected your wishes years ago about your baby's father, and I'm asking you to respect mine now about Kaegan."

Vashti didn't respond for a long moment, and then she said, "Okay, Bryce, I will respect your wishes. Do you want me to come over? I could bring some ice cream."

"Thanks, but I just want to be alone right now. I'll talk to you later. Love you. 'Bye." She clicked off the phone. Before she could put down the phone and go into the bathroom for her shower, both Ry and Duke called. She assured them she was fine but told them she wouldn't be coming into the café tomorrow morning as usual. Although Kaegan hadn't come into the café any mornings last week, she couldn't risk seeing him.

She needed time to pull herself together before she saw him again. That was the only way she could move on with her life and one day find a man whom she could love and who would love her in return just as much.

"I wonder if Bryce didn't get back yesterday as planned," Ray commented when another waitress filled their order.

"She got back," Kaegan said, staring into his coffee. He had arrived at the café early that morning after a sleepless night, only to find out from Mr. Witherspoon that Bryce had decided not to come in that day because she had a lot of things to do. A part of him knew that was just an excuse. She was avoiding him, and he'd been hoping to do just the opposite with her. He had wanted to see her. Apologize again.

More than once last night, he'd been tempted to get out of bed and drive over to her place to see her. But each time he would talk himself out of it when he remembered the look on her face when she'd said, "Don't you dare blame me for our breakup. You can only blame yourself for not believing in me..."

Again, he could only ask himself how he could have been so fucking stupid. He had spent all those years wanting to hate her. Despise her. Believing she had betrayed him, and as a result, he'd thought all sorts of mean things about her when she'd been innocent of all of it. Totally innocent. Instead she'd been being Bryce. The person who was always a champion for the underdog, the girl who would give you the shirt off her back, a person who was that friend when you needed one.

"And you know this how?"

He glanced over at Sawyer. For him to ask meant he hadn't heard anything. That didn't necessarily mean Bryce hadn't told Vashti, because he had every reason to believe that she had. It only meant Vashti hadn't told Sawyer. "I know because I saw her yesterday evening when I came in here for dinner."

"Oh."

That "oh" had come from Ray. Kaegan moved his gaze from Sawyer to Ray. He might as well level with the two men who were the closest things to brothers he would ever have. "I fucked up." There. He'd said it. He'd spelled out his torment in three words. Words he felt all the way to his gut.

"Would you care to tell us how?" Sawyer asked quietly.

So he did. He told them everything. About his father's lies. About what he thought he'd seen that night he'd planned to ask her to marry him. About how he'd treated her when she showed up at that club near the marine base. "For ten years I believed Bryce had an affair with another man and last night I found out it had all been a lie. A fucking lie. I've been trying to hate her when I could have been loving her."

For the longest time the table was quiet. Neither Ray nor Sawyer said anything. Then Sawyer spoke up. "The first step is admitting you were wrong."

"And the second step is making the wrong right," Ray added. "I recall when I fucked up with Ashley and you guys came looking for me. It was one of those you-better-get-your-ass-in-gear moments and I took heed. Grudgingly, but I did it."

Kaegan didn't say anything as he remembered that day. It had taken all he and Sawyer could do not to toss Ray off his boat into the water to wash some sense into him.

"I've had one of those moments myself with Vashti," Sawyer said. "When she tried to tell me about what had happened at the hospital. I didn't want to listen or accept it. I refused to believe her and accused her of all sorts of things."

Kaegan was hearing what his best friends were saying, but they'd had the sense to straighten things out with their women within hours. He'd let things fester for ten years. Ten long damn years. He took a drink of his coffee and said, "Getting things straightened out in less than twenty-four hours doesn't compare to ten years."

"True," Sawyer said. "But a man has to start somewhere and usually it begins with an apology."

"I tried to apologize but she walked off like she didn't want to hear it."

"And you're going to settle for that?" Ray asked him.

No, he wouldn't settle. He would apologize again, a thousand times more if he had to to show her how sincere he was. He had messed up, and if it took the rest of his life, he would show her just how much he regretted doing so.

A few hours later, Kaegan turned his SUV onto the street

where Bryce's real-estate office was located. He had passed by the place several times since returning to the cove. Had even done so at a time she had come outside to get into her car to leave for the day. He'd seen her but she hadn't seen him. At the time, just looking at her had elicited anger. Now he knew whenever he saw her that he would only feel regret. Regret for being such a stupid ass for believing the BS his old man had been feeding him. But then, he couldn't rightly place all the blame on his father. It was also what he'd thought he'd seen with his own eyes.

During his sleepless night, he had come to terms with how wrong he'd been. There had never been anything going on between Bryce and Samuel, and he owed her an apology. Hopefully she would find it in her heart to accept it.

He parked next to her car, unhooked the seat belt and got out of his vehicle. He took the steps two at a time, then sprinted toward the front door of the building and went inside. A young woman who looked to be in her early twenties sat behind a desk. She smiled when she saw him.

"May I help you?"

He nodded. "I'd like to see Bryce... Ms. Witherspoon."

The young woman nodded. "And what's your name, sir?"

"Kaegan Chambray."

"Just a moment, please, Mr. Chambray."

He glanced around when she picked up the phone to announce him. This was the first time he'd ever been here and he liked how Bryce had transformed the Cajun house into her workplace.

A door opened and Bryce walked out of it. His breath caught, as it usually did whenever he saw her. She was professionally dressed in a pair of black slacks and a short-sleeve printed blouse. Her hair flowed around her shoulders and he could tell from her reddened eyes she'd been crying. A lot. He felt a kick in the gut. He'd been the cause of her pain.

Without acknowledging his presence, she said to the young woman sitting at the desk, "You can leave for lunch now, Pia."

The young woman nodded. "Thanks." She got her purse out of the drawer and stood. Before walking out the door, she glanced over at him and smiled faintly. He figured it was her way of warning him that her boss was not in the best of moods today.

When the door closed behind the young woman, Bryce turned to him with narrowed eyes that were shooting daggers at him. "What are you doing here, Kaegan?"

He shoved his hands into the pockets of his jeans. "I came to see you." She crossed her arms over her chest. He wished she hadn't done that. That drew emphasis to a pair of perfect breasts. That was the last thing he needed to think about now.

"Why?"

"I said it last night and I felt the need to say it again today. I'm sorry, Bryce."

Her spine stiffened and the glare in her eyes deepened. "I don't want your apology, Kaegan. It doesn't matter. I stopped caring how you felt about me that night you walked out of that club with that other woman. Please leave."

He could tell her that woman hadn't meant anything to him. That the two of them hadn't slept together that night. But that couldn't erase the other women he'd slept with over the years. Women he'd used to eradicate Bryce from his mind and heart.

"Bryce, I—"

"No. Today is not a good day, Kaegan. Maybe one day I'll be ready to forgive you. But not now. Not today."

At that moment, although she didn't say it, the words *not ever* hung between them. He wasn't given a chance to ask because she turned toward her office, went inside and closed the door behind her.

He had been dismissed with a finality that he felt all the way to the bone.

★ ★ ★

"You look like crap, Kaegan."

He rubbed a hand down his face. Of all people, he didn't need Vashti to tell him that. Besides, he had news for her—he felt like crap, as well. When he left Bryce's office, he'd come here to Shelby by the Sea. He needed to see Vashti because she was one of his best friends. Always had been. More than anything, he knew he owed her an apology.

Since returning to the cove and finding out about his and Bryce's strained relationship, Vashti had, on more than one occasion, tried intervening. Now he wished more than anything that he would have heeded her advice. Hell, he wished she would have knocked some damn sense into him.

"I owe you an apology and you can go ahead and say 'I told you so,' Vashti."

She looked at him over her shoulder as he followed her to her office. "Apology accepted. You have to admit I tried."

"Yes, but now I wish you could have been a little more forceful with it."

Vashti went over to the chair behind her desk and sat down. "It's not easy being best friends with both you and Bryce. I felt like I was caught in the middle and at times I thought that I was the only sane person in the room. I was convinced the two of you were trying to drive me crazy."

Kaegan could only imagine. "How could you even put up with me, knowing what you knew?" he asked, taking the chair across from her desk.

"That's just it. I didn't know everything. I knew about what happened with Samuel, but until just recently I didn't know that she'd traveled all the way to that marine base to see you and tell you everything. In fact, it was the night of your party when the two of you had that little tiff. That's when she told me. You don't know how hard it was for me to even talk to you after that. If you noticed, I didn't for a week."

He'd noticed. "I've been such an ass."

"Yes, you have." She paused and then said, "She's hurting and I believe you're hurting, as well, because of the pain you know you've caused her. Just so you know, I promised Bryce I wouldn't intervene on your behalf, no matter what. I guess you know what that means."

Yes, he knew. He'd gotten himself into this mess and he was the only one who could get himself out of it. He met Vashti's gaze. "I intend to earn back her trust and love."

Vashti nodded. "Good luck. You are definitely going to need it because it's not going to be easy. But then, I have a feeling you know that."

He nodded. "Yes, I know it, but I am a determined man."

"I believe you. I love you both, you know."

"Yes, I know. Any words of advice?"

Vashti didn't say anything for a minute. Then she said, "Ten years is a long time, Kaegan. Earning back her love sounds good, but more than anything, I think you should let Bryce get to know the man you are now, and you should get to know the woman she's become."

CHAPTER SEVEN

Bryce sat cross-legged on the floor in her home with various papers spread out around her. Since she often worked half days on Saturdays at her office, she would normally close at noon on Wednesdays. More times than not, she would help out her parents at the café, but decided not to do so today. In fact, she hadn't been to the café since Monday, and had deliberately avoided being there the last two mornings. Because she knew her parents needed her help, she intended to shape up, get herself together and be there tomorrow morning. She had needed the last two days to stay busy and try to put things in perspective as much as she could.

In a way, nothing between her and Kaegan had changed other than he now knew the truth. It was up to him how he chose to deal with it as long as it didn't involve her. She'd had ten years to know he'd wronged her. Now he needed his ten years.

Her brothers must have mentioned something to her parents because her mother had called yesterday wanting to know if she was okay. In fact, she had been talking to her mom when Kaegan had shown up at her office yesterday. She had assured her mother she was fine and that her argument with Kaegan hadn't been a big deal.

She glanced up at the sound of the doorbell and wondered who would be visiting her. Very few people knew where to find her today, since she usually would be at the café helping her parents and brothers.

She got up and headed for the door. Looking out the peep-hole, she saw it was a young man with flowers. Surely he had the wrong address since nobody ever sent her flowers.

Opening the door, she smiled at Paul and Samantha Jenkins's oldest son, who'd graduated from high school last year and worked at his parents' flower shop. "Hi, Mellon."

"Hello, Miss Bryce. I have a delivery for you."

"You sure it's for me?"

"Yes," he said, handing her the flowers. She looked at them and knew who'd sent them. Only one person knew the kind of flowers she liked, calla lilies. Kaegan. He used to sneak into old lady Lula's flower garden to pick them for Bryce when they'd been teens. Once Ms. Lula discovered the mystery of the disappearing lilies, she would save him the trouble and have a bunch ready for him to give to Bryce each week. He'd said that he had wanted to make his last year in high school, the last year he would get to spend with her, special. There had been no doubt in either of their minds that once he graduated, he would be leaving town to join the marines.

"They're pretty, aren't they?" Mellon asked her, smiling.

"Yes, they are pretty." And they were. An assortment of different colors, some fully bloomed, others not, made up the stunning arrangement, which was in a beautiful ceramic vase with a huge purple bow. Purple was her favorite color and Kaegan knew it.

"Have a nice day, Miss Bryce."

"Wait. Let me give you a tip."

"No need. The sender covered it."

What she should do was tell Mellon that she wouldn't accept them and give them back to him, but she would accept
them. The arrangement was too beautiful for her not to. It
didn't matter if she didn't like the sender—she did like the
flowers.

She closed the door and went to place the vase in the perfect spot on the coffee table. They looked simply beautiful
there. Then she pulled off the card that was attached and
read it.

I hope that one day you will forgive me for not believing in you.
Kaegan

The message had been written in Kaegan's handwriting,
which meant he'd gone into the florist's himself and written
out the card. Bryce placed the card beside the arrangement
and stared down at the flowers. Moments later she picked up
the card again and reread it.

She fought back tears because, at that moment, she wasn't
sure if she could ever forgive Kaegan or not.

"Kaegan, you have a call on line three. It's Samantha Jenkins from Jenkins's Florist."

"Thanks, Wil," he said to his administrative assistant, Willa
Ford. "Please put her through."

When he heard the connection, he said, "Mrs. Jenkins,
how are you?"

"I'm fine, Kaegan. I wasn't here when you dropped by this
morning. I had to do a bank run. Paul took your order and
I want to make sure he jotted down the right instructions."

Kaegan leaned back in his chair. "Okay."

"You want a vase of calla lilies delivered every week to
Bryce Witherspoon. Is that right?"

"Yes, that's right. I pre-signed at least three cards already. When you run out I'll come in to sign some more." Not wanting anyone to know his and Bryce's business, he had stopped by the florist's himself, written out the messages on the cards and sealed the envelopes. For as long as it took her to forgive him, she would get the flowers and the card with that message.

"Well, all right. And we have your credit card on file, so there shouldn't be a problem."

"No, there shouldn't be."

"I'll talk to you later and thanks for your business."

"You're welcome."

"Wait! I just remembered something."

"Yes?"

"I'm selling tickets to this year's Catalina Cove charity ball. How many tickets would you like?"

In all the years he'd lived in the cove, not once had he attended one of those charity balls. He would support them by buying a handful of tickets for his employees, but he'd never felt comfortable attending those types of community functions himself. Kaegan wasn't one who did a lot of socializing with people he didn't know that well. Sawyer and Ray were the only men in the cove he spent any amount of personal time with. Reid had talked him into being a part of the cove's zoning board a few years ago, and that was as far as he intended for his community involvement to go.

He recalled both Sawyer and Ray mentioning they would be attending the event with their wives. The dance was a month from now. It was probably wishful thinking on his part, considering how she felt about him now, to even assume Bryce would go with him to the dance. It would be a miracle to think that by then he would have gotten in her good graces enough to at least get a dance with her. He, of all people, knew how much she liked to dance. The few steps he knew were ones she'd taught him.

It was a long shot, but it was a long shot worth taking. That meant he had to step up his game. But first, of course, he had to get her to forgive him. That was the most important thing to him right now.

"Yes, I'll take twenty tickets this year."

"Wow! Twenty tickets! Your support is definitely appreciated, Kaegan. Thanks."

He ended his call with Samantha Jenkins and went to the coffeepot thinking maybe he should go to the ball this year. There was a first time for everything. After pouring a cup, he moved to the window and looked out.

Kaegan knew Vashti was right. There was nothing wrong with sparking memories, but he and Bryce needed to get to know each other again to cultivate new ones, as well.

They were no longer in their teens, or young and in love. Now they were both in their thirties. It was time they saw things with new sets of eyes. Those belonging to mature adults. They couldn't change the past, but they could control their future. It would be up to him to help her see that and get her to believe in them again.

He knew why the pain of what he thought was her betrayal had hurt him so much. Because he had loved her so deeply. He could honestly say that other than his mother, Bryce was the only woman he'd ever loved. He had loved her and had never stopped loving her. Even when he'd thought bad of her there was something that still pulled at him. And that something had kept him going to the Witherspoon Café every morning because he knew she would be there.

Kaegan also knew that no matter how long he lived in Catalina Cove, it would never be home to him without Bryce. When he'd lived here before he had considered it home because she'd made it so for him. He'd been back awhile now, but a part of him hadn't truly thought of it as home. It would take Bryce to help him find home again.

She was the only one who could do it.

CHAPTER EIGHT

"Kaegan, there's someone to see you."

Kaegan looked at Willa, who'd stuck her head in the door. "Who is it, Wil?"

"Bryce Witherspoon."

He looked at his watch. She would have gotten her flowers by now. The third arrangement he'd sent her. "Okay, send her in. And go ahead and take your lunch now."

"I just came from lunch."

"Take another one." The last thing he wanted was his employees being privy to anything Bryce might say. Although he had his own office, he knew voices carried. Faith Harris, his other office worker, had taken the day off, and Toby Franklin was on vacation.

Willa smiled. "You won't get an argument out of me. I think I'll go back to that dress shop and buy me something to wear to a party I'm going to this weekend."

"Do whatever rocks your boat," he said, standing. "Please send Bryce in."

He came around to sit on the edge of his desk and had to swallow twice when Bryce walked in. He reached behind him to grab his coffee cup and take a sip since his throat had gotten dry.

She'd walked into his office with her head held high, lips tight and a mass of hair around her shoulders. She didn't look happy, he thought, as his gaze roamed over her. She was wearing a printed dress, with a stylish navy blue jacket and navy blue pumps. She looked so damn good.

He stood. "Bryce, this is a surprise. I missed seeing you at your parents' café during lunch the last few Wednesdays. Your mom reminded me about those real-estate classes you started taking in New Orleans." There—he'd let her know he noticed her absence, as well as the fact he'd asked about her.

She squared her shoulders. "We need to talk, Kaegan."

"Go ahead, Bryce. I'm all yours."

He doubted she knew just how much he meant that. In his heart he was hers and always would be. He'd had a few weeks to dwell on what he wanted out of his life and he'd decided he wanted Bryce. He was well aware accomplishing such a thing wouldn't be easy. First, he had to earn back her trust, and he was working daily thinking of ways to do that. He wouldn't rush her. As far as he knew, although she dated, she wasn't involved in a serious relationship. He intended to make sure nothing changed with the latter. He would do whatever was needed to make things up to her. He knew now what he should have known all along. She was his past as well as his future.

"I want to talk to you about the flowers."

"What about them?"

"They are beautiful and all, and I want to thank you for them. However, you don't need to keep sending them. You've told me that you're sorry."

He nodded. "Yes, but you've yet to say you've forgiven me."

She frowned at him. "Fine, Kaegan. I forgive you. Please stop sending the flowers."

"So we're friends again?"

"No. We could never be friends."

He'd figured they could start with friendship while he proved that he was worthy of more. That he wanted more between them. "Why not?"

"I don't want you as my friend. Friends trust each other. They believe in each other and they are there for one another. Samuel was my friend and you tried making it into something dirty."

He sighed deeply. "I regret that and my only excuse is that I didn't know the nature of your relationship with him."

"I tried telling you, but even if I hadn't tried, it should not have mattered. You should have trusted in the nature and depth of my relationship with you. My love. My commitment. Remember doing this?" she said, holding up the nick on the third finger of her right hand. "That should have told you how much I valued not only what you and I shared, but what you, me and Vashti meant to each other. But especially with what you and I shared. I would never have betrayed you. You should have known that."

He rubbed his hands down his face as he leaned against the desk. "I know, but when I saw you wrap your arms around Samuel's neck, I thought the worst."

"I placed a kiss on his cheek and that was all."

He shoved his hands into the pockets of his jeans. "I didn't stay around to see where you would kiss him. I just knew that you would. When I saw you lean up toward him on tippy toes, I turned and walked away. I thought I had seen enough. Surely you can see how I could have misunderstood the situation."

She shook her head. "No, I don't see. You should have trusted me."

"I didn't know he was gay. He was a star athlete and adored by all the girls at school."

"It was a front he put on for others. No one knew but me.

When he found out you had broken off with me because of him, he felt guilty and told me to tell you the truth. That's why I caught the bus to see you. But that's all water under the bridge now because you didn't want to hear anything I had to say. And then there was that woman..."

"I didn't sleep with her that night, Bryce. I only left with her to make you think I would. I wanted to hurt you the way I thought you had hurt me."

"You succeeded in hurting me, Kaegan. It took me years to get over you and move on with my life. And then you returned to Catalina Cove, still believing the worst about me." She drew in a deep breath. "None of it matters anymore. I only came here today to say that I forgive you, so you can stop sending the flowers."

She turned and walked out of his office.

"Are you okay, Bryce?"

Bryce looked over at her mother. "I'm fine, Mom. Why do you ask?"

"You've been quiet."

Yes, she had been. After leaving Kaegan's office, she had gone home and changed clothes and come to the café to help out. She'd known Ry had taken the day off to attend one of Lil Ry's football games and her parents would be shorthanded with the afternoon and dinner crowd. Her father had worked with Duke in the kitchen, and Bryce and her mother had waited on tables.

It had gotten busy very quickly. This was the first chance they'd gotten to talk, but she wouldn't tell her mother anything. The last thing she needed was her parents worrying about her...and they would. Regardless that she was thirty-two, she was still the baby in the family. Her family liked Kaegan, and because they didn't know all the details of why she and Kaegan had broken up, they merely saw it as a communication problem.

She knew the way her parents' minds worked. In Kaegan they saw the young man who'd looked out for their daughter while growing up. He'd appeared on their doorstep every morning to walk her to school and back, from the time she'd been in first grade to when he'd left town for the marines.

Then there was the time her father liked reminding her, and anyone else who cared to listen, how Kaegan had all but saved her life during a bad hurricane. Luckily the massive storm had deviated from its course, otherwise it probably would have destroyed the cove. But water surges had still impacted the town. And when she had gotten caught up in it, when she had been out helping others to evacuate, it had been a sixteen-year-old Kaegan who'd maneuvered one of his father's boats through the streets of Catalina Cove to rescue her. Why was she remembering that now? She wasn't sure, but she was determined to banish all thoughts of Kaegan from her mind.

Behind her she heard the café door open, alerting her of new arrivals. Her mother smiled at her and said, "I'll let you take care of him, Bryce."

She frowned, turned around and looked right into Kaegan's eyes. So much for banishing him from her thoughts. She looked back at her mother. "No problem."

She left and greeted Kaegan. "Hello, Kaegan," she said, as if she hadn't seen him earlier that day. As if she hadn't told him that they could never share a friendship again.

"Hello, Bryce. Good seeing you."

"Why?" she asked, as she led him to an empty table.

"Just is."

When he sat down, she handed him a menu. "You want a beer to start things off?"

"Yes."

She walked off while thinking she had to get a grip where he was concerned. More than ever she was looking forward to meeting Jeremy Skinner for coffee next week. Jeremy had called a few days ago and they realized he'd be in New Orleans the day of her class. Bryce had suggested meeting up for that cup of coffee she owed him. She needed to place her concentration on any man other than Kaegan.

Moments later, when she returned with his beer, she couldn't help but notice he had rolled up the sleeves of his shirt to expose strong hairy arms. Arms that used to wrap around her. Hold her tight. Arms her fingers used to stroke.

The memories had forbidden desire trickling down her spine. For crying out loud, that was the last thing she needed, but obviously, her body didn't know that.

She placed the beer in front of him. For some reason her hands were shaking and the beer nearly sloshed out of the glass. Kaegan reached out and covered her hands with his to steady the beer mug. "Easy," he murmured in a low, throaty tone.

As far as she was concerned, there was nothing easy about waiting on him, and definitely nothing easy about the warm hand covering hers on a cold glass. She shouldn't feel heat from that, but she did. "I'm good now, Kaegan. You can take your hand away."

He did so slowly and she removed hers. Then for some reason she just stood there and watched him lift the glass and take his first sip. There was something erotic about seeing him do that. Something so arousing. And when he put down his beer mug, he glanced up at her and licked his lips. "That was good and just what I needed."

Bryce was certain what she needed was to have her head examined. She should cross the room and tell her mother to finish waiting on Kaegan, but that meant she would have to explain why. Clearing her throat, she said, "Do you know what you'd like to have this evening, Kaegan?"

"Yes. I'll have pork chops—marinated, boneless center-cut, the way I like them—smothered in gravy with dirty rice, red beans, okra and corn. And don't forget the corn bread."

She wondered where he intended to put all that food. "I won't forget the corn bread." And knowing her parents, they would send extra.

"And for starters I'd like a bowl of she-crab soup."

"Fine." She turned to walk off when he said her name. She whirled back around. "What, Kaegan?"

"I'll be wanting dessert later."

Then as she watched him, he picked up his beer mug and took a sip while she was held captive by his dark brown eyes. Was he using code words on her? Code words they'd created years ago? Words only the two of them knew the true meaning of? She'd known exactly what he'd meant when he said he wanted dessert later. Those were the times when she'd been his dessert.

She lifted her chin and, without saying anything, turned and walked off.

"I think it's time we have a good talk, don't you think?"

Kaegan lifted his gaze to find Chester Witherspoon sliding into the seat across from him. "It's about time for you to close the café, isn't it, Mr. Chester?"

"Already done. Duke's dropping his mom off home. Bryce just left and Ry took the evening off."

"Oh." Kaegan had finished eating but was hanging around, hoping he would get a chance to talk to Bryce, maybe even walk her to her car. He hadn't known she'd left already. With everyone gone and Kaegan the only customer, it seemed that Mr. Witherspoon had planned the perfect opportunity for them to have a private talk.

Chester Witherspoon was a big hulk of a man, but for some reason Kaegan had never feared him. Probably because he had such a friendly attitude and liked giving huge bear hugs.

"You hurt my daughter," Chester said bluntly.

Kaegan hadn't expected that. There was no accusation in the words. There wasn't even a question. It was a matter-of-fact statement, which demanded a matter-of-fact answer. So he gave one. "Yes, sir, I did. I was wrong to think at some point she betrayed me. I only found out the truth a few weeks ago."

The older man nodded. "I never knew the reason the two of you broke up, Kaegan. Bryce never said and her mother and I weren't ones to pry. We figured sooner or later she would tell us everything, but she never did. I guess for her it was better to keep it to herself. All we knew was that whatever happened between the two of you had left her crushed. At one point her brothers wanted to come find you and demand to know what happened, but Debbie and I convinced them to leave it alone and not take sides...especially when Bryce wasn't telling us anything."

The older man shifted in his seat and then said, "I would admit that when you moved back to town I was tempted to do just what I'm doing now. Have a man-to-man conversation with you and find out what the hell happened when I knew just how much you had loved Bryce. Debbie felt since you and Bryce were adults that we shouldn't pry. I've seen what could happen when parents stick their noses into their grown children's affairs. Had I listened to Debbie's parents, we would never have married. Debbie and I believed you truly loved our daughter and whatever was keeping you apart was a huge misunderstanding."

Kaegan nodded. "Yes, it was mainly on my part."

Chester didn't say anything for a long while, and then he

said, "I can only assume you're taking the necessary steps to win her back...or at least you're trying."

"Yes, I'm trying. But at the moment, she doesn't even want us to be friends."

Chester nodded as he stared into Kaegan's eyes. "Don't give up trying. Hopefully, she'll eventually come around. I never told you but I messed up with Debbie some years ago."

Kaegan quirked an eyebrow. "You did?"

"Yes. Before we married. I had made plans to break up...at her parents' suggestion. They claimed she would never embrace the idea of leaving Canada to live in the United States. I believed them. I'd begun missing my family and no longer had negative thoughts about going to war. I was ready to fight for my country if needed. Only thing, Debbie was pregnant and I didn't know it. She didn't intend to tell me, either, because she knew if she had, I would have married her. Since I hadn't asked her to marry me before then, she felt I would have married her because of the baby and not because I loved her."

Kaegan nodded. "How did you find out she was pregnant?"

"I overheard a conversation between her and her best friend. I got mad because she hadn't planned to tell me. That she would let me leave and not know she carried my child. I thought what she planned to do was unforgivable. Then there was another major issue. She was a Canadian girl who I thought would never move away with me to the States. That was a lie her parents told. But still, trying to get her to believe that I loved her was nearly impossible."

"How did you get her to change her mind about marrying you?"

The older man smiled. "It took a while. But I convinced her I couldn't live without her, and if she wouldn't go with me, then I would continue to make Canada my home. That's when I found out it never had been about her leaving Canada.

But still, since I do know how much she loves her homeland, I promised to take her back to Canada to visit her family as often as reasonably possible. It made her parents happy. Made them tolerable."

The man paused and then said, "Bryce thinks she has every reason not to trust you and be your friend again. You need to make her understand one thing."

"What?"

"The two of you being friends isn't an option. You got a nick on your finger to prove it."

At Kaegan's surprised expression, Chester said, "Yes, I know about that, too, since it was my knife that was used. I missed it and then one day it miraculously returned to my toolbox. And then there was the fact that you, Vashti and Bryce were all walking around with a bandage on the same finger."

The older man shook his head, grinning. "When it came to doing things behind my and Debbie's backs, you and Bryce failed each and every time."

Kaegan didn't say anything, but he couldn't help wondering if perhaps the Witherspoons knew all of his and Bryce's secrets from the past. He always thought they were smarter than most parents.

"And another thing," Chester said, interrupting Kaegan's thoughts. "Bryce is a lot like her mother. Sweet as pie just as long as you don't cross her. When that happens she can be as hard as nails and stubborn as sin. Then you have to all but pour honey all over her to get her sweet again. You got your work cut out for you. Winning my daughter back won't be easy. She can't be rushed and she has to believe you're sincere in everything you say and do."

The older man then looked at his watch. "I've said my piece. The rest is up to you, Kaegan."

Kaegan nodded. Yes, the rest was up to him.

CHAPTER NINE

Bryce saw Jeremy the moment he walked into the restaurant, and when he saw her, he smiled. She smiled back and he began strolling in her direction.

The man was handsome, but he didn't have those drop-dead gorgeous features that Kaegan possessed. Not that she should be comparing him to Kaegan.

"Good seeing you again, Bryce," Jeremy said when he reached her table and extended his hand out to her.

"Good seeing you again, too, Jeremy," she said, taking his hand and immediately noting she felt nothing. Not that warm, sensual feeling she was hoping for from his touch. "I'm glad you could join me."

"Thanks for the invitation."

"Hey, it's the least I could do for your help that day," she said.

"I was glad to do it. Did you get that tire fixed?"

"Yes, I did. At least, one of my brothers did. He took it in and got it repaired for me."

"You got siblings?" he asked her.

"Yes. Two brothers, and you?"

"One sister, and trust me, she's a handful. In fact, she can be rather difficult at times."

"Older or younger?"

"Younger, thank goodness. I couldn't imagine how things would be if she was the older one. She's twenty-five and still has a lot of growing up to do."

Bryce wondered what he meant by that, but decided not to ask him. She, on the other hand, always thought that her brothers were more mature than they should be. That was why it hadn't come as a surprise to her or her parents when they'd married right out of high school. No need to say Ry and Duke had settled down since there was never a time they'd been unsettled. Her sisters-in-law were lucky women and they both knew it.

At that moment the waitress appeared to take their order. "They have pretty good pastries here, if you'd like to order one in addition to the coffee," Bryce said, smiling over at him. "Today it's on me."

He shook his head. "Thanks, but I ate a big lunch. Tomorrow is the last day for my business seminar and the firm I work for always throws a big luncheon the day before."

"Sounds nice. What sort of work do you do?"

"I'm an attorney. In addition to Shreveport, my firm also has offices in Baton Rouge, Houston and Phoenix."

"Sounds interesting."

"It is. I'm a multilicensed attorney in several states, so I travel quite a bit handling various court cases. What about you? From your business card I see you're in real estate."

"Yes, and one of the things I intend to do is be multilicensed so I can sell property in several states. That's the reason for the classes I'm taking. I take my exam next month. The instructor is covering a lot of material and I hope I will be able to remember it all."

"There's no doubt in my mind that you will."

"Thanks."

For the next thirty minutes he told her about various cases he'd handled and trips abroad he'd taken. She told him about her parents' café and how she spent her leisure time reading. Her life definitely seemed boring compared to his. He also told her his parents were deceased and his sister was his only relative.

She glanced at her watch. "I need to get going if I want to make it to class on time. I enjoyed sharing coffee with you, Jeremy."

"And I with you. How about if we do it again sometime?"

She smiled. "I'd like that."

He smiled, as well. "Good. How about if I call you in two weeks? I'll be back in this area then."

"Sounds like a good plan."

His smile widened. "Great. It sounds like a good plan to me, too."

"Tell me about the dress you bought for the charity ball."

Bryce chuckled. I can do better," she said, pulling her phone out of her purse. "I took a picture of it."

She pulled it up on her phone and showed it to Vashti. "It's gorgeous, Bryce. I love it."

Vashti had invited Bryce to join her for lunch at Shelby by the Sea. It was a beautiful day and the breeze from the ocean felt divine. They were enjoying apple cider and grilled turkey sandwiches on the gazebo. "Thanks. I knew I wanted it when I walked into that store in New Orleans."

"And you're still not bringing a date?"

"No."

"Why didn't you invite that guy you've met for coffee? He sounds nice and I would love to meet him."

"We've only met for coffee that one time, although we're supposed to meet again when he comes back through in a couple of weeks. Jeremy is nice but I'm not ready to take our relationship beyond the occasional coffee meeting."

"Oh."

What she hadn't told Vashti was that although Jeremy was handsome, intelligent and a good conversationalist, he hadn't done anything for her. She had felt nothing. Not even a twinge of an attraction.

Bryce glanced over at Vashti. "I ran into Marcel this week while in New Orleans."

Vashti lifted an eyebrow. "The one who dumped you for his ex?"

Bryce frowned. "Well, dang, Vash, do you have to sound so brutal?"

Vashti grinned. "I was just repeating what you told me."

Bryce knew Vashti was right. That was what she'd told her. "His ex-wife still had her hooks in him, but I didn't know it at the time. Now they've remarried and have two kids. In fact, he said she's expecting their third."

"You talked to him?"

"Yes. I have no problem doing so. I am so over him. I honestly doubt I was ever into him." She glanced over at Vashti. "You don't know how lucky you are. You go to bed with a husband at night and get the real thing, Vash. I depend on my dreams to keep me sane. My very hot dreams. I haven't had sex in almost four years. Do you know how hard that is for me?"

Vashti nodded. "I can imagine."

"That's why when I see Kaegan sometimes I get hot, remembering how things used to be between us. Isn't that awful considering what he thought about me?"

"All of us have wants and desires that are often hard for us to control, Bryce. With that said, I invited you here today for a reason. I have something to tell you."

Bryce looked at her expectantly. "What?"

"I'm pregnant."

"OMG!" Bryce excitedly got up, went around the table and gave Vashti a huge hug. "I am so happy for you. When did you find out?"

"This morning. I took an at-home pregnancy test, but Sawyer claims it was a waste of time and money because he already knew."

"Have you told the girls yet?"

"Not yet. They're flying in this weekend for the charity ball. Reid requested their presence since he's being honored there for all his charitable contributions."

"Well, this calls for a celebration. No wonder you suggested apple cider instead of wine today. You are living your dream, kiddo. You always wanted four kids. I am so happy for you."

"Thanks, and more than anything, Bryce, I want you to start living your dream, as well." And with a mischievous gleam in her eye, Vashti added, "Even those hot ones you say you're having."

CHAPTER TEN

Bryce glanced around the ballroom. The decorating committee had done a fantastic job in making the entire room look festive. Suddenly, she felt a tingling sensation in the pit of her stomach. She looked beyond where Vashti and Ashley were sitting and saw Kaegan. He had entered the ballroom flanked by Sawyer and Ray.

Curious as to what she was staring at, Vashti turned and smiled. "I don't believe it."

Bryce bit down on her bottom lip. Neither did she. Kaegan was the last person she'd expected to see here tonight. In all the years he'd lived in the cove, she'd never known him to attend one of these types of functions. It wasn't that he was antisocial, per se; it was that he just didn't feel comfortable with certain crowds of people.

She couldn't help it when her gaze singled him out and roamed over him from head to toe. He was wearing a dark suit and his hair was flowing around his shoulders. He didn't just look handsome—he looked dashing. It seemed as if all eyes were on the three men who together were cotton-candy extraordinaire. But it was quite obvious that Ray had his eyes directed on Ashley, Sawyer had his on Vashti…and, heaven help her, Kaegan's gaze was directly on her.

Emotions were at war within her. A part of her couldn't help the sensations flowing through her. Sensations only he could stimulate. That fact had been proved time and time again with other men she'd dated. None could arouse her the way Kaegan could. Over the years, even those she'd thought were top contenders had failed miserably.

She wanted to break eye contact but couldn't, so she sat there transfixed under his stare as she watched his approach. He would be sitting at their table, which was a logical choice since he was close friends with Sawyer and Ray and he felt comfortable with them.

She could easily go sit at the table with her parents, but why should she? She and Kaegan had no reason not to be cordial to each other. He had apologized for believing she had betrayed him, and she had accepted his apology. If nothing else, tonight would be the perfect place to show she had moved on and he wasn't on her radar.

Now she wished she had brought a date. At this point even the thought of Jeremy wasn't a bad one after all. He had called two nights ago to let her know he would be back in New Orleans again next week and to confirm their date. This time he wanted to do dinner rather than just coffee.

Unfortunately, her instructor had offered to give an extra instructional hour to the students to prepare them for the big exam in a few weeks. She told him that she couldn't take the time for dinner, but could make time to meet for coffee. She promised a rain check on dinner. So they would be meeting for coffee again next week. Now a part of her wished she would have invited him here tonight. Too late to think of that now.

"Look who we ran into in the parking lot," Sawyer said,

grinning. "I almost didn't recognize him without his jeans, T-shirt and fisherman boots."

"And don't forget the ponytail," Ray said, grinning, as well.

"Oh, yeah, the ponytail," Sawyer said. "I think you clean up well, Kaegan."

"Thanks." He then looked at them. "Good evening, Bryce, Ashley and Vashti. You ladies look nice."

"Thanks, Kaegan, for your compliment. You look nice tonight, as well," she said, after Ashley and Vashti exchanged greetings with him.

There—he'd given her a compliment and she'd given him one back. Maybe she'd be able to get through this night after all.

Kaegan tried not to stare at Bryce, but found himself doing so anyway. Even now as he sat there sipping his beer, half listening to the conversation going on around him, he was staring at her on the dance floor. He'd known the exact moment some man had approached the table and asked her to dance. He hadn't liked it one damn bit.

"You know you can cut in, if you want," Sawyer said in a low voice as he leaned over. "It's perfectly legal and not against the law."

Kaegan shook his head. Leave it to Sawyer to look at everything as a matter of law and order. "I'm fine, Sawyer."

"Okay. It was just a suggestion."

He didn't say anything. Instead he sat there and continued to stare at Bryce and the man dancing. Bryce didn't look his way and maybe it was a good thing she didn't. He knew he had no right to feel jealous or territorial. Hadn't she said they weren't even friends?

More than once, he tried looking away and couldn't do so. Instead his gaze was fixated on her. She was wearing a long red gown with the top and bottom covered in silver-covered sequins. And he thought now, as he'd always thought, that she was beautiful. Tonight, she had to be the sexiest woman he'd seen not just in a long time, but ever.

When the song came to an end, she smiled at her dance partner and turned to walk off the floor. The man caught hold of her wrist to bring her back to him as the live band began playing another song. This one slow. Kaegan felt his hand grip the wineglass he was holding, and then suddenly, he set it on the table with a thump.

When everyone looked over at him, he stood and said, "I think I'll go dance." He didn't say with whom and figured they all knew. If they didn't, they were about to find out.

Ray then said, "I wondered how long it was going to take you to come to your senses."

Kaegan frowned. Come to his senses? Had Ray been out on his boat too damn long today? He *had* come to his senses. It was Bryce who'd accepted his apology with conditions. Mainly, they could not be friends. He was still trying to figure out just how that was supposed to work when they had the same circle of close acquaintances. Maybe it was time he asked her.

When he reached Bryce, he tapped the man on the shoulder. The look he gave the man all but told him to haul ass. The man evidently got the message, because he nodded and walked off. Kaegan then drew Bryce into his arms.

She didn't say anything to him. Didn't even look at him. He was fine with that for now. If she was stewing because of the change in dance partners, he would let her stew. She was in his arms now and for him that was what mattered. It was his arms wrapped around her. But he wanted to get closer to her. A decent close, but close nonetheless.

"I don't think Herbert liked you cutting in," she finally said.

He was about to tell her that he didn't give a royal damn

what the man named Herbert liked. Instead he asked, "What about you, Bryce? Do you have a problem with me cutting in?"

When she looked into his eyes, he knew. She was struggling with emotions that she didn't want to feel. Only a man who knew Bryce as well as he did would recognize that a war was raging inside of her, and he understood. It had been that way when he'd thought she had wronged him. Although he'd tried to eradicate his love for her from his heart, he'd never succeeded.

There had been times when he'd looked at her and their gazes met, when he'd been close to her and they'd accidentally touched, that had let him know, even though he'd wished otherwise, that she was still in his blood. He figured it was the same way with her. She wanted to bar him from her life, her thoughts, her well-being, but doing so wouldn't be easy. He regretted the emotional conflict she was going through, but it gave him hope. Reclaiming her love would be a process and he had to be patient because he was going for keeps. More specifically, he wanted forever.

For a long moment he thought she wouldn't answer, and then she said, "No, I don't have a problem with you cutting in. I was getting tired of listening to him brag about all his achievements anyway."

"So he was trying to impress you?"

"Yes. I guess that's what he was trying to do."

He smiled because she'd said it with that but-I-really-didn't-want-to-be-bothered attitude, one she could use on everyone else, except him. The slow, seductive melody filled the room and instinctively he pulled her closer to him. She, in turn, pressed her cheek against his hard chest. Glancing down, he saw that her eyes were closed as they slowly swayed to the music. He could feel every inch of her curvaceous body plastered to his. The way he was holding her seemed to make every square inch of her body touch every square inch of his. The full awareness of her in his arms this way charged him with a heated rush through all parts of his body.

Resting his cheek against the crown of her head, he closed his eyes, as well, absorbing the music into his mind while holding the woman he knew he still loved close to his heart. Their movements were invigoratingly slow and stimulating to the point where he felt himself get aroused. There was no way she could not feel his erection pressing at the juncture of her thighs. Just like she had to know there was no way he couldn't feel the hardened tips of her nipples pressed into his chest.

It was quite obvious the sexual chemistry flowing between them was at a volatile point, which prompted him to give in to temptation and wrap his arms more securely around her. On the drive over he had wondered if she would dance with him because, more than anything, this was what he'd wanted. It was worth coming to an event he'd never been to before, one he'd shunned in the past. When he'd driven into the parking lot, just knowing she was in the building had made it worthwhile. When he realized the song was about to come to an end, he opened his eyes.

"Did Sawyer show you the gifts out in the parking lot that Reid bought his granddaughters?" she asked, tilting her head back to look at him.

He understood what she was doing. With the music about to come to an end, they needed to concentrate on unstimulated bodies. "Yes. I don't know who was more excited about those new cars, the girls or Sawyer."

She chuckled and he loved the sound. "According to Vashti, the cars were supposed to be Christmas presents, but Reid couldn't wait to give them to Jade and Kia."

"That's what I heard. I can't imagine having a grandfather

who's able to afford not one, but two Tesla sports cars. Must be nice," he said.

"Yes, he spoils them, but Sawyer and Vashti, along with the Harrises, help keep Jade and Kia pretty well grounded. They'd already told the girls the cars won't be parked on any college campus, but will remain here to drive whenever they are home."

"And I guess they know what happens if their father—who happens to be sheriff—catches them speeding."

Bryce smiled. "Yes, they know."

The dance came to an end, and Bryce moved to head back to where they'd been seated, when he tightened his hold on her hand. "Take a walk in the garden with me, please."

She looked at him and he wondered if she would deny his request. Nodding, she allowed him to lead her toward the set of double French doors that led outside.

"Any reason you wanted me to come outside with you, Kaegan?" Bryce asked the man walking by her side. So far they'd checked out a number of various plants known to grow in Louisiana soil. The night was filled with the sounds of crickets, frogs and katydids, and the scents of begonias, zinnias and birds-of-paradise.

"I needed some air and wanted you to join me."

She nodded, remembering another time he'd said those same words. It had been at her sixteenth birthday party and the first social event he'd ever attended off the bayou. Typically, the Pointe-au-Chien tribe kept to themselves and didn't feel the need to socialize with the townsfolk. There was nothing written in stone but it had been a practice evidently understood. Unfortunately, she and Vashti hadn't gotten the memo when they decided to make Kaegan their new best friend in first grade.

Bryce had been aware that a few people had frowned upon

their close friendship, but neither her parents nor Vashti's parents and Aunt Shelby had cared what those few single-minded people thought. She had to say it was one of the few times Vashti's parents had shown they really had spines. Most people in the cove genuinely liked Kaegan and had accepted that the three of them were inseparable as they were growing up. However, both she and Vashti had known Kaegan was uncomfortable attending social events. That was why he'd avoided such things in the past and she was surprised that he had shown up tonight.

"Thanks for dancing with me, Bryce."

She looked over at him, wanting to say he didn't have to thank her and that was what friends were for, when she remembered she'd told him they weren't friends anymore. She had truly accepted his apology, but he hadn't regained his friendship status with her. Her trust, once broken, was a hard thing to regain, and she didn't think she would survive if Kaegan broke it again. "You're welcome, Kaegan."

He didn't say anything for a moment as they continued to walk around the flower garden. She had a feeling that he had something on his mind. Knowing she wouldn't be fully prepared for whatever it was, she was about to suggest they go back inside, when he said, "More than anything, I'd like for us to get back together, Bryce."

She stopped walking and stared at him, not believing he would say such a thing. One dance where she'd foolishly lost herself in the moment, where she'd obviously sent out unintentional vibes, and he thought that was all it would take for a comeback. Okay, she would even admit for a moment she had enjoyed being in his arms a little too much. Four years without male contact could probably do that to you. However, with that being said, she felt it was time to reiterate her position.

"That is something that won't happen, Kaegan. We had

our time, but forever wasn't in our future like we'd thought. Accept it and move on, like I have."

He stared at her and then said, "Couples have problems, Bryce. Not making light of ours, but the key is they try and work things out."

She shook her head. "There is nothing to work out. Some things that are broken can't be repaired, Kaegan."

"Why are you willing to give up on us so easily?"

His question made something inside her snap. Ten years of hurt and anger came shooting out and she couldn't hold back her emotions. "You want to accuse me of giving up so easily? Well, let me tell you a thing or two, Kaegan. I had ten years to feel the hurt and pain of knowing the man I'd loved thought I was nothing but a slut. You were so convinced you had caught me red-handed with another guy. It was as if you wanted your father to be right about something, after years of being wrong. And you allowed him to use me to do it. Did you know he even called me a slut once to my face?"

She saw the stricken look that suddenly appeared on his face, but she didn't care. She felt tears trying to fall but refused to let them. "You gave Mr. Chambray that power because of your mistreatment of me. You'd conveniently forgotten about all those times I was there for you when he treated you like crap. Yet you allowed his lies and what you thought you saw that night to come between us and destroy what we had."

She sighed, not able to stop the tears now. "You didn't just break my heart, Kaegan. You destroyed it. You had been my only boyfriend ever. The one guy who was supposed to love me and believe in me, yet you didn't. You were quick to believe the worst about me and the very thought of that devastated me. I never thought you would do me that way. Reject me so callously. Make me feel like I was nothing to you. That all our years together meant nothing. I had nobody to talk to. Vashti was attending college in New York and I was too hurt to tell my parents or my brothers anything. So I went through that time alone."

She paused a moment, trying to collect herself, and then said, "Samuel, the same Samuel you accused of being my lover, was there for me. He became worried about me to the point where he persuaded me to go see one of the therapists on campus. The same one who'd helped him deal with a lot of things. In my senior year of college when I should have been happy because of my accomplishments, I was fighting depression and struggling with self-esteem. Because of you, my confidence took a nosedive."

"Bryce, I—"

"No, Kaegan. No more apologizing. I want you to stand here and listen. I graduated without you being there and I came back to Catalina Cove. Everyone wondered what had happened between us and I couldn't tell them that the man I'd loved all of my life thought I was shit."

She swiped at her tears. "So don't you dare say that I'm willing to give up on us so easily. You gave up on us ten years ago. And now that you find out the truth you want me to just fall in line. It doesn't work that way for me. You said you were sorry and I've accepted that, but I meant what I said about not wanting you in my life as a friend or anything else. You are a liability to me. You are the cause of so much pain. Pain that I simply refuse to go through a second time. We can never pick up where we left off because I doubt I could love you again. You destroyed my ability to not only love you, but to love anyone, Kaegan. A part of me will always resent you for doing that. Now if you will excuse me, I'm going back inside."

CHAPTER ELEVEN

Kaegan pulled his truck into Bryce's yard and came to a stop. He glanced at the package on the seat beside him. It was dinner her mother had prepared and asked him to bring. He knew Mrs. Witherspoon and figured she was well aware that he was the last person her daughter would want to see today, yet she'd asked the favor of him anyway.

After opening the truck door, he got out and grabbed the bag off the seat beside him. As he made his way to the door, he thought about the conversation they'd shared in the garden at the dance. She had unloaded a lot that night and she'd poured out the depth of her pain and her disappointment in him. Now he understood why she didn't want them to be friends. She didn't just not trust him with her heart—she refused to trust him with her well-being. Now, more than anything, he had to prove to her that he wasn't that young Kaegan who'd grown up with insecurities that he'd allowed his father the power to play on them. He was a much older, wiser and more secure Kaegan.

At least he'd gotten her to forgive him. Now reclaiming their friendship was the next step, and after that, her heart.

He had to prove to her that he valued her heart and that the next time she entrusted it to him he would take better care of it than he did before.

Reaching the door, he knocked, and soon it was opened. Bryce frowned at him. Regardless of her agitated expression, his breath left his lungs the moment he saw her. He'd definitely been unprepared for the raw beauty of the features staring at him in annoyance.

It looked like she'd just released her hair from that ponytail she sometimes wore, and it hung in a wild mass around her shoulders. That style brought out the beauty of her green eyes. The color of her eyes had always captivated him, along with her strong cheekbones and full lips. She wasn't wearing any makeup. She seldom did and none was needed. For a fleeting moment he was tempted to reach up and stroke what looked like flustered cheeks.

She was in her bare feet and wearing a pullover sweater and leggings. He always thought of her as beautiful, curvy and leggy.

"What are you doing here, Kaegan?"

Her tone matched the look on her face. "Making a delivery," he said, quickly easing by her to enter her home.

"Hey, I didn't invite you in here."

"No, you didn't, but like I said, I'm making a delivery. Your mom sent this," he said, holding up the bag. The aroma of the food filled the room. "Ms. Debbie said you were studying for some exam and wouldn't take time to eat and asked me to bring this to you."

"She did, did she?" she asked, taking the package from him.

"Yes. She also made me promise to hang around and make sure you eat it."

He could tell from her mutinous expression that that didn't go over well with her. "I don't need you to stay to make sure I eat, Kaegan."

He smiled. "Evidently your mom thought otherwise."

She glared at him for a minute, then said, "Well, I don't agree with her. You can let yourself out. Goodbye." She then walked off toward her kitchen.

He glanced around and saw the books spread over her coffee table. Studying had never been Bryce's thing. But it was his.

He glanced at Bryce in her kitchen. From where he stood he could see her taking down a plate from the cabinet. Watching her stretch her body while reaching into the cabinet was such a turn-on. Maybe he should leave, like she suggested. "Take a plate down for me. Your mom sent enough for the both of us."

She jerked around and her glare was back. "Why are you still here? I thought I told you goodbye."

He nodded. "You did, but I'm more afraid of Ms. Debbie than I am of you. Besides, I can help you."

She narrowed her gaze. "Help with what?"

"Your studying. I know how lousy you are at it and how good I am."

Kaegan saw the hint of a smile touch her lips. She was smart and intelligent, but when it came to studying, she struggled. They both knew it. Back in high school they would cram together the night before an exam to guarantee that they both aced it.

She didn't say anything for a long moment, merely stared at him across the breakfast bar. Kaegan held his breath and only released it when she turned, reached into the cabinet and grabbed another plate. "Why would you want to help me?" she asked, over her shoulder.

He chose his words carefully. "Because I can remember a time, many years ago, when you helped me."

She placed both plates on the table along with eating utensils. "Vash and I both did."

"Yes, and today I'm helping you out as a way to thank you.

Next week it might be Vashti, although I believe Sawyer's pretty much got his wife protected. We don't have to worry about her parents acting crazy with her any longer."

"Oh, they're still acting crazy. I guess you've heard about their latest stunt."

Yes, he had. "All I have to say is they'd never met the likes of Sawyer Grisham," he said, grinning. "They can act crazy, but if it means protecting his family, Sawyer will act crazier, trust me."

He heard her chuckle and the sound did something to his insides. Made him wish for something he was determined to one day have again; namely, her in his life. After he'd returned to the party from the garden it was as if she'd disappeared and he'd known she was trying to put distance between them for a while. He had gotten drawn into conversations with Ray, Sawyer and their wives—people he felt comfortable with.

Bryce had returned an hour later and claimed to everyone she had wanted to mingle a bit and to give her parents, brothers and sisters-in-law some of her time. At least she hadn't accepted a dance with any other guy during the night. Reid had been honored with a special award and he'd brought Gloria on stage to introduce her to everyone as his future wife. His granddaughters had also been called on stage with him, but they hadn't needed any introductions since that scandal was old news.

"Kaegan?"

He glanced over at Bryce, bringing his thoughts back to the present. "Yes?"

"Since Mom sent enough for the both of us and I'm tired of pulling my hair out while trying to wrap my mind around that real-estate exam…and since I recall that you do have a simpler way of studying, I'll take you up on your offer and appreciate you for making it. However, let's get one thing clear—there's nothing going on between us. Understood?"

He held her gaze while thinking more than anything he wished he could kiss that pout off her face. "Yes, I understand. May I use one of your bathrooms to wash up for dinner?"

She nodded. "Yes. There's a bathroom down the hall, the first door on your right."

"Thanks."

When he returned moments later he saw she had filled both plates with food, which consisted of red beans and rice, pork chops, Cajun cabbage and jalapeño corn bread. She had also poured iced tea into their glasses. She looked over at him when he entered the kitchen.

"I think my helping you study should get me more than just thanks," he said.

She glared at him and he could imagine what she was thinking. "Something like what?"

"Friendship. Don't you think I'm entitled to that at least?"

She sat down, and when he didn't join her, she looked over at him and said, "I need to think about that friendship piece, Kaegan."

Considering that a huge win, he decided not to press his luck anymore. Sitting down at the table, he glanced over at her and said, "Fine. You do that." It was all he could do to keep a smile off his face.

"Name at least three types of real-estate scams, Bryce."

Bryce scrunched up her forehead. "I should know this. I just read about it yesterday, Kaegan," she said, then ran frustrated fingers through her hair.

"Hey, just relax your mind while I give you a hint," he said, stretching out on her living-room floor.

"Okay." Bryce didn't mind that he'd made himself comfortable for the past hour. At the moment all she cared about was that, thanks to his good studying techniques, she was actually retaining most of the stuff.

"What were the first names of the three girls in our eighth-grade class who were bona fide bullies?"

She rolled her eyes. "Oh, that's easy. Rita, Monique and Faye."

"Right. If you remember that then you will ace that question."

She frowned again. "How?"

"I asked you to name at least three types of real-estate scams. If you can, remember Rita for rental, Monique for mortgage and Faye for foreclosure. Those are the three types of scams. Rental, mortgage and foreclosure. There are others, but if you remember at least three, you're good."

Bryce grinned, shaking her head. He'd been giving her word-association tactics for most of the answers to questions she would get stumped on. So far it was working. "Who would have guessed those three bullies would be helping me years later to ace an exam."

"From what I understand, they've changed. I ran into Rita when I was stationed in Mississippi. She's living in Biloxi and is a principal of a high school."

"A principal of a high school? After all the trouble she gave our principal, Mr. Harding? You got to be kidding."

Kaegan laughed. "No, I'm not. I asked if she kept up with Monique and Faye and she said that she did. Monique is a dentist, married, the mother of three and living in Texas. Faye is a divorced mother of two and lives in Oklahoma. She owns a chain of smoothie shops in that state."

He shifted his body into a more comfortable position and said, "I gather from what Rita said, they still maintain a close friendship and get together for a girls' trip every year. She admitted they aren't proud of their past, which is why they've never attended a class reunion since moving away for college."

Bryce shrugged. "That shouldn't keep them from returning home if they wanted to. I often wondered what happened to them. But then, I could never talk Vashti into coming back to a class reunion, either. When she left she swore never to come back. You did hear about the holiday class-reunion committee being formed, right?"

"Yes. I heard about it."

She wondered if he planned to attend. It wouldn't surprise her if he didn't. She recalled a time he hated Catalina Cove High School. The way some of the students, parents and teachers had treated Vashti when she'd gotten pregnant had infuriated him. Kaegan had always been loyal to his friends and at the time she and Vashti had been the only friends he had.

It occurred to her then why it bothered him that she could not accept a friendship between them. He'd had few friends in his life. Sawyer and Ray were his close friends now, but he needed the originals, as well. Namely, her and Vashti. They had been as protective of him as he'd been of them.

At that moment an idea formed in her head. "I'm thinking about joining the reunion committee. I think it will be fun trying to get others to return to Catalina Cove for the holidays."

"That's a good idea. I think you would be great on the committee. I hope Rita, Monique and Faye will come this time," he said. "At one time or another, all of us have done some pretty stupid stuff while growing up." He paused for a moment, glanced over at her and then added, "Some of us have done stupid stuff as adults, as well."

She knew he meant how quick he'd been to believe she'd betrayed him. To give him credit, at least he hadn't wasted time apologizing when he'd found out the truth. And he had sincerely been remorseful; she was sure of it. Still, a part of her hadn't been ready to accept his apology at the time. It had taken her a while but she'd come around. Forgiving didn't mean reconciliation, and she had rejected the idea that they could ever be friends again. Yet here he was helping her in an area where she needed help. He'd known, and in simple Kaegan Chambray style, he'd delivered. She'd retained more information studying with him than she could have on her own.

"What about you, Kaegan?"

He looked over at her. "What about me?"

"Would you consider going to the holiday class reunion?"

He shrugged. "Not sure."

She didn't say anything for a minute, and then she said, "I have an idea. Like I told you, they are asking for volunteers to work on the committee. I will work on it if you will."

He stared at her for a long moment and then he shrugged his shoulders. "Okay."

She lifted an eyebrow. "You would do it?"

He nodded. "Yes, I will do it. Now let's get back to studying."

An hour or so later, Bryce watched as Kaegan closed the book she'd been studying from. "That's enough studying for tonight," he finally said. "You don't want to overload your brain."

Knowing he was right, she eased off the sofa. "I appreciate you taking the time to help me study and I want to thank you again."

"No need to thank me. I enjoyed it and it reminded me of old times," he said, getting up off the floor and stretching.

She wished he wouldn't do that, since it placed a lot of emphasis on what a fine physique he had. She really shouldn't be thinking about stuff like that, but it was hard not to do so when such eye-candy masculinity was on display.

"Will you be studying tomorrow?" he asked her.

She nodded. "Yes. My teacher canceled class today so we could study as much as we can. That means I'll be studying the rest of this week, including the weekend."

"Isn't the exam on Wednesday?"

"No. That was my class night. The exam will be administered on Monday evening at one of the test centers on campus."

"Then if it's okay with you, I'll come back tomorrow," he said, moving toward her front door.

She followed. "It's fine with me if you have the time, Kaegan. You helped me a lot tonight, but I wouldn't want to infringe on your time."

"You won't be. Once I get home from work I usually don't have a lot to do."

She wondered if it must be lonely for him out there on the bayou by himself. Since his mother passed away a few years ago, he had no family, which was probably why he came into town and ate at her parents' café most of the time. "How are things going with your business?"

His lips tilted in a smile. "Good. We took on a big client this year, and I had to hire a couple of new guys, just to keep up with the orders."

They had made it to her door. He opened it and turned back to her. "Take a shower, drink a glass of wine to relax your mind, and then go to bed and get a good night's sleep."

She smiled. "I will. Thanks again."

He waved as he walked out the door and sprinted down her steps. When he reached his truck, he glanced over his shoulder and saw she was still standing there. "'Bye, Kaegan."

"'Bye, Bryce."

Bryce closed the door and leaned against it while listening to the sound of his truck's engine. Tonight he had helped her study the way an old friend might and she refused to think letting him do so was a mistake. And she had persuaded him to work on the holiday class-reunion committee with her. Nobody, not even Vashti, would believe he had agreed to do such a thing. Smiling at the thought, she decided to do as he suggested and take a shower and drink a glass of wine before going to bed.

She then remembered the missed phone call earlier. She'd been too absorbed in her studying to take the call, thinking it was probably Vashti. Going into her living room, she grabbed the phone off the coffee table, where she'd placed it earlier.

It had been from Jeremy. They had met for coffee again last week, and although she had enjoyed his company, she knew that was as far as things went with them. She listened to his voice message. He confirmed he'd gotten her message from earlier, letting him know her instructor had canceled the class today, and for that reason she wouldn't be meeting him for coffee before class, like they'd planned. He'd also said he would be in New Orleans for two more days and would love to see her and take her to dinner if she had the time. He asked her to text him if that could be arranged. Unfortunately, right now she didn't have the time.

Jeremy was a nice guy and she enjoyed their conversations over coffee the times they'd met. However, she knew she could never see him as anything more than a friend. She had a feeling he was hoping for more, but the vibes just weren't there.

Deciding to phone him instead of texting, she punched in his number only for her call to immediately go to voice mail. She thanked him for the invitation to dinner and then told him that although she had enjoyed her time with him, she would be busy studying for a while and after that she would be focusing on building her career as a multistate Realtor and wouldn't have time for much else.

She hoped he got the message since she hadn't invited him to come to Catalina Cove to see her or asked for a rain check. The one thing she refused to do was lead any man on. Jeremy was good-looking, had a nice personality and a good job. He was a good catch for any woman looking for a man she'd want to get serious about. However, for her something was missing.

She never felt any sparks around him. Not even strokes of sensations swirling around in her tummy, and she couldn't see anything serious ever developing between them. Satisfied with the message she had left him, she headed toward her bedroom to take a shower.

Kaegan brought his truck to a stop at a traffic light and smiled as he recalled the two hours he'd spent with Bryce. He thought of how he would throw several questions out to her to stimulate her mind and how she would pace the floor before answering.

He had eventually gotten her to quit pacing and focus...so that he could stay focused, as well. It had been hard watching her lithe and graceful movements and not concentrating on her hot-as-sin curves. She even had pretty feet with painted toes.

Watching her lounge on her sofa as she answered his questions had been challenging, as well. He was glad when she'd stretched her long legs out on the ottoman in front of him.

And when she'd smoothed a frustrated hand through her hair whenever one of his questions would stump her, her already tousled hair looked even sexier.

She would never know how he'd fought the urge to reach out and trace a finger along her ankles and take his own hands and rake his fingers through her hair. Then there were those times when he'd analyzed the shape of her mouth, remembering how he loved devouring her lips.

Drawing in a deep breath, Kaegan knew he needed to take the same advice he'd given her. When he got home he would take a shower, but instead of wine he would grab a beer out the fridge and then go to bed to get a good night's sleep. At least he would try. There was no doubt in his mind that he would be dreaming about Bryce.

He then thought about something else he'd done tonight.

He had actually volunteered to work on that committee with her. He, of all people, who hadn't even liked his high school when he'd attended. Only Bryce and Vashti had made the time bearable. He knew the kids but doubted they would even remember him. But he refused to let that stop him because he thought being on that committee was an essential piece of winning back his friend. He had to believe that stepping out of his comfort zone would be worth it. He'd done it that night when he'd decided to attend that charity ball. It hadn't been so bad and he had gotten to spend time with Bryce. She had even unloaded some stuff he had needed to hear.

Something Vashti had said stuck with him. She was right. It was time to let Bryce get to know the man he was now and for him to get to know her as the woman she'd become.

CHAPTER TWELVE

"I think you're ready, Bryce. You answered every single question I tossed out at you. You're going to ace it," Kaegan said confidently.

Bryce drew in a deep breath, not as certain of her abilities as Kaegan. If she did ace the exam, she would credit her success to his study techniques. For the last three evenings he had picked up dinner from her parents' café and shared a meal with her before hitting the books.

He drilled her endlessly, gave her word associations that she could remember and made up flash cards to use for those questions she still had difficulty answering. "I honestly hope so, Kaegan. I'm tired of studying so hard."

"It will be worth it to get your multistate-Realtor license, right?"

She knew the answer to that without thinking. "Yes."

"Then don't start doubting yourself. You know the material. All you have to do is apply what you know. Did your instructor give the class a hint of what the makeup of the test would be like?" he asked, shifting in his place on her floor. That was his usual place to stretch out on her floor. Hers was the sofa with her legs extended across the ottoman. It was hard to believe just a few months ago they couldn't stand to be anywhere near each other.

"Yes. There will be one essay question worth twenty points and the rest is multiple choice."

He nodded. "Multiple choice give you plenty to choose from. You just have to concentrate on what you know is the right answer. And as far as the essay, you're good with writing. If you recall, you helped me get my writing scores up when I was in my junior year. If it hadn't been for you, I wouldn't have passed to the twelfth."

"Liar."

"No, honestly. You know how old man Goldman felt about people living on the bayou."

His words gave her pause because she knew. Everybody knew and they still allowed him to teach until her mother, Debbie Witherspoon, forever the outspoken Canadian social activist, called for the man to resign at a PTA meeting. Her mother had gotten a standing ovation because she had stood up and done what no one else in the cove had had the guts to do.

"Well, you proved him wrong."

Kaegan didn't say anything and she wondered if he was remembering what all they'd been through together over the years. The good, bad and ugly. They had survived it all.

That was why his rejection had been so devastating for her, and caused her an incredible amount of pain. But it had also taught her something. You couldn't put all your hopes and dreams into one person. She had. Kaegan had been her world, and when he'd walked out of it, she'd thought her world had come to an end. It had taken her a while, but she'd recovered. Found out life went on and the world still existed.

She had made some changes in her life, got her self-esteem back, decided to go into business for herself and live for today and not tomorrow. She knew not to depend on a man for her happiness, not to believe any man was perfect, and she had accepted that nothing was forever. In a way, she owed Kaegan for being the one to stop seeing life in a fishbowl. She owed him for showing her that whatever she did in life, she had to do it to make herself happy because she could not depend on anyone else for her happiness.

Kaegan eased up off the floor and her gaze followed the movement. She couldn't help it. Since he'd come straight from work he still wore his jeans and T-shirt. He'd taken off his fisherman boots at the door and walked around in socked feet. He looked comfortable at her place. So at home. A part of her was glad to realize their friendship was still there after everything. It was time she told him that.

"You need to take a break from studying tomorrow for a while, Bryce. I suggest that you do something fun to clear your mind. Take a tour of the cove on one of Ray's boats or take the trolley car around town for a few hours. Then come back here and binge-study the way we've been doing the last three days. If you do that then you won't have anything to worry about when you take that test Monday."

She smiled. "You have so much confidence in me."

When he didn't say anything, and just hung his head, she could only imagine what had flashed through his mind. There had been a time he'd lost his confidence in her and it had cost them everything. It was a love that could never be recaptured.

But she knew now that there was one aspect of their past that could be restored. "Kaegan?"

"Yes?" he asked, while sliding into his jacket.

"I appreciate what you've done the last three days. If I pass that exam I will have you to thank."

He shrugged and said, "That's what friends are for."

He held her gaze, seemingly waiting for her to say something to deny their friendship. This time he would have a long wait because she wouldn't. But acknowledging their friendship wouldn't give either of them the right to think it went beyond that. There could never be anything more than friendship between them.

It was important they both understood they'd had their chance and there was too much hurt, anger and pain to try to recapture a love that was not only lost, but also dead and buried. He'd buried it years ago and so had she. It was too late for anything between them to ever be resurrected, but they could be friends.

She got out of the chair. "You're right. That's what friends are for and the past three days have shown me that we can be friends again, Kaegan."

She paused a moment and added, "I think we both understand and accept that friendship is all there can ever be between us. Agreed?"

"Agreed," he said, zipping up his jacket.

She was glad they were in agreement, but did he have to be so quick and eager to concur? She should be glad he had, but still… "I'll walk you to the door."

"Good luck on your test Monday. I hope you will take my advice about clearing your mind for a few hours tomorrow before doing any heavy-duty studying."

"Hmm. Instead of taking a tour on Ray's boat or riding a trolley around town, I've got a better idea."

"What?"

"Earlier you mentioned that tomorrow a group of volunteers would be helping you out."

"Yes. I have a huge order of oysters to net for an all-you-can-eat oyster chow-down in Oklahoma beginning next week. All hands are on deck for even my office staff. Ray plans on pulling an all-day, but you know Ray. He looks for any excuse to be on the water," Kaegan said, grinning. "Sawyer and Vashti have volunteered, as well," he added.

She nodded. "I wonder who will be keeping Cutter."

"Sawyer said Gloria volunteered to do so."

"That was nice of her."

"Yes, it was. I believe that she and Reid think of themselves as Cutter's grandparents, as well. For a man who a couple of years ago was living a very lonely life, he certainly has it all now. A future wife and grandkids he adores."

Bryce nodded. "I agree." Then she said, "Well, I want to volunteer to help you tomorrow for at least half a day. I've always wanted to go back out on a Chambray boat."

"How are your sea legs?" he asked as his gaze roamed down her legs.

Certain she was imagining things and his gaze hadn't been as intense on her legs as she'd thought, she said, "I admit I haven't been out on a commercial shipping boat for years. At least not since that time you sneaked me on board as a stowaway."

They looked at each other and simultaneously burst out laughing. After wiping tears from her eyes, she said, "You know it's a crying shame when two adults can remember one of their outlandish escapades as teens and laugh about it."

"Your parents didn't do anything to you when they found out, but my dad raised holy hell and grounded me for a week."

Bryce still giggled at the memory. "He only punished you because it was me. He didn't like me and didn't care who knew it." Bryce had known she was Mr. Chambray's least favorite person because he had wanted Kaegan to date one of the Pointe-au-Chien tribe girls living on the bayou. She could think about that now and not feel threatened by it.

"Well, I liked you, and that's all that mattered."

"Yes, but we should not have tricked your dad that way."

"He would not have found out the truth if we hadn't got caught in that storm and a search party hadn't been sent looking for us."

Bryce recalled that day as if it was yesterday. Kaegan was to master his own shipping vessel, the one she'd been a stowaway on. It was one of the smaller boats in the fleet. They thought they'd succeeded with their plan to outwit his father. Then out of nowhere a summer storm blew in and the two ships got separated.

Kaegan had skillfully handled the vessel and they had made it through the swamp to Eagle Bend Inlet. It was there Kaegan had taken her to his private place on the inlet, an abandoned bunker he considered his secret home. It had provided shelter from the wind and rain, and protection from the wild animals known to come out at night. The search party had found them a little after daybreak the next day.

He glanced at his watch. "It's late and time for me to go. Remember, no more studying tonight. Shower, drink some wine and go to bed."

"I will," she said, walking him to the door.

He stopped before opening it. "You sure about tomorrow?"

"Yes."

"Then meet us dockside at six."

"Okay. I'll be there, sea legs and all."

"Thanks."

"That's what friends are for."

Smiling, he nodded, opened the door and left.

Kaegan walked to his truck while whistling. He tried to recall the last time he'd been in such a good mood. He felt good about the amount of information he'd covered with Bryce over the last three nights. He was confident that she would pass that exam.

But what had really made his day was Bryce acknowledging their friendship. A friendship that had started close to twenty-five years ago. Of course, he'd told her that little white lie, agreeing there could never be anything but friendship between them. He intended to prove her wrong. She hadn't wanted to be friends, either, and here they were. He wouldn't rush her but would give her time to realize it for herself.

Because a delivery truck had been in Bryce's yard when he'd arrived, he had parked on the street in front of her home. As he got closer to his SUV, although it had gotten dark, he noticed something was wrong. One of his tires appeared to be flat. He frowned as he squatted down and studied the tire. It had been slashed.

Standing, he glanced around. Although Catalina Cove had low crime, no doubt some teens had very little to do other than get into mischief. No need to make a big deal of it and he wouldn't bother mentioning it to Sawyer. He glanced back at Bryce's house and figured he could use what happened to his tire as an excuse to go back inside.

Releasing a deep sigh, he remembered his decision to be patient when it came to Bryce. Besides, hadn't he suggested that she take a shower, drink a glass of wine and go to bed? The thought of her naked and taking a shower had a number of salacious scenarios running through his head. He recalled a time during their weekend hookups when they would shower together. Those memories suddenly had him feeling hot and aroused. That was the last thing he needed to remember right now.

Removing his jacket, he went to work changing his tire.

PART 2

The greatest healing therapy is friendship and love.
—Hubert H. Humphrey

CHAPTER THIRTEEN

"How are things going, Bryce?"

Bryce looked into the man's face and smiled. Vaughn Miller had been born in the cove and, like a number of others, when he'd left for college he hadn't returned. She'd heard that five years ago he was accused of a white-collar crime for which he served time but had gotten released after a couple of years for good behavior.

Last year he had returned to the cove to live. Some locals were aware Vaughn had served time and there were some who weren't aware of it. It honestly didn't matter since Reid LaCroix, the wealthiest man in the cove, had trusted Vaughn enough to give him a job as part of his executive team. That hadn't come as too much of a surprise since Reid's deceased son, Julius, and Vaughn had been best friends while growing up and the two had graduated from Yale together. Everyone knew if Reid LaCroix liked you, then everyone else living in the cove liked you. Few people went against Reid.

"Things are pretty good. What about with you?" she asked, sipping her coffee.

"Same here. It's a beautiful day and I think the weather is going to be perfect."

She thought so, too. Waking up that morning, she'd questioned why she had decided to come here. The only reason Bryce could come up with was that since she'd agreed to be friends again with Kaegan, she had to keep their relationship just that.

She figured the hardest part would be being around him and doing things they used to do that once had a significant meaning but didn't any longer. She'd decided not to shun those things but be in control of how she felt about them. Closure meant the ability not to let the things they used to do together control her mind. Some people had their way of moving on and she had hers.

Bryce had to accept that most people recovering from a broken relationship and finding closure didn't have to encounter their ex on a constant basis like she did. Knowing she didn't love Kaegan anymore, she was convinced one of the reasons she hadn't been able to move on was because Catalina Cove was a small town and everybody knew everybody. They frequented the same places and shared the same friends. Avoiding each other had been impossible. Instead of evading those situations when confronted with them, she needed to be strong and meet them head-on.

Vaughn stood beside her on the dock sipping his tea and looking out across the blue waters of the ocean. He was a handsome man and she tried remembering whom he'd dated in high school. He had graduated with her, which meant he was probably thirty-two or pretty close to thirty-three.

"You volunteered today, as well, I see," she said to him.

He smiled. "Yes. I don't get out much, and since I had nothing better to do today, I figured I'd come help. Kaegan has gone out of his way to befriend me since moving back home. He didn't have to do that and I appreciate him for it."

Bryce had heard that Vaughn didn't socialize much since moving back. He pretty much kept to himself. Her parents had mentioned that he would drop by their café on occasion for take-out dinners but had never dined in. She'd also heard he was determined to prove his innocence regarding that white-collar crime he'd served time for and had hired a team of private investigators to clear his name.

Vaughn's parents had been part of Catalina Cove's old-money elites. When Eugene and Vivian Miller moved to Paris after their son and daughter left for college, instead of selling their home, they'd kept it with the intention of returning back to the cove to visit on occasion. They never did and had since passed away. Vaughn was living in the huge house alone. The house had been one of the original homes built for one of Jean Lafitte's numerous mistresses, who happened to have been one of Vaughn's ancestors. Bryce recalled that Vaughn and his younger sister, Zara, had both been pretty likable, unlike their parents, who'd been total snobs.

"Are you going to volunteer to work unloading on the docks or did you volunteer to go out on one of the boats?" he asked her.

"I prefer going out on the boat, but I'll pitch in wherever I'm needed. It seems a lot of people showed up this morning."

"Yes, sure looks like it."

Bryce hadn't seen Kaegan since arriving and figured he was somewhere in his office getting things organized. However, she had seen Ray, who'd arrived at the same time she had. He'd said he was okay with leaving Ashley for a full day since her three best friends were in town visiting her this weekend.

Sawyer had come a few minutes later and told her that Vashti would be on her way after dropping off Cutter at Reid's place. Everyone appreciated Bryce's parents for sending over the complimentary boxes of blueberry muffins to go along with the kegs of coffee they'd also provided. She hadn't been surprised by her parents' generosity to Kaegan. They knew a lot of the volunteers would be out on the water most of the day and had wanted to do their part, especially since Kaegan had ordered lunch and dinner for his crew to be catered from her parents' café.

"Would you excuse me, Vaughn? I see Willa and Faith and want to say hello."

"Sure. No problem."

She moved away from Vaughn and walked to where Willa Ford and Faith Harris stood talking. Bryce knew Willa and Faith. Like Bryce, Willa had been born and raised in the cove. Instead of going away to college, she'd opted to marry her childhood sweetheart. She and Ron were still married and had two sons in college. Ron was a part of the Catalina Cove police force.

Faith was four years older than Bryce and had graduated from high school with her brother Duke. She had come to the cove to live with her grandparents during her middle-school years. Bryce knew that Faith's first husband had died three years ago. It was known around town that the man had cheated on her a few times but she'd stayed with him anyway. A year after he'd died of a heart attack in another woman's bed, Faith had managed to pull herself together and get married again. This time around she was married to a man who adored her and treated her like a queen.

"Hey, guys," Bryce said when she approached.

"Hello, Bryce," Willa and Faith said simultaneously.

"I see Kaegan talked you into joining the team this morning," Willa said, grinning.

Bryce chuckled. "No, I volunteered. I figured it was the least I could do for him helping me study for an exam I'm taking."

"So is it official now?" Faith asked, smiling brightly. "Are you and the boss back together again?"

Bryce shook her head. "No. Kaegan and I are just friends and nothing more."

"Honestly, Bryce," Willa said as she shook her head. "Do you think you and Kaegan can ever just be friends?"

Funny, her brothers had asked her the same thing that morning when she arrived at the café and told everyone of her plans for today. "I don't see why not. Ten years apart is a long time and we're not trying to rekindle anything but friendship."

She knew that might be hard for Willa and Faith to believe because most people in the cove had been aware that the two of them had made plans to marry one day. Of course, by the time she'd finished college and returned home, most had heard the two of them had broken up, although no one knew why.

When Kaegan had moved back to the cove, Bryce had known all eyes were on them and that most people thought whatever had broken them up would be patched up eventually. She'd ignored the erroneous assumptions and everyone's speculations.

Bryce figured they would be under everyone's microscope even more now that they were friends again. The assumptions and speculations would increase, but there was nothing she could do to stop them, other than deny there was anything between them like she was doing now.

"There's Kaegan now," Willa said, smiling.

Bryce turned and saw Kaegan. As if he'd known where she was, his gaze connected to hers. He smiled and she couldn't help but smile back.

"Now, what was that you were saying a few minutes ago, Bryce, about you and Kaegan just being friends?" Faith asked, reclaiming her attention.

She broke eye contact with Kaegan to glance at Faith. "What about it?"

"We haven't seen the boss smile like that in a very long time."

She was certain Faith was exaggerating. "He's probably smiling because he didn't believe I'd show up.

"I'm only volunteering until noon. I got more studying to do."

"Your mom told me you were taking that class in New Orleans at Delgado Community College," Willa said.

"Yes, and the exam is Monday evening," Bryce replied.

"Good luck and I hope that you do well," Faith said.

"Thanks."

"Good morning, everyone," Kaegan said, and Bryce wished the sound of his deep, husky voice didn't still stir sensations within her. That was definitely something she needed to work on.

Everyone returned his greeting and then he handed Willa a clipboard. "Here you are, Willa. I've assigned everyone positions and grouped them into teams for the boats. Let everyone know their placement and duties after they've signed those liability forms."

"Okay," Willa said, nodding. Before walking off, she scanned the list, looked over at Faith and said, "We're manning things in the office while everyone's out on the boat."

"Where am I needed?" Bryce asked Willa. "I'm only available for half of the day."

"You're on my boat," Kaegan said, before Willa could answer her. "I'll be returning to shore every four hours and can bring you back."

"Oh." Bryce noted Willa and Faith were smiling. Unknown to Kaegan, he'd filled their heads up with crazy ideas.

"You were right," Kaegan told Bryce after he placed a huge tub of oysters on the scale to be weighed.

She looked up at him after recording the weight in the log. "About what?"

"Still having your sea legs."

She threw her head back and laughed, and he loved the sound. He couldn't recall the last time Bryce had laughed over something he'd said. "Did you think I didn't? I was born in the cove, remember."

"I remember." In fact, he was remembering a number of things. Like the last time she'd been out on a boat with him. He hadn't been able to sleep most of last night, wondering if she would keep her word and show up today.

He'd been in his office before daybreak and had known the minute she'd arrived on the pier. Watching from his office window, he'd seen her arrive and he'd felt something he hadn't felt in a long time. Love. He loved Bryce. A part of him knew he'd never stopped loving her, even during that time when he'd believed she had betrayed him. That was probably why he'd felt so much animosity toward her. He hadn't understood how he could desire someone who had dishonored him the way she had. When it came to Bryce, love and desire went hand in hand.

It had taken him ten years to find out she hadn't betrayed him. He'd been wrong, and he didn't care how long it took—he was determined to earn back her love. He had to because he couldn't imagine living another ten years without her.

Maybe that was the reason he'd felt a territorial tightening in his gut when he'd seen her talking to Vaughn. Kaegan knew that Bryce had a tendency to be friendly to everyone; that was why she was so well liked in the cove. The only reason he'd been so quick to believe the worst of her that time was because he'd also known Samuel's reputation with the ladies. At least he'd known the one the man had perpetuated for years. On top of that had been the lies his father had been feeding him. He'd played right into his old man's hands and he would admit that losing Bryce was what he deserved for not fully trusting her. For not believing she would not betray him.

Feeling territorial when it came to Bryce was nothing new and it wasn't anything against Vaughn. He felt the same way whenever he saw her conversing with Isaac Elloran, or any other single man living in the cove, for that matter. More than once, he'd run into her out on a date. Either he'd been on a date, as well, or he'd been alone. Didn't matter. He'd still felt the need to ram his hand into the nearest wall.

Since they were playing the "remember" game, he said, "I also remember that I was the one who taught you and Vashti to swim."

"Yeah, but that was only after we begged you to do so."

"Yes, the two of you did get on my last nerve."

"Oh, we did, did we?"

They turned and saw Vashti standing there with her hands on her hips, while frowning at him. Instead of answering her, Kaegan asked a question of his own. "How was your nap?"

Vashti's grin told him she was aware he'd deliberately switched topics and would let him for now. "It was fine. I guess next time you'll think twice about letting me come along. I'm not much help today."

He winked at Vashti. "I invited you because I knew inviting you meant also getting your husband on board. That's not a bad deal. Besides, you're pregnant. I understand pregnant women sleep a lot. At least that's what Ray told me."

He glanced at his watch when he heard a smaller boat approach. "Perfect timing. Elton is here with the boat that will take you back to shore, Bryce." Elton was one of the old-timers who'd worked for the Chambray Company when Kaegan's father ran things.

"Okay," Bryce said, adjusting the straps of the backpack on her shoulders. He thought they were beautiful shoulders and could remember a time when he would rub his hands all over them. Use his tongue to lick them.

"I'll call you later," Vashti said to Bryce, breaking into his thoughts.

He studied Vashti. "You sure you don't want to leave, as well?"

She shook her head. "No. Now that I've taken my nap, I'm fine. What do you need me to do?"

"For starters," Kaegan said, grinning, while shaking his head, "stop staring at your shirtless husband over there. I'm sure he's not displaying anything out here that you haven't seen at home."

Vashti threw back her head and laughed. "For your information, Kaegan Chambray, it doesn't matter where or how my husband displays it—I still think Sawyer Grisham is a fine specimen of a man. Besides, what could be better than seeing a half-naked man with the ocean as a backdrop?"

CHAPTER FOURTEEN

Bryce smiled, always finding it fascinating as well as endearing how attracted Vashti was to Sawyer, even after almost three years of marriage. But she understood. Some things couldn't be denied, no matter what.

She still thought that Kaegan was a sexy man, as well. When he'd been a teen, approaching manhood, she'd drool over his body. When he got older she'd thought he was the epitome of masculine fineness. Now as a full-grown adult in his thirties, he was even more buff. He put his shirt back on, but when he'd taken it off earlier, she hadn't been able to keep her eyes off his chest without remembering a lot about it. Like how she would kiss him all over it, how his chest felt rubbing against her nipples those times when she would straddle him when they made love.

Bryce kept telling herself that acknowledging Kaegan's sexiness meant nothing. It was a woman's thing for her. She thought Idris Elba was sexy, too. She knew how to stay in her lane where Kaegan was concerned.

"You can take Bryce's place with the logbook, Vashti," Kaegan said, interrupting Bryce's thoughts. "If you prefer doing something else, just let Elton know. I'm leaving him in charge until I get back."

Bryce glanced over at Kaegan. "Until you get back? Isn't Elton the one taking me back to the dock?"

He glanced over at her. "No, I am. There are several things I need to do at the office before coming back here with lunch for everyone."

"Oh." Breaking eye contact with Kaegan, she lowered her gaze to the clipboard, needing to record the last bit of information regarding the weight of the netted oysters into the log. Moments later, she glanced up and saw Vashti and Kaegan with their heads together laughing. She remembered those times in the past when the three of them would goof off or share laughter over something they'd thought was amusing at the time.

At that moment he looked over at her and caught her staring. If she looked away now it would be like she'd been caught doing something she shouldn't. For all he knew, she could have been looking at both him and Vashti.

He smiled over at her. "I'll be back in a minute. I need to let the guys know I'm leaving, but will be returning with their lunch."

"That should make them happy," Bryce said, trying to sound upbeat but beginning to feel rather nervous at the thought of being alone on a boat with him. Why? They'd spent the last three evenings alone in her house while she studied.

"Yes, I'm sure it will." He walked off toward the rear of the huge commercial boat, where Sawyer and a few other men were hoisting nets over the side. She couldn't help it when her gaze followed him.

"Hmm, looks like I'm not the only one admiring a nice piece of male flesh today," Vashti said.

She rolled her eyes at her friend. "Whatever. Put a man with a great tush in a pair of jeans and I can't help but stare."

"Even if the man is Kaegan?"

Bryce nodded. "Even if it's Kaegan."

Vashti nodded. "Well, just so you know, I was glad to see you here this morning. I admit I was a little surprised."

Bryce drew in a deep breath. "I figured volunteering to help out today was a way to repay him for helping me study." She paused a moment, then added, "And just so you know, Kaegan and I are officially friends again."

She saw the huge smile that lit Vashti's face and her best friend all but jumped up and down and clapped her hands. Bryce figured she needed to clarify a few things for Vashti, like she had for Willa and Faith that morning. The last thing she wanted was for Vashti to get any crazy ideas. "I said we were officially friends again, Vash. Don't get anything more into your head."

An innocent look appeared on Vashti's face. "What makes you think that I will do something like that?"

Bryce gave her a look as if she couldn't believe she would ask such a question. "Because I know you. You're in love and married to a wonderful guy. You're pregnant. You have a son and two daughters. Other than your crazy-ass parents, your life is as close to perfect as it can get, and being the type of friend you are, you want mine to be just as glorious. It's not."

Vashti walked over to her and placed a hand on her arm. "But it can be if you'd take a chance on love again. If not with Kaegan then with someone else. Of course, I'm Team Kaegan. He was wrong in assuming what he did about you and not giving you a chance to explain when you tried doing so, but everybody makes mistakes. You, of all people, know how I felt when Sawyer didn't believe what I told him about Kia. He all but called me crazy. Yet I was able to forgive him."

Bryce recalled that time and how Vashti had called her crying her heart out because Sawyer hadn't believed her. Vashti hadn't been sure she could forgive Sawyer for lacking confidence in her after the drama she'd gone through with her first husband, Scott.

"Yes, Vash, but you didn't have ten years for your anger, humiliation and pain to fester. There was not a time—years, weeks and months—when you had to go to bed imagining what the man you love had done to another woman just to spite you."

"But didn't Kaegan tell you that he didn't sleep with that woman?"

"But he deliberately touched her in front of me. And he kissed her."

"That's what's hard for you, isn't it, Bryce?" Vashti asked. "You want to forgive him. You claim you have but you truly haven't, have you?"

Bryce drew in a deep breath, inhaling the scent of the water and momentarily turning her gaze away from Vashti. When she looked back at her best friend she didn't care if Vashti saw the tears forming in her eyes. "I forgave him, Vash, but I can't forget. I'm trying. Honestly, I am. But I'm afraid of letting my guard down. I had loved him so much that even being just friends with him is hard."

She swiped at her tears. "Whenever I look at him, study his hands, check out his body, I have to accept that, unlike how things were ten years ago, I'm not the only woman who has had a piece of him. I'm not the only woman he's taken to his bed. It's hard to accept what was supposed to be all mine isn't anymore."

"He could say the same for you, you know."

Vashti's words stung. "And what was I supposed to do, Vash? Not live my life? I had to move on to retain my sanity."

"And you were right to do so, Bryce. Sorry if it sounded as if I thought you shouldn't have, and just like Kaegan blames himself for losing you, I'm sure he knows and accepts what all losing you meant. I believe it's a tortured hell he has to go through."

"Good. Let him." Then she wished she hadn't said that, but it was too late to take it back because that was how she felt. Bryce could now admit that the only reason she'd hooked up with Marcel was because she'd been desperate to get over Kaegan. "I'm ashamed to admit I never loved Marcel, but at the time I needed to move on in my life. You don't know how it feels when you've been betrayed by someone you loved."

"Hey, excuse me. It's me you're talking to. Why do you keep forgetting about Scott?"

Bryce shouldn't keep forgetting about Scott Zimmons and the pain he'd caused Vashti during their marriage. Nor should she forget about Julius LaCroix, Vashti's first boyfriend and the guy who'd gotten her pregnant at sixteen. Both men had betrayed her in different ways. The main reason she kept forgetting was because Vashti was so happy now. Sawyer had come into the picture and eradicated all the pain both Scott and Julius had left behind.

"Maybe that's what I need, Vash."

"What?"

"A man who can help me forget the pain," Bryce said.

"You ever considered that maybe there's a reason you're still carrying around all that pain after nearly ten years?"

Bryce frowned. "Yes, there is a reason. I made the man I loved such a major part of my life that when we broke up, I discovered I no longer had a life. At least not one to call my own. Then six years later, when I thought I was finally getting over him, he returns to town. Do you know what that did to me each and every time I saw him?"

"I think I do. When I married Scott, I honestly thought he was my forever-after. How do you think I felt when I found out he only married me so his boss wouldn't find out he was having an affair with the man's wife? Not only did I feel betrayed, I felt inadequate. For a while my self-esteem took a beating."

Bryce remembered that time. She had flown to New York to spend a week with Vashti and had ended up staying for two. Her best friend had needed her. "At least you eventually met someone, Vash."

"Hopefully you will, too. What about that guy you were meeting for coffee before class? Do you think you might have given up on him too soon?"

Had she? She honestly didn't think so. An attraction between two people wasn't everything, but in her book it had to be there somewhere. She wasn't certain why she'd felt no chemistry where Jeremy was concerned. "I wasn't feeling anything with him. I told you that."

"Yes, but did you give yourself time to feel anything or were you too busy comparing him to Kaegan?"

Had she been? "You think that's what I was doing?"

"Only you can answer that, Bryce. Don't get me wrong, I'd love to see you and Kaegan together again romantically, but more than anything, I want you happy. Even if it means being happy without Kaegan."

Bryce gave her an appreciative smile. "Thanks, but don't you think you're jumping the gun somewhat here?"

"How?"

"By thinking Kaegan could even be interested in me that way again? Just like I fell out of love with Kaegan, I'm sure he's fallen out of love with me. How could he not when he thought the worst of me? I don't think he's any more interested in me than I am in him." She was convinced the night of the ball when he'd suggested they get back together had been nothing more than his libido talking.

Putting down the clipboard, she said, "Besides, I have a

feeling he'll be dating seriously real soon if Sasha Johnson has her way."

"Sasha Johnson? Why on earth would you think that?"

"Because I heard she has a thing for him. She's pretty, so there's no reason he wouldn't return the interest."

"Jealous?"

"Of course not." Bryce was about to say something else when she saw Kaegan headed back toward them. She knew Vashti had seen him, too. "We'll talk some more later."

Vashti nodded. "Okay, but I think we need a hug," she said, moving toward Bryce and wrapping her arms around her.

"Hey, like old times. Can I join in?" Kaegan said when he reached them.

They both looked at Kaegan, and Bryce immediately recalled their group hugs. Knowing Vashti wouldn't give him an answer, especially not knowing how Bryce would feel about it, Bryce said, "Sure. Just like old times."

The three friends embraced in a group hug, just like those days when they'd needed it. Kaegan for when he had to deal with his drunken father's treatment of him and his mother, and Vashti during those times she had to deal with her parents when she'd gotten pregnant. For Bryce, she'd never had parent issues like her two best friends, but she'd had her own inner turmoil. Especially when she'd gotten older and discovered the feelings she'd harbored for Kaegan were turning into more than puppy love. She'd been afraid if he found out that he wouldn't want to be her friend anymore.

No one said anything as the hug between friends continued, transcending time and distance. How had the three of them lost this? A closeness that was never supposed to end? At one time she'd known them better than they'd known themselves and vice versa. She had known Vashti was pregnant weeks before she'd told her. And she'd known what days to bring one of her brothers' clean shirts to school for Kaegan because he'd slept in a boat on the bayou the night before.

And just like she'd known them, they'd known her.

At least they should have. Vashti had. Kaegan had proved that he hadn't. The thought of that had her suddenly pulling away and stepping back, breaking their circle of love. In her defense, Kaegan had broken it first. Glancing over at him, she said, "You can take me to the dock now."

As Kaegan maneuvered the boat through the waters of the Gulf, he noticed that an annoying silence had fallen between him and Bryce since leaving the commercial vessel around ten minutes ago. Instead of looking at him, she was staring out over the water.

He had tried engaging her in conversation, but she'd barely said three words. And all because of the group hug they'd shared? Now she was withdrawing—retreating to where, he wasn't sure. He refused to let her push him away. He'd been making progress; he'd been certain of it.

While she studied the water, he studied her. He couldn't help the way his gaze was glued to her chest. He doubted he would ever forget the first time he'd touched her breasts, run his fingertips across a hardened nipple only to feel it harden even more to his touch. She had always been responsive to his fondling and he'd enjoyed introducing her to passion.

Passion...

She had to be the most passionate woman he knew. At least she used to be and there was no reason to think she still wasn't. In her senior year of high school, when he'd been stationed in Maryland, she would occasionally take the bus on the weekends to visit her father's aunt, who lived in the DC area. They'd been able to spend a lot of time together. And then when she'd gone off to college, they'd had those weekends together, as well. It suddenly occurred to him just how well they'd masterminded plans over the years to stay close, refusing to stay apart for too long. Yet all of that had come to a crashing end because of him. He now knew he could never apologize to her enough for destroying what they'd had.

"Aren't we near Eagle Bend Inlet?"

"Yes," he said, glancing over at her. "It's not too far to the west. Just a few bends away."

She still hadn't looked at him but was staring in the direction of where the inlet was located. He wondered if she was remembering the night they'd escaped from the storm and stayed there all night together. But then, more important, all those other times they'd returned. The last time had been the night before he left for the marines.

Not wanting to remember the intimate details of any of those times, especially that last one, he thought about the inlet itself. Most locals avoided the small island mainly because you had to travel through the swamps to get to it. Another reason was that over the years there had been numerous stories surrounding the inlet. Of course, most of them were fictitious, although some people thought going to the island for the first time would ultimately be your last time. There were tall tales of alligators larger than most men, bald eagles that could eat you alive and quicksand that could swallow you whole. And he couldn't forget the tales of the ghosts of several pirates supposedly buried there.

For years treasure hunters had believed some of Jean Lafitte's hidden bounty was there and they'd fabricated all sorts of lies to keep people off the island. The quicksand that people had claimed was on the island had merely been holes left uncovered by men digging for the pirate's treasures. After Hurricane Katrina, the state of Louisiana had decided to sell it, and Reid LaCroix had immediately purchased it with the intent of retaining its wildlife state. The first thing he did was forbid anyone from coming on the island, especially the poachers and treasure hunters.

When Kaegan returned to town and had made some profit from the seafood business, one of the first things he'd done was to make Reid an offer for the island. The man hadn't understood why he would want to buy the inlet, but he knew of Kaegan's love of the bayou and felt he would preserve the inlet and protect the wildlife there. Few people knew that Kaegan now owned the island.

"Have you been back there since returning to Catalina Cove?"

Now would be a good time to tell her that the island was his, and because of that reason, he would go there often to not only check on things, but also to just get away. He loved the bayou, and since the inlet was a part of that environment, he loved going there, as well. "Yes, I've gone back a number of times, and as you can see, I survived all my visits there. I haven't gotten eaten by an alligator yet."

"And we survived our visits there, too," she said softly, as if remembering. "Although that time when your dad found us, I think he was tempted to kill us and feed us to one of those alligators."

She paused and then added, "I honestly think he was afraid that since we'd been missing overnight that I'd been 'compromised' and my parents would demand that you marry me, which was the last thing he wanted."

"In a way I wish they had demanded I marry you," he said, without thinking.

She held his gaze a moment and then looked away. He wondered what sort of life they would have had if her parents had done such a thing. When silence ensued between them again, he said, "The bunker is still there."

She looked back at him. "Is it?"

"Yes."

He'd come across the underground bunker by chance when he'd been only twelve and trespassing on the property while hiding out from his father. Because he'd never believed any of the hype about the island, it had been his secret place. When he'd gotten older, he'd researched the inlet and discovered it was a Cold War–era civil-defense bunker. It had been built back in the 1960s by the government to use as a possible emergency-operations center in case of nuclear war. He would never forget the first time he'd taken Bryce there.

"I own it," he then said.

"You own what?" she asked him.

"The inlet."

She lifted an eyebrow in surprise. "You were able to talk Reid LaCroix into selling you some of the property there?"

"I bought the entire island from him and everything on it."

Her eyes widened and she stared at him, shocked. "You're kidding, right?"

"No, I'm not kidding."

Now she looked confused. "But why would you buy it?"

He shrugged. "Because I always loved it there."

Kaegan hoped she didn't have to wonder why the inlet meant so much to him. For years they'd thought of it as their special place. Their private home. Even when he'd thought he hated her, he would still go to the inlet and remember the times they'd spent there together. He'd convinced himself reliving the memories and being reminded of her betrayal was a way of exorcising her from his mind.

She tilted her head and looked at him. "Yes, but you own a large section of land on the bayou. Why would you want Eagle Bend Inlet, as well?"

There was no way he could tell her the real reason why, so he said what he knew was another truth. "Rumors were flying around that poachers had begun roaming the island again, killing a lot of the wildlife. That's the main reason Reid had purchased it from the state, to protect the wildlife."

He decided not to mention that it would only have been a matter of time before someone stumbled across the bunker. "Reid knew about the bunker and that was possibly another reason he purchased the inlet from the government. However, after his son was killed and his wife died, he didn't have the state of mind to care about too much of anything. I made him an offer and he took it."

"Oh, I see. Anyone know you own it?"

"I've told Sawyer and Ray, and I'm sure Sawyer has told Vashti. Other than that, very few people know. Most people in the cove assume Reid is still the owner, which is probably why the locals—the ones who don't buy all those wild tales about the island—are reluctant to go there and do anything that would result in his anger. It's mostly the outsiders, who like fishing there, I have to worry about. Thanks to Isaac, that's been taken care of."

"How?"

"I had him install security devices." Isaac once owned a high-tech computer company in Boston before he'd returned to the cove. He had installed a number of state-of-the-art security features on the inlet. At any point in time, Kaegan was alerted whenever humans trespassed on certain areas of his property.

"I'd like to see it."

He glanced over at her. "See what?"

"The island."

He quirked an eyebrow. "You would?"

"Yes."

A part of him was questioning why she would want to go to a place that had once been their lovers' hideaway. Deciding not to question her about it now, he said, "Okay." He steered the boat westward.

CHAPTER FIFTEEN

Bryce studied Kaegan as he straightened to his full height while maneuvering the boat around the bend. She knew this smaller boat was just one of several he owned. When his yacht had been docked at the pier one day she'd gotten a good look at it and thought it was a beauty. Her brothers had joined him for one of his midnight fishing excursions and had come back bragging about how nice and roomy it had been. Even when she'd not been on good terms with him, she'd been proud of his success.

Years ago Kaegan had told her that his father had taught him to operate a boat before he could walk, and watching him now made a believer out of her. He was definitely a man made for the sea.

"We're almost there. Here, spray this on your arms," he said, handing her a can of mosquito repellent.

She knew why. The swamp had mosquitoes that were almost as big as humans. "Thanks."

She removed the can's top and sprayed her arms. She then glanced over at him. He was wearing a pair of jeans and a T-shirt. She doubted Kaegan knew how good he looked or how he had the ability to fuel women's fantasies. Earlier he had removed his shirt and at first she'd shivered when she'd seen him shirtless. After all, October wasn't exactly a good time to walk around half-naked with a chill in the air. But he'd done so as if it hadn't bothered him.

"What about you?" she asked him.

"I'm good."

She forced her gaze from scanning over his body, while also thinking, he was most certainly good...and immediately regretted those thoughts. Deciding to focus on something other than him, she glanced around and saw that the beautiful blue waters of the ocean had gotten replaced by the dark, murky waters of the swamp.

The first time she'd come through here she'd been afraid. It had been storming and she'd been convinced their boat would turn over and they would be eaten by alligators. However, Kaegan had calmed her fears by telling her how important the swamp and bayou were to the habitat and inland areas, mainly against coastal erosion.

He'd helped her to understand the environmentalists who fought to keep out developers from invading the inlands—developers who didn't understand and appreciate the swamp's and bayou's contributions. And then he'd held her while singing to her. They'd made it through the swamp to the inlet and they'd spent the night in the bunker out of the rain. It was the first time he'd shared the bunker with anyone. That night they'd made love for the first time.

Bringing her thoughts back to the present, she saw the marker alerting trespassers to keep out. She looked at Kaegan. "Do you get many trespassers?"

He smiled. "Not anymore. Those who ignore the sign usually are greeted by Sawyer when they return to the docks. Even if they try to deny they'd been on my land, thanks to modern technology I can prove otherwise. Unknown to them, I have video cameras installed in several areas. By the time they pay a hefty fine they figure it's not worth the risk to come back."

He steered the boat out of the swamp. They passed by several low-hanging trees while heading toward the inland, where the water became a beautiful blue again. She heard the chirping sounds of several birds, the splashing of otters and the croaking of frogs. After passing through the trees, she saw it. Like Kaegan, she'd always thought it was a beautiful place. To her it had always been a sort of paradise.

"We're here."

As she gazed upon the beauty of Eagle Bend Inlet, she tried wrapping her head around the fact it now belonged to Kaegan. He had to be proud of that and was probably wondering why she'd asked to come here. The reason was simple. For closure. More than anything, she needed it, totally and completely. Hopefully then she could finally move her life forward. She'd honestly thought that she had, but a recent self-evaluation of her life was a good indication that she hadn't.

She was in awe of all she saw. Regardless of all the horror stories she'd heard about the island, not to mention her fear the first time she'd come here, she could now admit it was a picturesque wonderland.

"I'll help you out, Bryce."

She watched as Kaegan tossed his long legs over the side of the boat to stand on shore. It was on the tip of her tongue to tell him that she didn't need his help, but it was too late— he reached out and took her hand. The moment their hands touched, sensations swept through her, invigorating her senses.

At times she found it difficult to digest that even after all the hurt and pain he'd caused her, there was still sexual chemistry between them. And she'd discovered just how potent it was the night of his party, when he'd caught her from falling off that ladder. She'd hoped the incident had been a fluke but had been proved wrong the night of the charity dance. That night when he'd held her in his arms, she'd realized he was no longer the boy she'd danced with at the prom, but a full-grown muscular man. And she'd allowed herself to get caught up in the moment.

It had taken Vashti telling her a few days later just how caught up she'd gotten. According to her best friend, she and Kaegan had danced together like the dance floor had belonged to only them. Vashti further claimed that people had stared at how in sync their bodies had moved to the slow music, and how wrapped up in each other's arms they'd been.

"You okay?" he asked her in that deep, throaty voice that could be drugging to any woman's senses.

"Why wouldn't I be?" she asked, looking up at him.

"No reason, other than the obvious."

She wondered what he thought was the obvious. "Which is?"

He just shook his head and said, "Nothing."

He lifted her up in his arms like she was weightless and placed her on solid ground. Being in his arms caused all kinds of sensations to rush through her. At that moment, she knew she'd made a mistake in coming here.

Kaegan didn't say anything as he watched Bryce take in the island. He knew what she was doing, which was the same thing he was doing—using that time to compose themselves. She had responded to his touch. He'd felt it. He'd also felt the way his stomach had tightened when he'd responded to her touch. He wondered if she was now regretting asking him to bring her here.

While she was trying to make up her mind on her next move, he couldn't help but stand there and study her. Her jeans were slightly damp from being out of the ship, mainly caused by the spray of the waves. He'd tried to persuade her to put on rain gear but she'd refused, saying she liked the feel of the misty waters touching her. That might have been good for her, but now seeing her in a pair of damp jeans wasn't good for him. Especially how those jeans now clung to her perfectly shaped ass.

Kaegan felt sizzling heat shimmer all through him as he remembered that part of her anatomy well. Too well. He recalled how much he liked to touch it, mold his hands all over it when they would dance privately, and press the front of his body to it whenever he'd come up behind her...and those times whenever he had it naked and kissed it all over.

In his mind, that perfectly shaped ass had always belonged to him. It even had his name on it. The initial *K*. She'd had the tattoo done in New Orleans her senior year of high school. He wondered if it was still there, or if she'd hated him so much she'd since had it removed.

When she glanced back at him, he waited for her to tell him she'd changed her mind about coming here and was ready to go back to the dock. He was surprised when she said, "I'm ready to see the changes now."

He decided to be honest with her. "There weren't many changes made to the island per se, Bryce, because I tried keeping everything in its natural state. The last thing I wanted to do was disturb the environment."

She nodded. "What about the bunker?"

His breath seemed to stall with her question. "The bunker?"

"Yes. Does it look the same?"

He shook his head. "No."

She broke eye contact with him to look away and he wondered what was going on with her. "Why did you ask me to bring you here, Bryce?"

Weeks ago she'd said that she had forgiven him, but there were times he wondered if she truly had. Then last night she'd said they could be friends, yet today, when he, Vashti and she had done a group hug like old times, she'd been the one to break away.

When she'd asked to come here, he thought it was the last place she would want to be...and with him, of all people. She met his gaze and said, "I wanted to come here for closure."

He raised an eyebrow. "For closure?"

"Yes. More than anything, I need that."

"And you believe coming here with me, to a place that used to be special to us, will help you find closure?" he asked, trying to understand.

"Yes. It's hard to explain."

"Please try," he said, sincerely wanting to know. He watched her nibble on her bottom lip a minute and could tell she was gathering her thoughts.

"I need to say goodbye to my past with you, Kaegan. I need to close that chapter of my life once and for all. I've forgiven you and last night I agreed to allow you back into my life as a friend. A part of me knows that's all we can ever be. I've accepted that fact on several levels but one."

"And what level is that?"

She dropped her gaze from his for a moment, and then when she looked back at him, she said, "The level that started here on Eagle Bend Inlet."

Bryce didn't expect Kaegan to understand. How could she explain that for years she'd thought he was her soul mate, the one man created for her? Finding out he hadn't been had been hard. But at least she'd found out. And she'd moved on. Or she'd tried. Seeing him on a constant basis whenever he would come into the café had been a dent in those forward movements. Tying things up with Kaegan in a neat tidy bow was essential to her.

"How will that help you find closure?"

She'd expected the question. "Our situation is different than most, Kaegan. We went from friends to lovers and now we're trying to be friends again. I wish I could delete from my mind our years as lovers, but I can't until I make sure they don't mean anything to me anymore. Coming here will help me do that."

"You think so?" he asked her, studying her intently.

"Yes." She figured that if she could get through being here with him, then she could get through anything. "So, let's go."

He nodded and began walking, and she fell in step beside him. His watch began beeping. "It's the alert for when someone is on my island," he said. After turning off the alert, he asked her, "Do you remember this area?"

She glanced around. "It's changed with all the undergrowth and added trees, but, yes, I remember it."

They had walked around for about ten minutes and several of the trees that were once small were now so huge they seemed to touch the sky. One tree she recognized immediately because there was a marking on the side, one you could barely make out if you didn't know it was there. *K & B*. She recalled the day Kaegan had carved it there with his pocketknife. "The bunker is around here," she said.

"Yes. Think you can find it on your own?" he asked her.

She glanced around. "Yes, I think so."

Walking ahead of him, she headed toward the right, which was an area totally covered with trees that were larger than the ones they'd passed earlier. They were trees that looked to be hundreds of years old and large enough to rival the California redwoods.

She knew that few people would detect a panel of grassy moss and thick vines that covered the entrance to the bunker. Because New Orleans was a city below sea level, most people assumed Catalina Cove was below sea level, too. That was not the case. It sat on higher ground. That was why several of the historical homes contained secret underground passages. The rooms had been deliberately built by the pirates as an escape route to their ships, if and when the need arose. Bryce's parents' home had one such passage.

Walking behind the trees, she pushed back the mossy vines. One of the reasons no one would dare come near the tree was because the thicket covering the trunk resembled poison ivy. "I found it!"

Kaegan's watch went off again and she figured he'd been sent another alert. He glanced over at her. "Yes, you found it," he said.

No one would detect a secret door was here, of all places, inside one of these two huge trees. She hadn't believed it, either, until that day Kaegan had shown it to her. Proud of herself, she pushed a hand through her hair and looked up at him when he reached her side. "It was just where I remembered," she said.

He nodded and leaned against the huge oak and stared at her. "Now tell me again why you wanted me to bring you here, Bryce."

His stare was bold—too bold. His gaze roamed all over her body. She had to be imagining things because she was certain she looked a mess. Knowing she would be out on the boat, she hadn't bothered with makeup. At some point the band holding her ponytail had popped off, causing unruly strands to flow around her shoulders.

"I told you, Kaegan. I'm here for closure."

He nodded. "Okay. Then let's go inside."

CHAPTER SIXTEEN

Kaegan stood aside and let Bryce go down the stairs first. He read the question in her eyes and said, "Yes, I had new stairs installed when it became too hazardous to use that old rusty ladder."

"Do others know about this bunker now?"

Was she wondering if he'd brought another woman here? Not only had this been a secret place for them, but it had also been one for him. It had been his refuge from the wrath of his father when sleeping outside on the boat at night or walking to town to sneak underground through the passageway into Bryce's parents' house became too risky. Especially after that night when one of Sheriff Phillips's officers had stopped him and asked why he was out so late and off the reservation.

He'd been only fourteen and full of anger at the way his father had been treating his mother yet again. That night Kaegan hadn't been able to contain his anger and told the police officer he'd asked a stupid question because Native Americans in Catalina Cove didn't live on reservations. They lived on the bayou, but only because they chose to do so. He was cer-, tain the red-faced angry cop would have hauled in his ass if

Bryce's parents, who'd been returning from the movies, had not seen the police with him on the side of the road.

Chester Witherspoon, like Reid LaCroix, demanded respect. Everybody knew him and when he spoke everybody listened, even one of Sheriff Phillips's men. He had demanded to know why Kaegan had been stopped. When the officer gave some lame-assed excuse, Mr. Chester had called it just that and accused the man of harassing Kaegan. He'd further stated if he heard about it happening again, he would have him fired from the police force. The man knew not to test Mr. Chester's threat and had even given Kaegan some flimsy apology before he got into his police cruiser and took off. The Witherspoons had taken him to their home...as if they'd known he'd been headed there anyway. He discovered later that they had.

Bryce and her brothers had been up watching television, and when her parents had walked into the house with him in tow, a twelve-year-old Bryce had run to him and hugged him. She had always been his safe haven from whatever storm that had been in his life. That night the Witherspoons told him and Bryce they were fully aware that he'd been using the secret passageway under their home and would sleep there on occasion. They had no problem with that, but preferred that he knocked on their front door because they would always have a guest room for him to use that was better than one of those drafty rooms underground. He had never taken them up on their offer because he feared being stopped by another cop on the streets of Catalina Cove. So he'd risked going through the swamp instead to Eagle Bend Inlet.

"No. For the longest time only Reid, Sawyer and Ray. I told Isaac last year when he installed all the security equipment."

"What about the builder who made all the changes?"

He knew she was trying to see if he'd missed naming anyone; specifically, a woman. "There wasn't a builder. Sawyer and Ray helped me with the stairs and everything else. Ray even knew how to hook up a generator so I could have lights in here. No more candles. I discovered Ray and Sawyer were pretty useful with their hands and a hammer." During that time his friendship with the two men had grown even closer.

"Oh, I see."

"And, Bryce?"

"Yes?"

"Not that you might care to know this, but I've never brought another woman here other than you."

"You didn't have to tell me that," she said, before moving down the spiral steel staircase.

Kaegan hung back, watching her. He had a gut feeling that he had needed to tell her that. He continued to stand there, wanting her to experience the full effect of seeing the changes he'd made. Before it had looked like a civil-defense facility, complete with the solid steel ceilings and cement floors. Now she was seeing he had since changed it into something else.

It was only when Bryce's feet touched the floor did he move down the stairs behind her. He saw her gaze moving all around, taking in all the changes. When he'd made the alterations he had no idea she would ever see them. At the time he'd been determined to change how it used to look, and make it different from those times he'd brought her here.

"It doesn't look the same," she said, looking over at him. Then she glanced around before turning back to him and asking, "Where's the cot? The table and chairs? The—"

"They were replaced," he interrupted. "There's a Murphy bed I had built into the wall and the breakfast bar serves as the sitting area. The pantry revolves now and I've installed compact kitchen appliances."

He watched her walk around the place, and when she

glanced down at the floor, she looked back at him. "You even tiled the floor."

"Yes."

She nodded and headed toward the area he used as a kitchen with the mini appliances. Without asking for permission, she opened the refrigerator and saw it filled with beer. She closed it and said, "You transformed it into a man's cave."

"If that's what you want to call it." No need to tell her that there were times he could swear he could still smell her scent, imagine hearing her laughter here. "I still have the covering you knitted for the table."

She glanced over at him. "You do?"

"Yes." He leaned against the breakfast bar and watched her walk around, taking in the different textured walls. The section of the room that used to look like a command center was now the area where he kept a lot of his electronics.

Kaegan wasn't sure how long she walked around and he wondered if she was somehow getting closure. Finally, she turned to him. "I'm ready to leave now."

He walked over to her, feeling emotions that she was trying to hide. This place was a part of her past, like it was to him. It had meant something to them once. "Talk to me, Bryce. Tell me what you're feeling. What you're thinking."

She looked away and then she looked back at him. "I came here today to find closure, but it appears that you beat me to the punch. Obviously, you needed closure here, as well."

He hadn't seen it as closure but more as survival. It had been time for changes and he'd made them. But nothing— and he meant nothing—could erase memories of her presence here. There hadn't been a single time when he'd come here that he hadn't thought of her, remembered bringing her here, making love to her here.

"No, Bryce, making changes was not my way to find closure. It would have taken more than removing pieces of furnishings and installing a staircase to do that. No matter what you think I might have transformed this place into, I never lost sight of what it had meant to us. Nothing can ever replace that."

She lifted her chin. "It should."

"Why?"

She glared at him. "Coming here was a mistake. I'm ready to go."

She moved to walk by him but he reached out and grabbed her hand, gently holding it in his. Her hand was trembling, but she didn't pull it away. She wasn't looking at him but was staring down at the tiled floor.

"Bryce?"

She slowly lifted her head and met his gaze. He felt a punch to his gut when he saw those eyes, which always had the ability to take his breath away, were filled with tears. When one fell and trickled down her cheek, on instinct he reached up and wiped it away with the pad of his finger.

"I can't say enough how sorry I am for what I did to us, Bryce. I take full responsibility for hurting you, for costing us the last ten years, the future we'd dreamed of."

He paused, fighting back the urge to tell her here and now that he knew he loved her and that closure was the last thing he wanted with her. The only reason he held back was because she wouldn't be ready to accept that yet. Bryce was a show-me kind of girl and he intended to show her that she was the only woman who had his heart.

He stared into her eyes and she stared into his. He was aware of the moment her gaze shifted from his eyes to his mouth. She used to do that when she wanted him to kiss her. Did she remember? Deciding not to waste time pondering it, he lowered his head to hers.

The moment their lips touched, ten years of denial, hunger and craving took control. He slid his tongue in her mouth like he had every right to do so. Like he *had* to do so, or die right then and there. There might have been other women after her but none had ever meant anything to him. None had ever made him feel the way she had. Only Bryce had the ability to not only rock his world, but also tilt the universe in his favor if she chose to do so.

And at that moment, he intended to give her a reason to do that very thing.

Deep in the recesses of her brain a warning light was going off. Bryce knew she should heed it. But she couldn't. She was too far gone and had been the moment Kaegan's mouth had closed over hers, almost eating her alive. Shivers of passion were flowing through her and she groaned when he deepened the kiss.

At sixteen she'd thought nobody could kiss like Kaegan and felt the same way when he'd celebrated her twenty-first birthday with her in a hotel room in Atlanta. He'd made all the arrangements and all she'd had to do was show up. She thought the same thing now that she had then. A twenty-three-year-old Kaegan definitely knew how to use his mouth and tongue. Now, fast-forward and her mouth was being taken by a thirty-five-year-old Kaegan.

The way he was kissing her was sending blood rushing through her veins and unleashing a degree of passion within her that had her wondering where it had come from. Her senses were on full alert. She was totally and completely reeling from the skilled and adept use of his mouth.

And then she felt his hands. They were roaming over her backside, molding to her like he used to do, and on instinct her body curved into his. And just like the night they'd danced together, she felt his aroused state. Knowing he still desired her did something to her and she reached up and wrapped her arms around his neck, cradling his erection at the juncture of her thighs.

Her mind was suddenly flooded with memories of how good things used to be between them, when he had been her world and she had been his. When they'd shared love, secrets and then more love. At this very place. He deepened the kiss even more and she could feel heat flowing from his body to hers. The strength of his thighs pressed even harder against her, and she could feel his thick, hard shaft getting bigger, more aroused.

She wasn't sure how long the kiss would have lasted because at that moment his watch beeped. He disengaged their mouths but kept his arms wrapped around her waist. Her hands fell from around his neck and she tried taking a step back but his hold around her waist tightened.

Clearing her throat, she asked, "Was that an alert letting you know someone is on the island?"

He shook his head. "No. That was a text from Willa. I need to get back to deliver lunch to my men."

His words made her realize he'd gotten behind on his schedule today to bring her here. "Sorry that I asked you to—"

"Don't apologize for asking me to bring you here, Bryce," he interrupted.

Yes, for all the good it had done. She'd come here for closure but instead what she'd gotten was awakening passion. "Why, Kaegan?" she asked him.

He lifted an eyebrow. "Why what?"

"Why did you kiss me?"

Releasing her, he shoved his hands into his jeans and she wished he hadn't done that. Doing so made the solid and enlarged shape of his erection that much more defined and pronounced. The area between her legs twitched in response to seeing it.

"You might want closure, Bryce, but I'm not sure that I do."

She frowned. "B-but you said we could never go back to being the way we were."

"No, you said that."

Yes, she had. "But you agreed."

"What I did was go along with what you wanted, but that kiss was a game changer."

Her frown deepened. *Game changer?* Lifting her chin, she said, "Nothing has changed, Kaegan. We will never be anything more than friends."

"Okay."

Okay? She lifted an eyebrow. "So you agree with me, right?"

He shook his head. "No, at the moment I'm going along with what you're saying."

At the moment? "I think we need to talk about this."

He shrugged massive shoulders and she noted his erection hadn't gone down—not one iota. "What is there to talk about? We want different things. You want closure and I want you."

She placed her hands on her hips. "So, is that what this is about, Kaegan? Sex?"

It seemed her question made something snap within him and he pulled his hands from his pockets and took a step closer to her. She could feel anger radiating out of his every pore. What was he mad about when she'd spoken the truth?

His eyes were flaring fire and his jaw was twitching. Then he said, "Let's get one damn thing straight, Bryce. I've never had sex with you. Every time I entered your body it was to make love to you, to cherish you as my mate. Don't try and cheapen what we shared together, no matter how things turned out between us. Don't ever do that again. Now let's go."

CHAPTER SEVENTEEN

Kaegan pulled the boat up to the dock. Turning off the boat's ignition, he offered his hand to Bryce to assist her out the boat. Instead of taking it, in a brusque voice, she said, "I can manage. Thank you."

"Don't mention it," he said with the same gruff tone as he watched her climb out of the boat onto the dock.

He watched her leave, which was fine because he needed a few minutes to himself to reflect on the kiss they'd shared. A kiss he knew would keep him up at night thinking about it, reliving the moment. Whether she realized it or not, that kiss had told a story of its own. She might want to deny it, but he'd felt her response. And she wanted closure? Well, he had news for her. If she thought the kiss was one-and-done, then she needed to think again. And he intended to do just that— give her time to think without crowding her. She needed to finally accept he wasn't going anywhere. Their lives were entwined. She belonged to him and he belonged to her.

Kaegan believed they were soul mates. What other reason could there be for them coming full circle? Hopefully, in time she would accept they could never be just friends.

They had ticked that box and moved beyond that when she'd turned sixteen.

Although today hadn't turned out quite like he would have liked, he believed them going to Eagle Bend Inlet had been something that was needed. There was nothing wrong with returning to the place it all started. The place where they'd first made love and where he'd told her he loved her and committed his life to her.

That was how it was and that was how it would always be.

That night Bryce closed her books, stood and stretched. In the far reaches of her mind she could hear Kaegan saying the words "take a shower and drink a glass of wine before going to bed." She intended to do just that. At least she was thinking of something else and not that kiss, which still had parts of her body tingling with sensations.

If there had been any doubts in her mind that Kaegan could still rock her world, they had been obliterated today. He was even better than she'd remembered. He had kissed her like the grown man that he was and she'd responded like the woman she'd become.

So much for wanting closure…

Her mouth had known him the moment he'd touched it. The same thing with her tongue. He had wrapped his around hers and sucked gently as he'd always been prone to do. But now there was a hunger within him that she detected. A hunger that had aroused her just as much as it had him.

Bryce knew that she and Kaegan were at odds again for now. During the ride back to the dock from Eagle Bend Inlet they hadn't spoken one word. He had definitely been quick to let her know making love to her had meant more than sex. She appreciated that, although at the time she hadn't because she'd been angry with herself for returning the kiss. Instead of blaming herself, she had blamed him.

Standing, Bryce was about to go into the bedroom to shower when her phone rang. She recognized the ringtone as Vashti calling. It was then that she recalled her last parting words to Vashti were that they would talk later. Now was later.

"Hello, Vash."

"Well, well, well, would you like to tell me how you and Kaegan happened to get lost at sea for two hours after you left the ship?"

Bryce rolled her eyes. "We were not missing for two hours. We took a detour that only took thirty minutes."

"That's not the way I heard it. I got sleepy again and caught a ride back to the dock with Elton after lunch and that's what I heard."

"Well, you heard it wrong." There was no need asking Vashti where she'd heard it from. It didn't matter since it could be from a number of people. Unfortunately, news traveled fast in Catalina Cove even when the news was not factual.

"So where did the two of you go?"

Bryce knew Vashti. Her best friend wouldn't let up until she spilled her guts. Besides, she could use another friendly ear and Vashti did owe her for all those times she had counseled her about Scott and even about Sawyer.

"We went to what used to be our secret place," she said, hating to admit such a thing.

"Really? Whose idea was that?"

"Mine," Bryce confessed.

"Could I ask you why?"

"I need closure."

Vashti didn't say anything for a moment, and then she said, "Let me get this straight. You want closure, so you asked Kaegan to take you to a place that used to be your private place, where the two of you would make love, make promises and whisper words of forever?"

"Yes."

"Excuse me, Bryce, but closure usually doesn't work that way."

Bryce dropped down on the sofa. "Not for most people, but I thought Kaegan and I should use a different approach. He went along with it."

"I just bet he did. He was probably hoping the place would have the opposite effect on you. Once you got there, instead of closure it would remind you of what the place meant to you both."

If that was what he'd thought then she'd really burst his bubble. On the other hand, he'd pretty much burst hers with that kiss. Locking lips with the fully grown Kaegan still had blood rushing through her veins. Now she wasn't sure if she still wanted to have closure or not. If not closure then what? Hmm…a kiss from him every now and then would work. Her cheeks reddened and she couldn't believe she could think such a thing. Of course she wanted closure. But then, from the way she'd kissed him back, she'd wanted him, too. She couldn't have it both ways.

"Bryce?"

"Yes?"

"So what happened? Did you find closure?"

She paused a moment and then admitted, "No."

"And it took the two of you two hours to figure that out?"

Bryce rolled her eyes. "We were not gone for two hours, Vash. I told you that."

"Okay, then how do you feel about that closure thing now?"

She drew in a deep breath. "Not good, because instead of closure I think something else got initiated."

"What?"

"An opening."

"Meaning what, Bryce?"

Bryce rubbed her hand across her forehead and thought

that was a good question. "We kissed…and do you know what, Vash?"

"What?"

"Like fine wine it's gotten even better over time."

"Hot diggity! Sounds like you've gotten yourself in a fix, girlfriend."

She didn't want to agree with Vashti, but she had a feeling that she had. But it was a predicament that she was determined to work out on her own. Bryce was about to tell that to Vashti when she suddenly heard a noise coming from her backyard.

"Hold on, Vash. I think I heard something."

"Heard something like what?"

"A noise coming from my backyard. It's probably Mr. Chelsey's cat trying to get into my garbage can." Alton Chelsey was the eighty-year-old widower who lived next door alone with his cat, Butterball.

"Wait! You don't know that. Don't you dare go outside and investigate. I'm sending Sawyer over. He just got back from being out on the ship and hasn't gotten ready for bed yet."

Bryce rolled her eyes. "Honestly, Vash. It's close to midnight. Like I said, it's probably Mr. Chelsey's cat."

"And like I said, you don't know that."

"Get real. This is Catalina Cove and not Amityville. Nothing sinister or crazy ever happens around here. You lived in New York too long."

"That might be the case, but I'm not taking any chances. I'm sending Sawyer over."

CHAPTER EIGHTEEN

When Bryce heard the sound of her doorbell, she crossed the room and, after taking time to make sure it was Sawyer, opened the door. "Sorry Vashti sent you out tonight, Sawyer, after being out on Kaegan's boat all day. You have to be tired."

"It doesn't matter. Until I make sure everything is safe here Vashti won't go to sleep, so let me check out back. Lock the door behind me until I return."

He went back out and she locked the door behind him as instructed. She went back into the living room to drink the rest of her wine. Tonight she'd done things in reverse. Wine first, then she would take a shower. Although she hated Sawyer coming over to her place for nothing, at least Vashti had sent Sawyer and not called the police station for one of his deputies to come and investigate. While out on the ship Bryce had heard Sawyer mention that he'd traded shifts tonight with Deputy Bob Fireside. Everybody in the cove knew Deputy Fireside would find any excuse to flash the blue lights on his patrol car.

She stood when she heard the knock at her door that signaled Sawyer's return. She put down her wineglass, quickly went to the door and checked out the peephole before opening it. "Mr. Chelsey's cat, right?"

Sawyer shrugged. "Not sure. Your garbage bin had been turned over and there were footprints near your back patio."

"Footprints?"

"Yes."

Bryce nodded and smiled. "They're Mr. Chelsey's. It wouldn't be the first time Butterball got out and he had to come in my backyard to get him. The footprints looked like a pair of sneakers, right?"

"Yes."

"Then the case is solved. It was Mr. Chelsey's footprints since he always wears sneakers."

"I'll go next door and verify it was him."

Bryce rolled her eyes. "Honestly, Sawyer, you've been hanging around Vashti too long or vice versa. The two of you are getting paranoid in your old age. If it makes you feel better, I'll ask Mr. Chelsey about it tomorrow when I see him."

He stared at her for a minute with that Sheriff Sawyer Grisham look, and she stared back and saw for herself how tired he was around the eyes. It was near midnight and Vashti said he'd just gotten home a short while ago. That meant he had stayed out on Kaegan's boat for over fourteen hours.

"It embarrasses Mr. Chelsey whenever people know he's outside at night looking for his cat. How do you think he's going to feel if you show up on his doorstep questioning him about anything tonight?"

Sawyer rubbed a hand down his face. "Fine. But if you hear any more noise tonight, call me or the station. And don't assume anything and go out to investigate on your own."

"I won't, Sawyer. I promise."

"Now lock your door."

Then he was gone. She locked her door and went back into the living room to finish off her wine.

★ ★ ★

The next morning Kaegan rolled out of bed and made it into his bathroom to start his day. He figured it would be a nice day to fish from the pier in his backyard. The bayou was brimming with over sixty species and he hoped that he'd luck up and catch a few bass, which were his favorite.

He left the bathroom moments later and got dressed for the day. When he'd gone to bed last night he should have been too tired to do anything but sleep. However, thoughts of Bryce stayed on his mind. Dreaming about her and reliving that kiss had taken precedence. He also thought about her silence on the ride back to the dock, as well as his own.

Kaegan needed time to think. Although he didn't regret kissing her, he wondered if he'd crossed the line in doing so when she'd made it clear all she wanted between them was friendship. He'd been determined to change her mind about that but hadn't intended to rush her. Now he was wondering if that kiss would have her scampering in another direction. One that was far away from him.

He was about to fix his breakfast when his cell phone rang. He picked it up and saw the caller was Walter Kerner. Why would his attorney be calling him on a Sunday morning? He clicked on the phone. "Good morning. What's up, Walt?"

"Today might be your lucky day. I need you in Boston as soon as possible."

Kaegan was surprised. "Boston? Why?"

"That warehouse on the harbor that I was telling you about might be going up for sale. If and when it does, you need to jump on it."

Kaegan leaned against his kitchen counter. His business was doing great in this region, but after taking on the Chappell Group as a client and seeing how profitable such a venture had been, he'd decided to expand his business to other areas. He now had the capital to do it and had more than one willing investor. Not only did Reid LaCroix think expanding was a good idea, but Ray also did.

Ray had discovered he was just as wealthy as Reid, thanks to a business deal he'd closed in his final days as Devon Ryan. Ray had let Kaegan know if he ever decided to expand, he would gladly come on board as a silent partner. Kaegan would admit that he was excited at the prospect of Chambray Seafood Shipping Company doing business in a New England state.

"I need you to take a look at it and talk to the present owners. And if that doesn't work out, I think you still need to check out the area. The Boston Harbor is the place to be if you want your business to expand to include lobster."

Kaegan was well aware that although the Gulf had several species of lobster, it was a known fact lobsters in the Atlantic, around Boston, were more plentiful and tastier. It was a market he was ready to explore. "That sounds good to me."

"Then I need you on the next plane. Just get to the airport around three. I've made all the arrangements and you'll probably be gone for at least three days."

He raised an eyebrow. "That long?"

"Yes."

That meant he needed to let Willa know that he would be out of the office. Of course, he would also let Ray and Sawyer know. His thoughts shifted to Bryce. She probably wouldn't want to know. At this point she probably didn't care. Besides, after yesterday maybe distance was what they needed more than anything.

She had that exam tomorrow and he could call and wish her luck. But he'd done that already. He would wait and congratulate her on passing the exam when he got back, since he was certain she would ace it.

"Okay. I'll leave for Boston today." After jotting down the pertinent information, he ended the call.

CHAPTER NINETEEN

Bryce held her breath as she punched in the control number on her laptop for the exam she'd taken yesterday. She had walked out of the testing center feeling confident about how she'd done. However, by the time she'd gotten home, she'd been a nervous wreck. She'd told everyone not to call her until after ten this morning because she couldn't check her grade until then.

After entering the number, she briefly closed her eyes, too nervous to look just yet. When she opened them, she smiled and then threw her fist up in the air in victory. She had passed with a ninety-eight.

At that moment she was both happy and relieved. It was over. She would now be able to sell, negotiate and market real estate in other states. That meant she wouldn't just be confined to Catalina Cove. She leaned back in her chair, staring at her test score again. The test had been hard and there had been tricky questions. But Kaegan had taught her how to focus on the key words.

Kaegan…

Bryce owed a lot of credit for her passing the test to Kaegan's study techniques, not to mention the time he'd spent drilling her for three nights straight. She owed him and would thank him when she saw him in the café in the morning. Because she'd needed to study, she hadn't helped out at the café for the past few days. This morning she'd known not to even think about going anywhere until she'd seen her grade results.

She couldn't wait to tell everyone. However, she knew the first person she wanted to share her good news with was Kaegan. She was about to pick up her phone to call him when her phone rang. It was her mother.

Bryce smiled—she'd told everyone not to call her before ten, and here it was barely ten fifteen. "I passed, Mom!"

After her mother's call, she received calls from Vashti, Ashley and several other friends in town. Even Jeremy called to see how she'd done and to congratulate her. He told her he was in court this week, but had taken the time to call her while on recess. That had been thoughtful of him and she told him how much she appreciated him calling.

She thought about calling Kaegan, like she'd intended to do earlier, but was a little disappointed that although she hadn't reached out to him yet, he hadn't called like the others. She could only think of one reason for him not doing so. He was still upset over their tiff on Saturday. In that case, she would wait for him to call her when he'd gotten over it. She refused to feel disappointed about anything today. It would be an upbeat day for her since she had a reason to celebrate. She had studied hard, passed the exam, and now the next chapter in her life presented endless possibilities. She would talk to Vashti on how she could market herself. Her best friend was good at that sort of thing and had Shelby by the Sea to show for it.

Bryce decided to eat breakfast, then go into the office. Pia had been holding things down for the last week while she'd studied.

A couple of hours later Bryce was leaving her house to go

into the office. She saw Mr. Chelsey outside in his yard and waved to the older man. She then remembered the incident on Saturday night and asked, "Did you ever find Butterball Saturday night?"

Mr. Chelsey smiled brightly. "Yes, I did. I hope that I didn't disturb you while I was out looking for him."

"No, you didn't bother me. I'm just glad you found him."

"Me, too. Have a good day, Bryce."

Kaegan entered his home. He was happy to be back, although he was glad he'd made the trip to Boston. He'd been busy from the minute he'd landed. Walt had made sure every minute had been used wisely and to his advantage. He was embarking on a whole new phase in his life and a part of him couldn't help but be excited.

Boston Harbor was a beautiful place but he was concerned whether or not he and the owner of that warehouse could reach a satisfactory agreement. Just in case, he would look at other properties near the harbor.

Kaegan's thoughts shifted to Bryce. He had thought about her every day he'd been gone and had been tempted to call her more than once but knew she would have been studying on Sunday and Monday. A part of him felt certain she'd passed her test and couldn't wait to see her to find out.

A couple of hours later he was walking into his shipping company. Willa smiled when she saw him. "Hey, boss, welcome back."

"Thanks. Any problems while I was gone?"

"None that we couldn't handle. We got that shipment off in time for the Oklahoma Oyster Chow-Down this weekend. The committee sends their thanks for such prompt service."

Kaegan smiled. "We want to keep our clients happy."

He glanced at his watch. "I'm only here for a few. Then I

have an off-site meeting." He'd talked to both Reid and Ray and both wanted to meet with him in a few hours.

"I'm sure Kaegan is happy that you aced your test," Vashti said.

Bryce tossed a file in the inbox of her desk while talking to Vashti on the phone. "I wouldn't know since I haven't heard from him. According to my parents, they haven't seen him in two days. Of course, they are concerned since he usually drops in at the café almost every day. They figure that he must be pretty busy."

"Sawyer mentioned he left Sunday to go out of town on an unexpected business trip."

Bryce sat up straight in her chair. "He did?"

"Yes. I thought you knew. Otherwise I would have mentioned it."

No, she hadn't known. "We didn't exactly part ways Saturday the best of friends."

"Oh? You didn't tell me that part."

Bryce rolled her eyes. "Mainly because you got hung up on the part I told you about—the kiss. Then if you recall, I heard noise in my backyard and we ended the call when you sent your husband over to investigate."

"Sawyer mentioned he'd found footprints in your backyard."

"Belonging to Mr. Chelsey. I spoke with him yesterday. Butterball got out again and he was looking for him."

"Well, still, you can never be too careful."

"I just hate Sawyer came over here for nothing. He looked tired."

"Hey, don't have pity on him. He might have looked tired but he wasn't too tired to rock my world and his own when he got back, trust me."

Bryce couldn't help but giggle. "I guess being pregnant hasn't slowed you guys down."

"Not at all."

"Well, I need to get back to work. It's going to take me the rest of the week to get caught up in my office. And I appreciate you and Ashley taking the time to meet with me next Thursday for lunch." She had reached out to Vashti for marketing tips and Vashti suggested she include Ashley. Ashley and her business partner, Emmie Givens, had founded StayN-Touch, a highly successful social-media-network firm. Hopefully the two of them could give her suggestions on how to jump-start her career.

Ashley had been kind enough to invite them to lunch. Presently, she and Ray were living in the house Ray owned before they married while their new home on the ocean was being built. According to Ashley, they expected the house to be finished before the babies arrived.

A few hours later Bryce was entering her home. She'd just placed her purse down when her phone rang. She dug it out of her purse and clicked it on without glancing to see who was calling. "Hello."

"Hello, Bryce, this is Kaegan."

The deep, throaty sound of his voice was like a long, sensuous stroke down her spine. Sliding down on the sofa, she said, "Yes, Kaegan, how are you?"

"Fine and I understand congratulations are in order. I'm glad you passed your exam. I told you that you would."

"Yes, you did. Thanks for your help, Kaegan. I'm convinced I would not have passed without your study tips."

"Glad I was able to help. Sorry I didn't call sooner but I had to make an unexpected trip to Boston. I just got back in town around noon today." He paused then added, "I started to call you on Sunday to let you know I was leaving but didn't want to interrupt your studying."

His words lifted her spirits because she'd assumed he was still upset about Saturday. If he'd thought of calling her before leaving town that meant he hadn't been.

"How was Boston?" she asked him.

"Nice, as usual."

"I've never been there, but it's on my bucket list of places I'd like to visit."

"Really? I'll be going back next month. Would you like to go with me?" he asked her.

Bryce arched an eyebrow. "Why would you ask me that?"

"Well, you just said it was on your bucket list of places to visit and I extended the invite to you as a friend. The thought of us staying in the same hotel room never entered my mind, Bryce, if that's what you're afraid of."

She swallowed. "I'm not afraid of anything."

"Okay then, consider the invitation out there. In fact, now that I think about it, you coming with me might be a good idea."

"Why would you think that?"

"You're the first person I've told other than my investors, but I'm expanding my business to the Boston area. There're a couple of warehouses on the harbor that I'll be looking at. Since you've passed your exam that means you'll be licensed to handle the sale when it's made, right."

"Yes." She couldn't downplay the excitement that began flowing through her. "You would actually hire me to represent you?" she asked, trying not to sound too enthusiastic at the prospect.

"Any reason why I shouldn't hire you as my real-estate broker? Vashti always said you did an outstanding job with trying to sell Shelby by the Sea. It wasn't your fault the deal fell through."

He was right. It hadn't been her fault that the Catalina Cove zoning board wouldn't approve the permit for a new tennis resort. Things turned out for the best when Vashti decided not to sell and, instead, run the inn herself. "It will take a week for my passing grade to be registered in the system with other states and then I can begin practicing as a broker."

"I can wait until then."

She tried not to feel all happy inside. "You sure?"

"Yes, I'm sure. Think about it, Bryce," Kaegan said. "If you aren't able to do it then I'll connect with a broker in Boston."

"I'll be able to do it," she said quickly.

"That's great. Are you free Saturday of next week to discuss it more?"

"Yes."

"Great. I'd like to invite you to meet me at my place."

"Your office?"

"No, my home. I'd rather not anyone know about my expansion plans yet. You can present me with locations on the harbor you feel might interest me."

She could definitely do that, although it meant going out to his place on the bayou. She couldn't help but recall what happened the last time she was there and what he'd said. But this time he was inviting her for business and not a party. "Fine. We can meet at your place next Saturday morning, around eleven. Will that time work for you, Kaegan?"

"Yes, that time will work for me. Goodbye, Bryce, and congratulations again on passing your exam."

"Thanks and goodbye."

After clicking off the phone, Bryce summed up in her head what had taken place over the call. She was smart enough to take advantage of a business opportunity when it knocked on her door, but it would mean working closely with Kaegan for a while, and it also meant a business trip with him to Boston.

She drew in a deep breath, confident that she could do both as long as they kept things in perspective, and there was no reason they couldn't.

CHAPTER TWENTY

"You actually volunteered to be on your high-school holiday class-reunion committee?" Sawyer asked Kaegan, surprised. They were walking toward the parking lot after attending the zoning-board meeting.

'Something like that. In fact, I'm on my way there now, so the zoning-board meeting ended right on time. We're meeting in the high school's library at seven."

"Now, that's interesting."

Kaegan glanced over at Sawyer. "What is?"

"Vashti mentioned Bryce was on that committee, but I have a feeling you knew that."

"Yes, I knew it. In fact, she's the one who suggested I join it."

Sawyer shook his head, grinning. "When a man loves a woman, he will do anything to stay within her good graces."

Kaegan smiled. "Hey, I'm still in the friendship state with Bryce. She's not ready to move beyond that."

"Don't give up on her, man. True love will prevail each and every time."

Kaegan remembered Sawyer's words a short while later

when he walked up the steps to the high school. When he'd been a student here, this place used to seem bigger than life and now everything looked small. He had Vashti and Bryce to thank for making his life tolerable while attending school.

He opened the door and went inside. He hadn't seen Bryce's car parked outside and wondered if she'd gotten here yet. She used to be a stickler for time and he wondered if that had changed over the years. He strolled past the rows of student lockers and several classrooms as he headed toward the library.

Over the years things had been renovated and the place looked different inside. He then realized that this was the first time he'd been in the school since graduating. He'd never had a reason to return. He wouldn't be here now if it wasn't for Bryce.

When he got closer to the library he heard voices. He remembered the one thing the librarian, Mrs. Tinkersley, wouldn't tolerate was anyone talking in the library. It was the one place he'd never heard voices, unless they were whispered ones. But even those weren't allowed by Mrs. Tinkersley.

Following the sound of the voices, he headed toward what he recalled as one of the smaller conference rooms. When he entered it seemed everyone sitting at the table looked up. "Good evening," he greeted them, feeling nervous somewhat.

"Kaegan, come on in," a woman he knew as Susan Langley said as she smiled broadly. "You know everybody here."

Yes, he did. All former classmates. He moved around the table and shook hands with Laura Crawford, whose family owned several businesses in town, and Charlette Hansberry, who owned a nursing home. Moving to the other side of the table to shake more hands, he remembered Derrick Conyers, who played on the football team, and Doug Bostic, who played basketball and who'd been their star swimmer. They smiled as if they were glad to see him.

He checked his watch, wondering where Bryce was. He

hoped she hadn't talked him into joining the committee, only to back out. As if Susan read his thoughts, when he slid into one of the vacant chairs at the table, she said, "Bryce just texted me that she's on her way and will be here in a few."

The woman's words released a load of pressure that had been building in Kaegan's chest. Just knowing Bryce was on her way meant everything.

Bryce glanced at her watch as she raced up the steps to the school. She hated being late when going anywhere, although she still had five minutes. She had intended to get here with time to spare, but had gotten stuck on the phone with a client.

When she entered the library she heard voices, so she moved toward the conference room where the voices were coming from. The door was open and she smiled as she walked inside. She was about to greet everyone when she saw Kaegan. He had come. She had wondered if he would. More than once she'd been tempted to call him to remind him of tonight's meeting and decided that, since he'd been the one to accept her offer to join, he should care enough to make sure he kept his word and remembered to come. He had.

"Come on in, Bryce. You arrived with two minutes to spare, but since you're here we can go ahead and get started," Susan said.

"Hello, everyone," Bryce said, as she swiftly moved to sit in the only vacant seat, which happened to be across from Kaegan. She forced herself not to glance over at him and instead tried to focus on what Susan was saying as she called the meeting to order.

One of the reasons she'd decided to be a part of the committee was because Susan was known to be a very organized individual, who didn't believe in wasting time. That meant the meeting would follow an agenda and they would be leaving at the allotted hour.

Although she'd tried really hard, she hadn't been able to resist temptation, and more than once she'd glanced over at Kaegan. Thankfully, he'd been paying rapt attention to what the others were saying, as if she hadn't been there.

"Anyone want to work on the music committee to assure we have a blend of all types to satisfy everyone attending?" Susan asked. "Like I said, the response has been overwhelming. Since we're encompassing five graduating classes instead of just one, we'll have a large group coming. Music will play an important factor."

"I suggest we get a band," Charlette said.

Susan nodded. "Any more suggestions?"

Bryce raised her hand. "Since this reunion will encompass several classes, I thought what would really be neat is that, in addition to getting a band, we hire a DJ to play a few songs that were popular during the year we graduated. It will be fun to hear them."

Derrick nodded. "I think that's a good idea."

"Well, I don't," Laura said. Even in school, she was the most argumentative person around. People usually gave in to her just to shut her up. "I suggest we do neither and just make our own playlist. That way we can save on hiring a band and a DJ."

Everyone stared at her, but then, they really weren't surprised. Laura was tight with her money and didn't like spending it on anything. The thing was, the committee had the money to spend from the tickets they'd sold to the reunion. People were expecting something a little more special than just a playlist and the committee could afford it. When nobody said anything, probably too shocked to speak, Laura smiled and said, "I'm glad everyone agrees with me, so now we can move on to something else."

Bryce waited to see if anyone would stand up and tell Laura

they didn't agree with her. When it seemed no one would, she raised her hand. Susan looked over at her. "Yes, Bryce?"

Bryce stood. "Thanks for making that suggestion, Laura, but I don't agree. From what Susan indicated we have in the treasury, we do have the money to spend toward music, so we should. Some people are coming a long way and the least we can do is to have good music playing at the event."

"I suggest we spend less on music and more on food," Doug said.

Bryce drew in a deep breath when she saw a few of the others speaking up to side with Laura. Bryce knew one of the reasons was that Laura's dad, although not as rich as Reid, was still a major employer in town. It bothered her that everyone would so easily accept whatever Laura wanted.

Instead of being one of them and sitting down like she figured everyone expected her to do, she remained standing and said, "I think we should spend more money for music."

For a minute nobody said anything, and then, surprisingly, Kaegan spoke up and said, "I agree with Bryce. For years the reason I never attended a reunion was because I never felt included."

Bryce knew what Kaegan was referring to had nothing to do with the music, and from the looks on some of the faces in the room, they knew that, too.

Kaegan then added, "Bryce is right. Music has a way of bringing people together. It transcends all levels of communication. People are coming a long way and we are their hosts. Now is not the time to concentrate on money if we have it to spend. What are you going to do with it if you don't use it?"

Bryce glanced at the faces around the table. Kaegan had spoken. Once everyone had gotten over the shock of him doing that, they listened to what he said. Even Laura had been shocked into silence. While in school Kaegan rarely voiced his opinion about anything. He was seen but not heard. He couldn't help but be seen when most of the girls at school used to drool over him, including Laura Crawford. He'd thought Samuel was the heartthrob, but it had been him. And Bryce had been proud that, of all the girls at Catalina Cove High, she had been the one—and the only one—he'd wanted.

Bryce looked back at Susan, who said, "I think we should take a vote. All those in favor of varied types of music that includes both a band and a DJ, please raise your hands."

To Bryce's surprise, the majority of the hands went up in her favor. She released the deep breath she'd been hold-ing when Susan said, "The majority of everyone agrees, so, Bryce, are you willing to be the one to make sure we get the different kinds of music everyone wants to hear?"

Bryce nodded. "Yes."

"Thanks, Bryce. And, Kaegan, since you agreed with Bryce's position, can we count on you to work with her on the music?"

Bryce turned her head to look at Kaegan. Before answer-ing Susan, he met Bryce's gaze and said, "Yes, I will work with Bryce."

Bryce broke eye contact with Kaegan as she sat back down. She'd come close to saying that she could handle everything on her own without anyone's help. However, she recalled she'd been the one to talk him into being a part of his reunion, too. She would welcome anyone's help, even his.

"That's great, Kaegan. I appreciate you doing that," Susan said, smiling.

Bryce glanced back over at him, smiled and said, "Yes, thanks, Kaegan. I will appreciate the help."

CHAPTER TWENTY-ONE

"Good morning, Kaegan, Ray and Sawyer. The usual?"

"Yes, the usual," all three men replied to Bryce before she walked off.

Ray grinned. "Hmm, some things never change."

"And some things do," Sawyer added.

Kaegan shifted his gaze away from Bryce when she disappeared into the café's kitchen. It had been almost a week since the night they'd met for the class reunion meeting. He had contacted her earlier in the week to arrange a meeting to discuss the music for the class reunion. She had agreed with his suggestion that they meet on his yacht when she mentioned she would be in the area near the pier this evening.

He looked over at Ray. "What never changes?"

Ray smiled. "The way you still check out Bryce every morning when we come in here. Even when the two of you were at odds with each other, you used to look at her like you wanted to eat her alive...after making senseless love to her."

"You're imagining things."

"No, I'm not," Ray said.

Deciding not to argue with Ray, Kaegan shifted his gaze to Sawyer. "And what has changed, Sawyer?"

Sawyer chuckled. "There was a time Bryce didn't even acknowledge your presence. Now not only does she acknowledge it, you get first dibs. Now when she greets us in the mornings, she puts your name first."

A smile touched Kaegan's lips. He had noticed that. Was it because he'd offered her the job as his broker or that he'd backed her at the class-reunion meeting? Either reason didn't matter because he knew she would be good as his broker, and he agreed with what she'd said about the music. He hadn't been trying to score brownie points with her.

"Interesting," Sawyer added.

Kaegan chuckled at his friend. "Jealous?"

"No. In fact, I'm glad to see the two of you are now on friendlier terms. At one point I thought I was going to have to make some arrests. Put you and Bryce in the same cell and have you fight it out, get it out of your system."

Ray laughed. "A fight isn't what they need to get out their system, Sawyer."

At that moment Bryce returned with their muffins and a pot of coffee. She smiled at them. "Anything else, guys?"

"Nope. We're good," Kaegan said, smiling back at her.

"I forgot to ask if you spoke with your neighbor to verify those were indeed his footprints," Sawyer said to Bryce.

She looked over at him. "Yes. He said Butterball got out Saturday night and apologized for the noise. I told him there was no need to apologize, so, Sheriff, the mystery has been solved." She smiled and then walked off.

"What was that about?" Kaegan asked.

Sawyer grabbed a blueberry muffin out the basket and began buttering it. "Apparently nothing now. Bryce and Vashti were talking on the phone late Saturday night, that same weekend we all helped you net oysters. Bryce heard a

sound coming from her backyard. Although she tried assuring
Vashti it was probably just her neighbor out looking for his
cat, Vashti wanted me to go over to Bryce's place and check
anyway. I did and found footprints in her backyard. Bryce
was convinced they were her neighbor's and said she would
check with the man the next day. Evidently she did check
and the footprints belonged to him."

Kaegan didn't say anything for a minute as Sawyer began
talking to Ray about how Ray's tour-boat business was coming along. When there was a lull in the conversation, Kaegan
said, "I'm glad you went to check anyway, Sawyer. My tire
got slashed at her place."

Sawyer's head snapped up from looking down into his coffee cup. "What? When?"

Kaegan shrugged. "Friday of that same week when I went
over to her place to help her study. It was after eleven, and
when I came out I saw my tire flat, and after checking further, I saw the tire had been slashed."

"Slashed? And you didn't call the station to report it?"

"I didn't see the need. I figured it was kids with nothing
better to do."

"On a Friday night? When the Livewire serves free pizzas
every Friday night to the local teens?" Sawyer asked, frowning. "I can't see any teen missing a free pizza to slash a tire."

The Livewire was a hangout spot for the teens in town.
It was a decent place that provided a safe environment for
them to play arcade games and fill up on hamburgers, fries
and milkshakes. There was even a quiet corner in the back
for those who wanted to get an early start on their homework
during the weekdays. On Friday nights they always served
free pizzas and hosted talent night so the teens could show-
case their skills. Usually the place was packed but always or-
derly. "I changed the tire myself and kept moving. I didn't
even mention it to Bryce," Kaegan said.

He took a sip of his coffee and studied Sawyer. Anyone who'd been around Sawyer long enough knew how his mind worked. He was thinking. Personally, Kaegan thought he was thinking too hard, but a part of Kaegan understood. Sawyer was sheriff of Catalina Cove and he liked staying on top of things. He was ex-military and ex-FBI, and being suspicious of anything and everything was part of his makeup. Since Sawyer had been sheriff, the residents of Catalina Cove had a positive regard for the law. Sawyer was fair and crime was almost nonexistent. Cops now treated the people with respect.

Before Sawyer there had been Sheriff Phillips, who'd finally retired after his son was killed in a hunting accident. For as long as Kaegan could remember, there had been a Phillips enforcing the law in Catalina Cove. It had been a foregone conclusion that if a Phillips ran for sheriff he would win and always did. As far as Kaegan was concerned, Sheriff Phillips had been a lazy sheriff and rarely left the station. His deputies did all the work and some weren't all that nice to people.

Sawyer was totally different from Phillips. He was a hands-on sort of sheriff and he got out of his office more than he stayed in. He knew how to connect with the people. He didn't act like his badge was a sign of privilege, but rather, it was a badge of honor. And he definitely didn't act like he made the law, like Sheriff Phillips and his regime had. Most of the men who worked for Phillips either quit or joined the New Orleans police force when Sawyer took over. They couldn't stomach having an outsider come in and run things.

Sawyer looked over at him. "If any craziness happens again, let me know. I don't like the idea there might be kids going around slashing tires."

"Okay, I'll let you know if it happens again," Kaegan said.

He shifted his gaze from Sawyer to Bryce. A man whom Kaegan didn't recognize had entered the café and he immediately knew the guy wasn't from around here. However, from the huge smile of recognition on Bryce's face, they obviously knew each other.

Kaegan tried downplaying the jealousy he felt that suddenly rushed through his body. He didn't recall making a sound, but obviously he had because both Sawyer and Ray glanced up at him and then followed his gaze across the café.

Ray looked back at him. "Like I said earlier, some things never change. Whenever Bryce talks to a guy, steam comes out your ears."

He continued watching Bryce and the guy chat it up while he responded to Ray. "Steam does not come out of my ears."

Ray chuckled. "Yes, it does. More is coming out now and I don't know why. She's not your girl."

It was then that Kaegan aimed a narrowed gaze at Ray. "Not my girl but she's my friend, and I don't know the guy. Do either of you?"

Both Sawyer and Ray shook their heads.

"He's probably someone passing through or visiting someone in the cove. Chill, man," Ray said. "You're acting territorial again."

Kaegan glanced back at Bryce and the man. At that moment he didn't care how he was acting. He didn't like how friendly Bryce and the man seemed to be.

Kaegan looked back at Sawyer. Although he hadn't said anything, it was obvious from Sawyer's smile that he'd agreed with everything Ray had said. Okay, maybe he *was* acting territorial, and he didn't have any right doing so because Bryce wasn't his girl. But little did his friends know that he intended to change that soon. Real soon.

"It's good seeing you again, too, Jeremy. What brings you to Catalina Cove?" She had spoken with him when he'd called last Tuesday to congratulate her on passing the exam.

She didn't recall him mentioning that he would be in the area this week.

"I'm visiting someone and remembered you once said your parents owned a café here and served the best blueberry muffins. I decided to stop by and see if you knew what you were talking about."

Bryce threw back her head and laughed. "You'll see how good they are. Do you want anything else to go with the muffins and coffee?"

"What do you suggest?"

"Depends on what you like. Some people like to eat bacon or sausage with their muffins."

"That sounds like a winner. I think I'll take an order of bacon."

"Okay," Bryce said. "I'll be right back with your coffee." Smiling, she walked off, glad to see Jeremy, but she knew nothing had changed. She still wasn't interested in him and was pretty sure he'd gotten the voice message she'd left on his phone letting him know how busy she would be if she passed her exam. When she'd spoken with him on the phone last week he hadn't asked her out.

She wondered whom he was visiting in the area and had been tempted to ask, but knew it wasn't any of her business.

After placing his order on the counter for one of her brothers to pick up, she glanced over at Kaegan. He was staring at her and the heat from his gaze made sensuous currents flow through her as if she was holding a live wire. She broke eye contact with him to grab the coffeepot so she could pour Jeremy's coffee.

Bryce was tempted to look back over at Kaegan but didn't. Instead she walked back to where Jeremy sat to serve his coffee.

Back at the office Kaegan could barely get any work done for thinking about Bryce and that guy this morning. Even after Ray and Sawyer had left he'd hung back, getting more muffins and refills on his coffee and pretending to check messages on his cell phone just to linger around. There was something about the man he hadn't liked. Namely, the man's interest in Bryce. And like he'd told Ray and Sawyer, it was obvious they knew each other. How? Had the two of them dated before?

When she brought over his refill of coffee, he'd been tempted to ask but didn't. Like Ray had said and Sawyer had reiterated before leaving, Bryce was not his girl and he needed to stop acting territorial where she was concerned.

The beeper on his desk went off. He pressed the button on his desk. "Yes, Willa?"

"Ray is here to see you."

"Okay, send him in." He stood and walked around to the front of his desk, leaned against it and waited for Ray to walk in. "And what brings you here for a visit, Ray? Bored with being tour-boat captain and want your old job back?"

"No. First, I wanted to make sure you hadn't gotten into trouble this morning after Sawyer and I left. You were pretty ticked off."

Kaegan went back to sit down in the chair behind his desk, thinking about that morning and feeling frustrated. "Yes, I was pretty ticked off, although I know I don't have a right to be, like both you and Sawyer pointed out. I was the one who screwed up, Ray. I should have believed in Bryce, had more faith in her. I loved her. She'd been my best friend forever, but in that space of time I forgot all about that."

Ray sat and didn't say anything for a minute. "I recall getting mad with Ashley when I thought she'd betrayed me. Something you said is what kicked my ass into gear."

"And what did I say?"

"You basically told me that I could continue to feel sorry

for myself, or I could grow some balls and be thankful for Ashley and do something to make sure I kept her."

"Grow some balls? I'm sure I didn't use that terminology."

Ray grinned. "No, but what you said meant the same thing. I think it's time you take heed of your own advice."

Kaegan rubbed a hand down his face and then met Ray's gaze. "I love her, Ray."

"Hell, you don't think I know that. I've always known that. You loved her even when you swore you couldn't stand her. Nobody believed you, by the way. Not even the women in town, those who slept with you and those who didn't. Those sleeping with you did it just to get a piece of you and for you to get a piece of them, hoping you'd be impressed. You weren't. And those who wouldn't waste their time sleeping with you refused to do so because they wanted more and knew your heart belonged to Bryce."

His heart belonged to Bryce... "Too bad they know and she doesn't."

"Have you told her?" Ray asked.

Kaegan shook his head. "No, it's too soon. I'm working out a strategy with Bryce. For us to make a comeback, she has to want it as much as me."

"Yes, but at some point you might have to turn up the heat," Ray said. "How you handle your business is your decision. However, there's a quote someone at the hospital gave me the day I checked out to come here. At the time I wondered if I would ever get my memory back. Would I ever recapture the love I was convinced I had prior to my accident? The quote said, 'No matter where your path may take you, you can always find your way back home.'"

Ray paused, as if he was giving the quote time to sink into Kaegan's mind. "Home for you has never been Catalina Cove, Kaegan. Home for you is the love you have for Bryce. The two of you need to find your way back home together."

Kaegan didn't say anything. His mind was absorbing the quote like he figured Ray wanted him to. His friend didn't know it but he'd pretty much stated what Kaegan had concluded a while back. Only Bryce could make Catalina Cove home for him. Then to make light of the situation, he said, "You came all the way over here to get my confession of loving Bryce?"

Ray grinned. "No, but I'm glad you finally gave it. The other reason for my visit is because for the last few months I've been thinking like Devon Ryan."

Kaegan rolled his eyes. He'd discovered that Devon Ryan used to be a business-suit-wearing, suave, debonair and sophisticated sort of guy. Someone too smart for his own good and who had an IQ the likes of which most people couldn't even dream of ever having. Aside from the smarts, the man had been the total opposite of Ray. "Please don't tell me you're going to start wearing expensive business suits and Gucci shoes around town."

Ray chuckled. "No. Those days are totally over for me. I was thinking more along the lines of how I can grow my assets."

Kaegan leaned in closer to listen. Ray was the one who'd planted the idea in his head to expand his business and the results were paying off big-time. So whenever he spoke about finances, Kaegan listened. "All right, so what do you have in mind?"

"A water-taxi service from here to New Orleans. I had Ashley conduct a survey and there are a number of people living in the cove who work in New Orleans. They prefer living here for the small-town feel, but the bigger job opportunities are in New Orleans. Those same people have started complaining, and rightfully so, about the commute into work, which usually takes an hour or so on a good day. We can do a water-taxi service and get them there in half the time and it would be a relaxing trip since they won't have to drive."

Kaegan rubbed his hand over his chin, already liking the idea. "I can see it working."

Ray smiled. "So can I. We can even serve a complimentary breakfast from Witherspoon Café. Something simple like blueberry muffins and coffee. That would boost sales for the Witherspoons, and the increase in blueberry sales will be good for Reid's blueberry plant. It would help out with traffic jams whenever the cove hosts one of their festivals. A big bonus is that there will be less auto fumes on the road from here to New Orleans. And it might even increase home sales for people who prefer living in a small town."

Kaegan nodded. "I'm sure you've talked to Reid about it. What about Sawyer?"

"Yes, and like you, both think it's a great idea and are surprised no one has thought of it sooner. Of course, we'll have to get permission from the state, but Reid doesn't think there will be a problem."

Kaegan chuckled. "I'm sure he doesn't. We're voting for a new governor next year, and any candidate would love to have Reid's support and the nice campaign contribution that goes along with it."

Ray shrugged. "Hey, whatever works." He eased out of his chair. "Well, I'm glad you like the idea of the water taxi. Once more details are worked out, I'll bring it before the Catalina Cove zoning board."

He paused a moment and then said, "And think about what I said about Bryce, Kaegan. She's a beautiful woman and men are going to want to talk to her. Instead of getting jealous, do something about it and make her yours permanently."

Kaegan was still thinking about what Ray had said when he and Bryce met later that evening to discuss music for the high-school holiday reunion. It didn't take a rocket scientist to know she hadn't wanted to meet with him. She'd tried getting him to agree to a discussion over the phone. He turned down her offer both times.

It still bothered him whenever he thought about the guy who'd come into the café that morning, but like Sawyer and Ray had said, he had no rights where Bryce was concerned, so he needed to get over it. Besides, the last thing he needed was for her to think he was being territorial.

He had everything set and when he saw her strolling down the pier toward his yacht he couldn't help but feel the love he had for her. She looked comfortable in a pair of warm brown slacks and a beige blouse. It was mid-October and the weather today was rather warm for this time of year.

He stood on the deck of his yacht and studied her. She'd always had a regal walk but had never been one to hold herself apart from anyone. Unlike him, she was a people person, but she'd always included him in everything, making it clear that, along with Vashti, the three of them were a team. And during that time when Vashti had been sent away to have her baby, the two of them continued to bond and their bond had transformed into love.

That she was even communicating with him after what had happened was a miracle in itself. But he knew that, although she'd forgiven him and had now reclaimed him as a friend, she still guarded her emotions where he was concerned. He knew that and for now he accepted it as the price he had to pay for hurting her the way he had.

"Nice yacht," she said when she came aboard. He had reached out his hand to assist her, and the moment their hands had touched, he'd felt full sexual awareness. A part of him knew she had, as well, but was refusing to acknowledge it.

"I admit one of the reasons I accepted your offer to meet you here was because I've been dying to see around your yacht for a long time. It's beautiful. Ry and Duke brag about it every time you invite them to go night fishing with you."

He chuckled, thinking how much fun he had with her brothers whenever they all went fishing at night with Ray and Sawyer. "Now you can take a look around for yourself. Spencer's will be delivering our pizza shortly."

"Okay, but you didn't have to order food. I only need to be here for a minute to go over the music ideas with you. I made a list."

"It's just something light."

"Pizza?"

He grinned. "I know how much you like pizza. By the way, I checked out a number of bands that perform in the area. Only two were within the committee's budget."

"Figures. Good bands aren't cheap these days." She glanced up at him. "Well, are you going to show me around?"

"No, feel free to look around. I have no secrets where you're concerned." He could see the surprise in her eyes at what he said. There. He'd planted that thought in her head and he wanted it to take root.

She didn't say anything. Instead she turned and, out of the corner of his eye as he began setting the table for their meeting, he could see her looking around. She was right—his yacht was a beauty. His dream come true...behind her, of course. Bryce was his first dream and would always hold that position.

When she left to go check out other parts of the yacht, he released a deep breath. Her scent alone could render him weak. It was such a luscious fragrance. His phone went off and he checked the caller. It was a number he didn't recognize, so he let the call go to voice mail and then listened to it.

"Kaegan, this is Sasha. I was wondering what you would be doing Friday night. A girlfriend of mine is in town and I would like her to meet you."

Kaegan frowned. Why was she calling when she didn't

know him like that? Some women had a lot of nerve. A better question to ask was, how had she gotten his number? Since Farley Johnson was one of the team leaders on his boat, Farley did have his personal number, but Kaegan couldn't see him sharing it with his sister.

Twenty minutes later Bryce returned, all smiles. Undoubtedly, the smiles were for what she'd seen on her tour of the yacht. "I've never seen anything like this before," she said, her smile widening. "I am so proud of your accomplishments, Kaegan."

He knew her words were sincere. "And I am proud of yours. You did great on your exam."

"With your help."

"Then I can also say that I got all of this," he said, spreading out his arms wide, "with your help. You, your family and Vashti were always there for me in my early years. You know my history better than anyone, Bryce."

He'd deliberately mentioned a connection between them that would always be there. "What do you think of the upper deck?" he asked her.

"Oh, I loved it. I could spend a whole day up there while out in the middle of the ocean."

"So can I and usually I do. That's normally where I am on Sundays when I'm not doing my volunteer work."

She lifted an eyebrow when she sat down at the table. "You do volunteer work?"

"Yes."

"For who?" she asked him.

"One of the soup kitchens in New Orleans."

"Oh? How did you get involved with something like that?"

He shrugged as he sat down at the table after pulling out his music list. "While in the marines a group of us began volunteering on our days off-base. Rick Astor, one of my team members, gave us the idea. He said while growing up that was the only place he got a decent meal. Rick was killed in Iraq eight years ago, and in his memory, we all agreed to continue what he'd encouraged us to do."

He didn't say anything for a minute and then said, "Rick's story showed me that no matter how bad you think you had it growing up as a child, there is a kid out there somewhere who had it even worse."

When he heard a knock on the cabin door, he stood. "That's probably our pizza."

Over pizza and beer they covered their music lists, satisfied that what they would present to the committee at the next meeting would please everyone, including Laura. He even had sound equipment on the yacht that they used to listen to some of the songs Bryce had selected that he could not recall.

"I can't believe you don't remember Prince."

He shook his head, grinning. "Let's not get it twisted, Bryce. I remember Prince, but not that particular song."

By the time she gathered her items to leave, he was already looking forward to Saturday. That was the day they would meet again when they discussed his company's expansion plans in Boston.

"I take it you're registered with the state of Massachusetts now?" he asked her when he walked her back on deck to leave.

"Yes. Everything is done electronically these days and I got my paperwork in a week."

"Good. You haven't changed your mind about working for me as my broker, have you?"

"No, and you haven't changed your mind about hiring me?" Bryce asked him.

"No."

"Good, because I've been doing my research already."

He threw back his head and laughed. "Now, why am I not surprised."

She chuckled as she glanced at her watch. "I need to go."

He wondered why the rush. Did she have a date for later? Was it the guy who'd come into the café that morning? He bit back asking why she was in such a hurry to leave. Instead he said, "Okay. Enjoy the rest of your evening."

She smiled over at him. "Thanks. I will."

"Surprise!"

Bryce threw her hand to her chest in total disbelief. The last thing she'd expected when she arrived for lunch at Ashley and Ray's home was to find balloons and a cake.

She looked at Ashley and Vashti. "Surprise? What for? It's not my birthday or anything."

Ashely laughed. "No, but you've been studying hard for that exam and you aced it, so we decided to celebrate your achievement. You did it, girl, and Vashti and I are proud of you!" she said, giving Bryce a hug. Vashti gave her one, as well.

"We got a bottle of wine, although neither of us will be able to share a glass with you. We're drinking apple cider."

Bryce didn't want to get all emotional, but she was definitely feeling it. Vashti had been her best friend forever, and since moving to town and marrying Ray, Ashley was someone who'd become a dear friend to her.

"Don't you dare start crying, Bryce," Vashti warned.

Bryce smiled. "I won't but this is so special."

"Because you're special. I made sandwiches for lunch and a fruit tray. The weather is nice, so we can sit out on the patio and smell the apples," Ashley said, maneuvering around the room pretty easily for a woman who would be giving birth to twins in a month's time.

Ray had purchased the two-bedroom, two-bath home a year after moving to the cove. It was a beautiful house and ideal for one person. There was a screened-in porch on the back that faced an apple grove. The grove was beautiful and the scent of apples filled the entire house.

Over lunch Ashley told them the house that she and Ray were having built on the ocean was supposed to be finished before the twins were born. "Ray and I want to lease this place instead of selling it. When that time comes we'll contact you to handle it for us," she said to Bryce.

Bryce smiled. "Thanks, and I'll be glad to do that. It should be an easy rental."

"Since you were busy playing catch-up at your office last weekend, do you have big plans for this weekend to celebrate?" Vashti asked, taking a sip of her apple cider.

Bryce shook her head. "No. I just plan to take it easy and chill. However, I am meeting with Kaegan on Saturday morning."

Vashti looked at her, surprised. "You are? Why?"

Bryce smiled. "Kaegan is expanding his business and is presently eyeing Boston Harbor." She figured she wasn't telling them anything they probably didn't already know since their husbands were Kaegan's best friends. "He hired me to find potential properties for his business in Boston and handle all the arrangements, whether he decides to buy or lease."

"That's a strong way to kick off this new phase of your career as a real-estate broker. It's pretty nice of him to select you for the job," Ashley said, smiling.

"I think it was, too," Bryce agreed.

Vashti looked at her curiously over the rim of her glass. Bryce knew that look. "What?" she asked her best friend.

"Nothing," Vashti said, smiling.

Bryce leaned in toward Vashti. "Oh, no, there *is* something, Vash. I know that look."

Smiling, Vashti propped her fists under her chin and rested her elbows on the table. "Does the job require any traveling?"

Bryce knew what Vashti was getting at and leaned back in her chair. "Yes," she said softly.

Vashti's smile widened. "What did you say? I can't hear you," she said, singing the last sentence.

Bryce glared playfully at Vashti. "Yes, it requires traveling."

"You and Kaegan together?"

Bryce rolled her eyes. "It's not what you think."

"Okay," Vashti said, straightening up and picking up her glass.

Bryce knew that meant Vashti didn't believe a word she said.

"Am I missing something?" Ashley asked, looking from Vashti to Bryce.

"Nothing other than Bryce and Kaegan might be traveling out of town together quite a bit."

"That's interesting," Ashley said, smiling.

Not looking at Vashti, Bryce spoke to Ashley and said, "And those times when we do, he'll have his hotel room and I'll have mine."

Vashti grinned. "And probably with a connecting door in between."

Bryce rolled her eyes again and took a sip of her wine. "Like I said, it's not what you think."

Vashti nodded. "That's right. You and Kaegan are good friends and nothing more. I got it."

Bryce stared at Vashti, knowing her friend hadn't gotten it at all. Deciding to change the subject, she turned to Ashley. "So what happened with your folks? I thought they would be hanging around for a while."

Ashley shook her head. "Ray asked them to leave. He would have let my father stay but he knew he wouldn't do so without my mother, so he asked both of them to leave and not return until they are invited. Ray also told them when they say they're coming to visit for two weeks, the welcome mat will only be out for two weeks and not three or more."

"Wow," Bryce said, not believing the unflappable Ray had done that, and that Ashley didn't seem bothered that he had. "You're not mad at Ray? After all, they are your parents."

Ashley shook her head. "I know my parents better than anyone. Dad is great, but Mom is controlling. Devon Ryan knew how to handle her, which is the way Ray handled them three days ago. He had to remind my mother why they never got along. He knows how she operates, and he didn't tolerate it as Devon and he's not putting up with it as Ray. Dad had things under control for a while with Mom, but then he got lax and now she's trying to call the shots again. This time she's telling us what to name our kids."

Vashti sighed. "At least it sounds like there's hope for your folks. I can't say the same about mine. They have yet to apologize for what they did and the lies they told."

She paused thoughtfully, then continued, "Sawyer is a big proponent of forgiveness and heaven knows I tried. They came to our wedding and met the girls but it's as if they're ashamed of them because they were conceived out of wedlock. They act as if Kia and Jade aren't good enough to be their grandkids for that reason."

"You honestly think that?" Ashley asked, as if she was finding it hard to believe parents could feel that way.

"Yes," Vashti said sadly. "They are happy about Cutter and consider him their legitimate grandchild. They call every week to see how he's doing and said they would love to come see him for Christmas. They never ask about the girls. Just like Ray, Sawyer finally had enough, and last week he told them unless they can accept all our kids as equals then don't bother accepting any because he would not tolerate them playing favorites between our children."

"Good for him," Bryce said, loving the stance Sawyer had taken.

"How do the girls feel about it?" Ashley asked.

Vashti took another sip of her cider. "They both know the story about their births, and I think they'd reached the conclusion that my parents aren't wrapped too tight. The girls have the attitude that if they don't want to accept them as their granddaughters, then that's fine. They won't accept them as their grandparents. They aren't little kids but eighteen-year-olds who can make up their own minds about things."

Her eyes brightened as she smiled. "Besides, they are perfectly happy with Reid as their lone grandfather. He had no problem claiming them from the start and they get more than enough love from him. And they give it back. They simply adore him. And now that he's getting married to Gloria, Kia is happy to share her grandmother with Jade."

"I propose a toast," Ashley said, holding out her glass. Vashti and Bryce did the same. "To Bryce, on expanding your career as a real-estate broker. May it bring you success in both your business and personal life."

Bryce smiled, shaking her head. Evidently Vashti had put ideas into Ashley's head about her and Kaegan. Soon enough they would both see just how wrong they were about that.

CHAPTER TWENTY-TWO

Bryce opened her car door and stared at the monstrosity of the house erected before her. Usually when she came here for a party or cookout it was always at night. Now she was seeing the place in all its splendor in the daylight. When the builders had completed this place, Kaegan hadn't wasted any time tearing down what had been his parents' home. She knew that house had held very few good memories for him.

She wondered how he liked living in the huge house alone. The one thing she did know was that he loved the bayou. He said leaving here when he moved away had been hard. She was not surprised this house took full advantage of the view of the bayou.

One of her favorite things about the house was the wrap-around porch that faced the water. The chairs on the porch looked so inviting and she could see herself sitting in one for hours while reading her favorite novel. No sooner had the thought entered her mind than she shook her head. No, she couldn't see herself sitting in one for hours. This was Kaegan's home and not hers. A home until just last month she hadn't been welcomed to.

Walking up to the porch, she hoped he remembered she was coming today. When she'd seen him at the café for breakfast yesterday, he hadn't mentioned it. And it might have been that he hadn't wanted anyone to know. She knew what a private person Kaegan was, but couldn't see him not mentioning that he'd hired her as his real-estate broker to Sawyer and Ray. She had certainly mentioned it to their wives.

Reaching the door, she knocked.

"The door's unlocked. Come on in."

The deep, rich huskiness of Kaegan's voice reached out to her, and when she opened the door it all but lured her inside. She glanced around. Kaegan always had this thing for neatness and it seemed he still did. There were even fresh flowers on a table in a massive foyer that had to be at least ten feet wide with the prettiest wood floors she'd ever seen.

"Kaegan?"

"I'm in the kitchen. You know the way."

Yes, she knew the way and remembered what had happened the last time she'd been in his kitchen. When she reached the massive kitchen, which was any cook's dream, she paused in the doorway. He was standing at the sink cleaning fish. She had heard from her parents he'd gone fishing with Sawyer yesterday, and from the looks of it, they'd had a good day.

She drank in the sight of him, shirtless and in a pair of jeans. She shouldn't have been surprised by the missing shirt. Kaegan never liked covering his chest. It wasn't uncommon once they were out of the schoolyard for him to whip his shirt over his head and stuff it in his backpack.

He glanced over his shoulder at her and smiled, and she suddenly felt weak in the knees. "You're in time to join me for lunch," he said.

She glanced at her watch and then back at him. "It's a little early for lunch, isn't it?"

"Nah. By the time I get these babies seasoned and fried and prepare the hush puppies and salad, it will be noon."

Bryce had expected something like this, for him to invite her to lunch or to go out on the bayou in his boat or something similar that would require them to spend unnecessary time together. She had rehearsed all morning what she would say. "Thanks for the invite but I need to decline."

He quirked an eyebrow. "Why? Do you have plans for lunch?"

"No, but I'm here to discuss that Boston opportunity with you."

"And we will. Over lunch. If you want to get started while I prepare everything, then check out the websites I've written down on the paper by my computer."

"I've done research," she said, holding up the folder in her hand.

"Good, then I'm curious to see what you got, and I want you to see what I came up with. We'll compare." He returned his attention to the fish in the sink.

She sighed, deciding not to get in a tit for tat with him about anything. The one thing she did wish was that she wasn't drawn to his male magnetism. It had been that way when he'd helped her study and then when they'd been together at Eagle Bend Inlet.

Now, why was she remembering their time spent there? Especially their kiss. Had it been a week ago today? More than once on the drive here, she'd questioned whether she was making the right decision about taking him on as a client.

"Fine. Where is your computer?" she asked him.

He looked over at her again. "In my private office, which is connected to my bedroom upstairs. Once you reach the landing, it's the room with the double doors. You have to go into my bedroom first to get to it."

She felt an intense throb at the base of her throat. He had to be kidding. "Your bedroom?"

"Yes."

"Could you bring your laptop down here so I sit at the kitchen table and use it?"

"I can't."

She frowned. "Why can't you?"

"Because it's a desktop." He turned around to face her, leaned against the sink, crossed his arms over his chest and did the same for his legs at the ankles. That was when she noticed he was in his bare feet. There was just something about a laid-back look on a man.

"You aren't afraid of going into my bedroom, are you?" he asked, staring at her. "I promise there's not a thing in there to bite you."

She straightened her shoulders. "That's not the point."

"And what is the point, Bryce?"

"You knew I was coming here for business and you—"

"Did nothing," he interrupted. "Other than be nice enough to invite you to lunch and then suggest you get a head start with the *business* you came over here to do on my computer. Now you have a problem as to where I keep my computer?"

"I don't have a problem with it. It's just that your bedroom is your bedroom."

"And?"

Bryce huffed out a deep breath, and refusing to waste time with him any longer, she said, "And nothing. Tell me where your bedroom is again. I really wasn't listening the last time you said it." She refused to go wandering upstairs through his house looking for it.

"Turn right upon reaching the landing and you will see the double doors."

Bryce left the kitchen and headed to the living room, where the stairs were located. She absolutely loved his spiral stair-

case and liked how you had a view of the bayou while climb-
ing the stairs.

She reached the landing and veered to the right and saw the
double doors that opened to his bedroom. She pushed open
the doors and slowly entered the room, and the first thing
she saw was the massive bed. She couldn't imagine anyone
sleeping in the huge bed alone. An inner voice reminded her
that for all she knew he didn't sleep alone.

Trying to ignore the bed, she couldn't help noticing just
how tidy the room was. Nothing was out of place. She saw
the alcove and headed in that direction after seeing the computer sitting on an oak desk that faced a window. Now she
understood why he'd claimed this particular spot as his private workplace. His bedroom was enormous, and the private
alcove didn't distract from the design of the room and was
perfect for the size of the desk. And then there was the gorgeous view of the bayou. For her the view would be a negative since she wouldn't ever get anything done for gazing out
the window in front of the desk.

She put aside her purse and sat down at the desk. Kaegan
had jotted down several websites, which meant he'd done
his homework. She wasn't surprised about that. For someone
who'd been two grades behind in school most of his life, with
a father who hadn't cared if he graduated at all, he had worked
hard, done all his homework and any special assignments to
get in his right grade by the time they'd reached high school.

After perusing the sheet of paper, she noticed a few were
the same ones on the comp list she'd compiled. *Smart minds
think alike*, she thought, smiling. She'd worked for a good
twenty minutes going down the list, marking off duplicates,
before she leaned back in the chair and reached her arms over
her head to stretch. Glancing around the room and admiring his furniture, she suddenly froze. There on his nightstand
was a framed photograph of her. She remembered it as one

she'd given him years ago, when they'd meant something to each other. Why would he still have it and why was it here in his bedroom?

She stood and her gaze scanned the room, certain there was a photo of Vashti somewhere in the room, as well. Then her picture in here, of all places, would make sense. Or at least kind of make sense.

Drawing in a deep breath, she tucked a thick curl of hair behind her ear, refusing to let that photo affect her. If his purpose for sending her in here was so she could see that photo, then fine. She saw it and would ignore it.

She booted up his computer and in no time was checking out the various sites that showed warehouses at the Boston Harbor. The sale prices on all the places were enormous, but she could see why Kaegan would want to expand to this northeastern market. Her job was to help him find a place and then advise him on best practices and pricing strategies to get what he wanted.

She heard a noise and glanced out the window to see Kaegan in the yard below setting up the cooker for the fish. And he still wasn't wearing a shirt. Muscled shoulders. Hard jeans-clad thighs. Long legs. A totally buff body... Did someone forget to remind him this was October? Although the temperature outside was fairly decent, no one walked around shirtless this time of the year. Doing so was pneumonia waiting to happen. She shook her head, wondering why was she even concerned. He was a grown man who should know how to take care of himself. Her days of caring about him that way were over.

She took a deep breath and sighed loudly as she turned her attention back to the computer screen. At least she tried to, but seeing a sexy shirtless man, with his hair flying in the wind while standing there holding a cup of steaming hot coffee in his hand with the bayou as the backdrop, was one hot pose. One worthy of being on the cover of a romance novel.

He knew where she'd be sitting at the window and had probably intentionally drawn her attention. Yet he hadn't as much as looked up in her direction. He kept on doing what he was doing, as if cooking that fish was the most important thing for him to do. A part of her felt annoyed that although he was holding her attention, she undoubtedly wasn't holding his. But wasn't the latter what she wanted? He hadn't acted unprofessional in any way since she'd arrived, although being shirtless and sending her to work in his bedroom was a little too much. With a house this big, you would think one of the rooms would have been a designated office.

She fought to concentrate on the task she needed to do, and before long, a good hour had passed. Glancing out the window, she noticed Kaegan was no longer there.

Suddenly, she heard the sound of his voice and realized he had an intercom system in his room. "Lunch is ready, Bryce. Come and get it."

The moment the invitation was issued her stomach growled. She was hungry. Standing, she stretched and was about to walk out of the room when something prompted her to move toward the photo of her. She remembered the day she had taken it on the college campus and buying this particular frame and mailing it off to him. It had been her senior year, just three months before they'd broken up. Why had he kept it for the past ten years? Given the way he'd felt about her, she would have thought he'd tossed out every single thing that reminded him of her. But then, didn't she still have a lot of the things he'd given her? Yes, but they were stored in a trunk in her attic and not out in plain view.

Did he expect her to question him about why he still had it? If he did then he would be disappointed because she wouldn't.

Walking out of his bedroom, she decided that she was going to pretend she hadn't seen it.

Kaegan glanced over at Bryce. They were sitting out on his back porch enjoying the view of the bayou while enjoying the fried fish, salad and hush puppies that he'd prepared. One thing he'd always appreciated about her was that she was not a finicky eater. She'd always loved food and it appeared she still did. He recalled those days when she ate too much, she would talk him into running around the track after school to work it off. He knew she was still an avid runner. More than once, he'd seen her jogging around the cove.

He recalled what Ray had said earlier in the week. Bryce was a beautiful woman and he couldn't go around getting mad at every man who found her gorgeous, as well. After breaking up they'd both moved on, but here it was ten years later and neither had found someone else. Yes, they'd dated and had been in relationships they might have thought were serious, but in the end here they were, in their thirties, single and not seriously involved with anyone.

He thought she looked pretty today. Hell, he would admit to thinking that she looked pretty every day. But especially today. There was just something about a woman with gorgeous legs and curves in a pencil skirt. And she smelled good, too. She'd tied her hair back from her face, which showcased the cutest pair of ears. He liked her loop earrings—they made her appear sexy.

She glanced up and caught him staring, and he quickly asked, "Food's okay?"

She smiled over at him. "It's better than okay, Kaegan. Everything is delicious. I'm all but licking my fingers. Whatever seasoning you used on the fish is to die for and tastes better than the fish served at my parents' café. But you better not tell them I told you that."

"I won't. Scout's honor," he said, holding up his hand.

"You never were a Scout."

"I was hoping you wouldn't remember that," he said, grinning as he pushed aside his plate. "So did you see any real-estate properties that might interest me in Boston?" he asked, knowing she would prefer if they stuck to the business at hand.

She nodded as she pushed away her plate, as well. "I saw quite a few available that I think will work for you. Will you maintain your place here as the primary headquarters?"

"Yes. I am a Louisiana guy through and through."

She nodded again. "You'll be making a big step for your company, Kaegan."

Was that caution he heard in her voice? "Yes, but Reid thinks I'm ready. The first place he expanded LaCroix Blueberries was in Boston and he has done well there. I'm ready to tap into that market."

"I think what you're doing is wonderful. Good luck."

"Thanks. Now show me the comp listings you've come up with."

After clearing off the table, they spent the next two hours going over listings before he selected two for her to check out. "I checked comps in the area, and I think we can negotiate for both."

"Good, but, of course, I'd want to see them. When can we take a trip to Boston?"

He noticed her hesitation. Then she asked, "When would you like to go?"

"Preferably within the next two weeks."

"Okay." She checked her watch. "I can't believe I've been here for four hours."

"We had a lot to go over."

"Yes, we did," she said, standing.

He stood, too, as she stuffed the papers into her folder. "What are your plans for the rest of the day?"

She glanced over at him. "I don't have any. Why?"

"After I straighten up things here, I'm driving to New Orleans. There's a jazz show that's starting around five."

"Jazz?"

"Yes," he said, grinning. He knew her. You said the word *jazz* and automatically her toes would start tapping. As proof, he glanced down and her feet were moving to some inaudible beat. When he glanced back to her face, she laughed.

"I can't help it."

He nodded. "I know you can't. That's why I believe in another life you were a jazz musician." He'd always told her that. "That's also why the band I recommended to the high-school-reunion holiday committee was big on jazz."

"I noticed and appreciate you for it."

"So will you go with me to listen to some jazz?"

She nibbled on her bottom lip, as if she was trying to make a decision. He then said, "You spent two hours with me on my yacht this week, so you should know I don't bite."

He thought that at least he used to not bite, but now he could imagine putting all kinds of passion marks all over her while branding her his. That way other men would know whom she belonged to because they would see his imprint. Kaegan's woman. For years he'd thought of her as his girl, but over the years she'd developed into a woman.

"Would I need to go home and change?"

He shook his head as his gaze scanned over her. "No, what you're wearing is fine. You look great, by the way." She had come dressed for business in that stylish pencil skirt and collared blouse. In his book she'd still managed to look sexy.

"Thanks."

"So what's your decision?"

Drawing in a deep breath, she nodded. "Yes, I'll go to New Orleans with you."

CHAPTER TWENTY-THREE

This is not a date, Bryce kept telling herself as she and Kaegan left the club after listening to two hours of jazz music. It
had been wonderful, and more than once instead of tapping
her feet, she'd gotten on the dance floor to sway her body
to the music.

He had surprised her when he'd gotten out there with
her. Second time in a month that he'd done so. In the past,
he never danced. He preferred just sitting back in the corner
while watching her. It had felt good having him out there on
the dance floor with her. However, she would admit she'd
liked those times when he'd sat watching her and she would
intentionally move her body knowing just how much he liked
seeing her do it. Kaegan's dark eyes had always been read-
able to her. She could recognize anger in them and could also
recognize desire.

She loved New Orleans as a place to visit, but not a place
to live. For her there was nothing better than Catalina Cove.
It was a nice, peaceful town with great people who looked
out for each other. Thanks to Reid and a number of citizens

on the planning board, the cove retained that small-town atmosphere.

"Hungry?"

She glanced up at Kaegan. Why did he have to look so handsome in his shirt and jeans and with moccasins on his feet? He had a rawhide jacket with frills and with the way his hair was down and flowing around his shoulders made it obvious he was Native American. Full-blooded. Hot-blooded. Sexy as hell. She noticed more than one woman eyeing him at the club. Now women that they were passing on the sidewalk were openly staring.

"Yes, I'm hungry. What about you?"

He smiled down at her. "Yes, I'm hungry, as well. I suggest we go to Finley's."

She glanced at her watch. "Close to seven on a Saturday night? Good luck."

He grinned down at her and she felt her stomach stir. "I have connections. I'm one of their biggest suppliers. We'll be able to get in."

She laughed. "Okay, let's do it."

Less than an hour later, good to his word, Kaegan had gotten them in, bypassing the extremely long line. Not only did he get them in, but they also had special seating in a small private room, where the sound of jazz music was playing through the speakers. Automatically, she began tapping her feet.

The food was delicious. Not only was the huge seafood platter they shared very good, but Kaegan also boasted that everything on their plate was his catch. "I don't think I can eat another thing," she said, leaning back in the chair and rubbing her stomach.

He looked at her and laughed. "Take a look, sweetheart. There's nothing left to eat. You ate it all, even that last crab cake I was eyeing."

She threw her hand to her mouth to keep from laughing

out loud. He was right. She'd definitely eaten a lot. "Okay, I owe you a crab cake and will cook it for you one day."

"Soon?"

She tilted her head. "How soon do you want it? I have to buy the ingredients and crab meat isn't cheap."

"Oh, but you have connections," he said, grinning. "I happen to know this terrific guy who owns a company that goes out and pulls the crabs right from the ocean. They can't get any fresher than that."

She grinned over at him. "No, they can't."

Bryce could honestly say she had enjoyed her day spent with him. If anyone would have told her this time last year that she and Kaegan would be out together in New Orleans, she would not have believed them. Hiring her meant he believed in her abilities and she appreciated that. Just like she had appreciated Vashti when she'd hired her to sell the inn. Although the deal fell through, just knowing her friend had trusted her judgment had meant a lot.

"I think I need to get you to dance with me before you tap a hole in that floor," he said, glancing at her feet.

She laughed, and when he stood and reached out his hand to her, she automatically took it. She was glad this was a private room and that they were the only couple in here, which was probably why he felt comfortable dancing with her. The moment their hands touched, she'd known it had been a mistake but couldn't do anything about it. In all honesty, at that moment she didn't want to do anything about it. And when he drew her into his arms, she was reminded of the last time they'd slow danced together at that charity ball. Tonight they were not in a crowded room and the music was jazz. Swaying to the music, she leaned in and placed her head on his chest, inhaling the masculine aroma of his scent that was totally Kaegan.

His body, long, hard and muscular, pressed against hers and

she could actually feel him in every nerve, pore and pulse of her body. He wrapped his arms tighter around her and she closed her eyes, moving to the jazzy rhythm while remembering a time, a rare moment, when they'd danced in their hotel room. It had been his twenty-fifth birthday and she'd wanted to dance with him. Naked.

He had obliged her, and every time during the dance that their naked bodies had met, touched, stroked each other, coiling arousal had invaded her core. She could vividly remember wrapping her arms around him, gliding her hands up and across his muscled back, loving the curve of his shoulders and arms. Desire had clawed at her that night, and at twenty-two, she hadn't fully understood the magnitude of what had been taking place between them.

Oh, she'd known how the night would end because they had made love over the years plenty of times. But that night had been special because it was his twenty-fifth birthday, and she had been determined to make it one he would never forget. She wondered now if he remembered that night. It had been the last night they'd slept together before their split.

"You okay?"

His question made her quickly open her eyes. Had she said something or made a sound? She glanced up at him, saw the look in his eyes. *That* look. Her breath nearly caught in her throat. They stopped dancing when he reached out and cradled her face in his hands and lowered his mouth down to hers.

Kaegan had to kiss her. Whether she'd been aware of it or not, she'd given the code, a secret language they had developed between them years ago. The tip of her fingernail had written it in the crevice of his back. Even with clothes on he'd known what she'd engraved. *I W Y.* I want you.

He wanted her, too, in every cell in his body. He wanted

her with a need he'd denied himself for ten long years. A need that only she could take care of. He wanted her to know his response, to feel it in the way his tongue was taking her mouth. Boldly, hungrily, ravenously, while clamoring at the last of his control. But then, he'd never had any control where Bryce was concerned. She had been his from the first, on the day in elementary school when he'd sat beside her in class and she'd shared her box of crayons with him. That had been the beginning. Over the years she'd shared her mother's blueberry muffins when he'd missed breakfast, and had shared one of her father's sandwiches after discovering on some days he didn't have lunch of his own. And she'd shared her brothers' clothes those days when his had been too dirty to wear to school. Even as a kid she'd shared her parents' underground passageway by leaving the door unlocked for him to get in for shelter when things had been difficult for him at home. And she'd shared her heart with him, and her body at seventeen.

Now he fully understood what Ray had meant that day. Home for him was not Catalina Cove or the bayou. Home for him was here in Bryce's arms. Home was kissing her, tasting her, knowing she was kissing him in return. He loved her. He'd always loved her and would always love her. He had loved her through all the hate he thought he'd felt. Loved her when she would glare at him with a gaze that all but told him to shove it and where. Then there were the times there had been fire in her eyes when he knew he'd risked pushing her to the limit and he could very well end up with a pot of coffee thrown in his face. But he had needed that fire to stay his distance. But now he wanted to close the distance, and reclaim everything that he'd walked away from ten years ago.

His mouth was eating away at hers with a hunger he felt in his groin and she was kissing him back with a greed that matched his own. He was convinced his testosterone was out of whack, causing every nerve in his body to bring him to full awareness of her, even in the air he was breathing. Her scent was driving him insane. Before they got arrested for indecent exposure, he broke off the kiss and breathed in deeply. Leaning close to her ear, he whispered, "I think we'd better leave here now, don't you?"

Instead of answering, she nodded and he took her hand in his. After going back to the table to sign the check, they walked hand in hand out the restaurant.

Bryce knew this was crazy. Absolutely, unconditionally, unequivocally crazy. But at the moment she couldn't help it. Even while sitting in Kaegan's car with the night's wind hitting her in the face, it wasn't putting any sense back into her brain. She was too far gone for that. Her mind and body were ruled by something she hadn't counted on. A deep sexual need.

After going without a man for nearly four years, her body was protesting. It had taken as much as it would take and those damn battery-operated boy toys weren't enough. It wanted the real thing, from the real deal. It wanted the man who'd ruined her body for any other man.

Tonight was tonight. What would happen tomorrow? The day after? Then the day after that? She had no idea and, honestly, at the moment she didn't care. Bottom line was that she needed Kaegan to make love to her. Tonight. She would deal with tomorrow *tomorrow*.

He wasn't saying anything. He hadn't said anything since they'd left the restaurant. Music was playing on his radio. No longer jazz but a sultry sound of soul. The lyrics spoke of love, making love and endless love. She tried ignoring the words and concentrating on the music.

And on the man driving the car.

It no longer mattered what women he'd made love to after her. She'd had him first. She and Kaegan had taught each other to kiss, to feel, to touch. Nobody could ever take those things away from her or from them. She realized they were not the teens and young adults they once had been, where their worlds revolved around each other and no one else. They were mature adults who saw things differently than before.

Tonight she was definitely into her feelings, and what she was feeling more than anything was Kaegan Chambray. There was something she needed to know, though. "Did I give you a code back there, Kaegan?" she asked.

He only took his eyes off the road for a quick second. That was enough. Even in the moonlight shining in the car, she could see a flash of heat in those dark eyes. "Yes, you coded me."

She swallowed. "And what was the code?" While dancing with her eyes closed, she had thought of several erotic things. And he'd been the leading man in all of them.

"You coded that you wanted me." He paused a moment and then asked, "Do you?"

No need to play games, act coy or change her mind since she was definitely having a Kaegan Chambray moment. "Yes, I do." Things were moving fast. They'd just officially become friends again recently. "How do you feel about that?"

They'd come to a traffic light. He glanced over at her and said, "You will know exactly how I feel once I'm inside of you again, Bryce."

Lordy...thanks to his words, she was threatening an orgasm right then and there and tightened her legs together. Frissons of fire raced all through her womanly folds. There were just some things a boy toy couldn't do, but Kaegan knew how to do it all, and she had a feeling this older, mature and ripe Kaegan would likely blow her away.

She barely recalled when they reached the Catalina Cove city limits; could vaguely remember passing through town and definitely didn't recall when they were on the road that led to the bayou. But she had full recollection of when they pulled into his yard and he parked the car. And she would never forget when he told her to stay put in that deep, husky voice, before coming around to open the door for her, then unhook her seat belt before he swept her into his arms and carried her inside the house.

Her memory would forever be filled with recollections of him closing the door with the heel of his foot, before taking the stairs two at a time with her in his arms. What other man could do that?

Then he was entering his bedroom and placing her on the bed. Instead of taking off her clothes, he stood back and stared at her. "Ten times, Bryce."

She looked up at him, confused. "Excuse me?"

"We've been apart ten years, so do you know what that means?" he asked her, holding her gaze intently.

She shook her head. "No." She watched as he slowly stepped out of his moccasins.

"That means an orgasm for every year we've been apart. That's what I want, Bryce."

She blinked, thinking he definitely wanted a lot. "Over a period of when?" she asked.

"How I'm feeling now, I would have to say a few hours," he responded.

She had to keep her mouth from dropping open. Had he forgotten that she was a one-orgasm-a-night girl? And with Marcel she'd even faked it a few times.

"Not sure I can accommodate you, Kaegan."

He smiled and that dimple in his chin nearly made her moan. "It's not about you accommodating me, Bryce. It's all about me accommodating you. It's not about me telling you what I want for myself, but me telling you what you'll be getting."

Bryce stared at him as he removed his shirt, thinking of the result of what he was alluding to. A lot of sore muscles. She figured now was the time she needed to speak up, to make something clear to him. "News flash. I need to be able to walk out of here, Kaegan."

He shook his head as he began easing his jeans down muscular legs. "No, you don't. I will carry you."

CHAPTER TWENTY-FOUR

Kaegan wished he could kiss that shocked look right off Bryce's face. It was obvious that, over the years, while his level of sexual experience had increased, hers had not. After they'd broken up, he had bedded a number of women to ease his pain and to try to make him forget she'd ever existed. When he'd found that impossible to do, he'd settled down to just bedding women whenever he needed to relieve primitive urges.

The women knew what to expect and what not to expect, and the one thing they understood was that love and forever were not in the picture. Since returning to the cove, the women he'd bedded weren't bothered by his lack of commitment because they weren't looking for love and forever any more than he was.

Bryce wasn't saying anything, and he could just imagine what she was thinking. He figured he needed to address her fears...on more than one level. He was naked and she was staring at him below the waist like he'd exposed something she hadn't seen before, when she had. Several times. However, he would admit it had grown in size. He was no longer in his early twenties and a lot of changes had taken place in his body since then.

"Bryce?"

She slowly tore her gaze away from his groin area to look up at him. Was she too shocked to speak? He found out that wasn't the case when she suddenly exclaimed, "What happened? You weren't *that* big."

Kaegan would have rolled over in laughter if the expression on Bryce's face wasn't totally serious. Now he had two things to address to calm her fears before they could move forward. When he moved toward the bed, she actually backed up a little. The last thing he wanted was for her to be afraid of him or think his size would physically harm her in any way.

Sitting on the edge of the bed, he said, "First of all, we don't have to make love ten times for you to enjoy ten orgasms."

She tilted her head like she didn't totally agree with him on that, and that was fine. Those would have to be one of those I-will-just-have-to-show-you moments. "And as far as my size…"

"Yes?" she asked, leaning closer as if whatever explanation he gave her was something she just had to hear.

"Most guys reach their full penis size by the time they're twenty-one or twenty-two. However, a man's penis size is determined by his genes."

"Oh."

"In case you're worried about anything, just keep in mind that size doesn't matter because a woman's body is built to adjust."

She tilted her head and frowned at him. "Says who?"

"Says experience."

He saw a flash of something that appeared in her eyes and recognized it for what it was. Something else they needed to address. The thought of him sleeping with other women was something she had to get beyond, like the thought of other men sharing her body was something he had to deal with and accept, as well. For them the important thing was not what happened during the ten years they were apart, but what was happening now.

"Bryce?"

"Yes."

"Like I told you, I didn't sleep with that woman you saw me with that night at the club. I did go back to her place, and although I was angry and hurt, I couldn't do it. However, there have been other women I've used to ease the pain of losing you."

She glared at him. "You used them?"

"I didn't mean to insinuate I took advantage of them, Bryce," he said. The last thing he wanted her to think was that he'd become a selfish bastard over the years. "Any woman I slept with knew up front that I wasn't in the market for a serious relationship of any kind."

She nodded and then said, "And the guys I slept with knew that I *was*…in the market for a serious relationship. I honestly thought they were serious relationships, but evidently they weren't serious enough."

He wasn't going to ask her what happened, because he honestly didn't want to know. All he cared about was that she was not involved with anyone now and that tonight she was in his bed and he would be the one to make love to her.

"Now getting back to my size, will you believe that I won't hurt you, Bryce?"

He wondered if she recalled that was the same question he'd asked her the very first time they'd made love on Eagle Bend Inlet. They'd been young and inexperienced. He had refused to physically hurt her then and wouldn't do so now.

The smile that appeared on her face at that moment let him know she had remembered. "After all this time I'd think you would have come up with a better line by now, Kaegan."

He couldn't help but chuckle. "You think? But seriously, I won't hurt you."

She nodded and then said, "I think we do need to get an understanding, though. About this. I want you tonight, Kaegan. I need you tonight. However, I don't intend for it to happen again."

He reached out and cupped his hand at the back of her neck. "Then it will be up to me to make sure you'll want it to happen again."

He saw the mutinous look in her eyes—eyes that would always be beautiful to him. Deciding they'd talked long enough, he leaned in and captured her mouth with his.

Bryce figured she hadn't made things absolutely clear to Kaegan—that tonight would be all they would have together. Regardless of what he might assume, there could not be a repeat of this. With that thought firmly embedded in her mind, she concentrated on the kiss he was plying to her mouth.

Leaning in and wrapping her arms around his neck, she molded herself to him, wanting to feel as much of his naked masculine body as she could. She was the one still wearing clothes. He was not. Bryce knew the moment his hand touched her thigh to slowly raise up her skirt. Air fanned her thighs and she knew he was about to remove her clothes, as well.

She was so into the way he was kissing her that she hadn't been aware he was removing her blouse until he suddenly broke off the kiss to tug it over her head. Then his mouth was back, taking hers and using his tongue to masterfully stroke the insides of her mouth. She moaned and tried to participate by twirling her tongue around his and sucking on his the way he was sucking on hers.

She was convinced that nobody kissed as well as Kaegan. Nobody could make her moan this way, make her body ache and want something it really shouldn't have. Ten years without him and dealing with men who weren't even second best was driving her over the edge. When she felt air touch her breasts, she knew he'd removed her bra.

"Wow, Bryce. Would you like to explain these babies?" he asked, reaching out and cupping her breasts in his hands and staring down at them with amazement in his eyes.

"In case you're wondering, yes, they are the real thing, and I guess like what happened with you, it's a genes thing."

"And one I definitely like," he said, running his fingertips over the hardened nipples. When he did so, she felt a pull between her legs.

"And if they're bigger that means they are sweeter. Only one way to find out." He then buried his head to her chest and captured a nipple between his lips.

"K-Gee."

He didn't seem bothered by her calling him that. It was what she'd called him whenever they'd made love in the past. He'd always been K-Gee. Another reason that he hadn't reacted was because he was too busy licking her breasts and driving her insane in the process. He moved from one breast to the other and she could feel the area between her legs throb. The magnitude of sensations made her shudder all over, and she reached out to run her fingers through the silky strands of his hair and hold his head to her breasts.

Suddenly, the area between her legs began throbbing with an intensity that had her moaning. As if he'd suspected such a thing would happen, his mouth latched even more firmly to her nipple and he began sucking with imposing need.

"K-Gee!"

And then she threw back her head and closed her eyes as a multitude of sensations swept through her and all around her. She was having an orgasm just from him sucking her nipples. That had never happened to her before but she would admit he'd done some things with his tongue that he'd never done before. She wasn't sure if she could handle this new Kaegan. She'd been satisfied with him all those years before, but it seemed he was determined to make up for lost time.

"Now for the rest of your clothes," he said, leaning back to slide the skirt off her body and reveal a pair of black lace undies that matched the bra she'd been wearing. "You're one sexy lady, Bryce Witherspoon."

He leaned in and took her mouth again.

Kaegan loved kissing Bryce. Whether she knew it or not, that orgasm was just the beginning. Like he'd told her, there was another way to ten orgasms instead of one at a time. One benefit to joining the marines and being around a lot of guys 24/7 was that some men liked talking about sex, especially their conquests. Another thing they liked to do was share tips on pleasuring your woman.

What Bryce didn't know and what he didn't intend to boast about was that, over the years, he'd become the MOM, the Master of Multiples. The key was to not only concentrate on your partner's G-spot, but also to know how to pleasure it, which some men failed to do because they couldn't hold back on their own pleasure. He didn't have that issue because whenever he'd made love to Bryce, her pleasure had always been more important than his own. Making sure a woman got hers before he got his was second nature to him.

Now that she'd had her first, it was on to the second. Already, she was pretty wound up and she greedily returned his kisses, lick for lick, stroke for stroke. Her tongue was tangling with his and she was feasting on his mouth with a hunger that astounded him. That made him wonder when the last time she'd been fully pleasured by a man had been.

She'd admitted she needed this tonight. Did she not know that she might be needing it tomorrow night and the next night, as well? Did she honestly think this could be one-and-done? He would let her discover on her own that when it came to them making love, there was no such thing as one-and-done.

He pulled back from the kiss and looked into her eyes. They were hazy with desire and he loved seeing them that way. The sight gave him even more of a boner. He lowered his hand to the juncture of her thighs and gently began stroking her there while watching the look in her eyes fill with even more desire.

"What are you doing to me, K-Gee?"

Instead of answering, he asked a question of his own. "What do you think I'm doing?"

He inserted a finger inside of her and she moaned. He liked the sound. "Torturing me. Trying to drive me crazy," she said on a ragged breath.

"None of those things. What did I tell you about multiple choices?" He'd given her the rule when she'd been studying for her exam.

"That I need to concentrate on what feels right."

He was glad she remembered. "Yes, and tonight it's all about feelings."

Kaegan grazed his lips across her chin, moved to the corner of her lips and then licked across her entire mouth. He did all those things while his fingers were busy at work inside of her. Maybe he should have told her he was a master at multitasking, as well. He knew the location of her G-spot and planned to deliberately drive her insane to the point where she would want to make love to him again.

From the sounds she was making, she was enjoying his form of foreplay. The best was yet to come. He intended to make her initiation back into their brand of lovemaking so pleasurable that she would barely be able to stand it. *Torture?*

No. *Drive her crazy?* No. However, he did intend to drive her over the edge time and time again.

When her moans became louder, more intense, he knew he'd located her spot, but hadn't realized now just what a passionate woman Bryce was. Years ago he'd been too young and inexperienced to know much about G-spots, a woman's clitoris and the wide wonders of oral sex. Now he did. More than anything, he wanted their first time back together to be so memorable that she would think about it even when she didn't want to.

"K-Gee!"

She screamed his name when another orgasm hit her, and he was okay with that. He didn't have neighbors for miles. This was the first time any woman had slept in his bed and had spent the night in his house, and he had every intention of convincing Bryce to stay overnight.

"K-Gee," she said, this time in a whisper. A satisfied awe filled her face. And then, as if even saying his name had zapped every ounce of strength from her body, she collapsed back on the bed, closed her eyes and tried regulating her breathing.

Removing his finger from inside her, he slid onto the bed to lie beside her. "You okay?"

As if it took all the strength she had, she slowly reopened her eyes, stared at him and smiled. "You are wrong on so many levels, Kaegan."

He reached out to wrap her in his arms. Now they were both naked. "How so?"

"You have turned into a bad boy."

His smile widened. "Bad boy? You think so?"

"Yes."

He leaned up to loom over her and said, "Baby, you haven't seen anything yet." And then he eased down her body and began planting kisses all over her belly.

CHAPTER TWENTY-FIVE

Bryce was convinced Kaegan was trying to kill her and she was dying a slow, passionate death. Sad thing about it was she couldn't do anything about it. She didn't want to do anything about it. Not with the way his tongue was licking around her navel and sending all kinds of erotic feelings throughout her.

She closed her eyes. Her entire nervous system was going on a wild race and was taking her heart right along with it. All this was new to her—the sensations of a magnitude she'd never felt before. He was touching her in places other men never touched and making her realize that, with him, even the sky wasn't the limit. He intended to take her to the furthest hemisphere and back.

"Bryce?"

She opened her eyes and stared down at him. He was lying sprawled between her spread legs. She remembered other times she'd been in this position with him and knew what always came next. She didn't know how but she was ready. She should be drained, completely exhausted, after having two orgasms in less than an hour.

"Hmm?"

"I want to reacquaint myself with your taste."

In other words, he wanted to drive her mad yet again. She knew what he was saying and already her body was responding to the very thought. Hadn't she had enough? And why was he intent on just giving her pleasure without seeking his own?

"May I?"

That was the one thing he'd never done, which was to assume he had more control over her body than she had. He would always remind her that it was her body and he could only do what she allowed him to do, so he always asked. "Yes." And then she closed her eyes to get the full effect.

She felt the way he was nibbling along her inner legs and licking his way upward, and knew the exact moment he'd reached his intended target. When she felt the silken strands of his hair brush across her inner thighs, she knew his head was between her legs. Suddenly, a hot tongue slid inside her womanly folds at the same moment his hands began slowly skimming along her hips.

Sexual excitement started circling around her insides as he began licking around her clitoris, driving to the point where she reached down to grab a fistful of his hair. That didn't deter him one bit. He continued making a feast of her and she was convinced he had the ability to grow his tongue to an extraordinary length. Kaegan began moving his tongue in a way that sent pleasurable shock waves through her, making her move her body when she couldn't keep still.

He gripped her hips to slow down her movements, and when he did, his tongue became even more aggressive, causing a relentless throb deep inside of her. Over and over, his tongue pushed her toward the edge, then snatched her back before she could free-fall. Over the years he'd acquired several stellar techniques and plenty of sinfully erotic skills that he was using on her. In response, her body was emitting hot sparks.

Suddenly her pulse kicked. Ragged heat invaded her entire

being. A rush of desire rocked through her veins. She tried to hold back but couldn't and lifted her hips off the bed to shove the lower part of her body closer to his mouth. Then it happened. Shock wave after shock wave tore into her and she began shivering all over as she convulsed with sensuous energy that kept slamming into her.

Before the last spasm rushed through her body, she opened her eyes to see him sheathe himself. Then he was back and easing his body over hers. She looked into his eyes when he whispered, "Now for the beginning."

Beginning? Didn't he mean the ending? Her body felt hot all over and continued to throb. Before she could question what he meant, he leaned in closer to her mouth and breathed against her lips. "Take me in, Bryce. Take all of me."

Her heart slammed erratically in anticipation. "I will."

He slowly began entering her, inch by inch, giving her body time to adjust to his size. She was surprised at how her body automatically adjusted to him as he continued to push deeper inside of her.

When Bryce felt him buried to the hilt, making her feel full and complete, he gave her time to breathe in deeply before he began moving his body to mate with hers. She lifted her body to meet his every thrust and, in return, he pressed down to meet her. Urgent need consumed her and her muscles began tightening around his thick shaft. It seemed he knew exactly what spot to hit to make her moan, get deliriously insane. She needed more, hoped for more.

Her body surged with his heat as she felt yet another orgasm building. Shocks of pleasure began claiming what breath she had left in her lungs. More fiery sensations tore through her as she continued to arch up to meet him. The ritual continued over and over, as her body relentlessly milked him as he'd taught her to do years ago. Sensations swept through her. Suddenly, she couldn't last any longer and her passion reached its peak. Contractions hurled all at once to her womb, and she tumbled over, realizing that, this time, Kaegan was tumbling with her.

"Brycie!"

She couldn't scream. What she did was whimper in ecstasy, knowing while he'd given pleasure to her, she'd done likewise to him. The drugging scent of his masculinity invaded her nostrils at the same time she heard him growl a ragged murmur of satisfaction.

When their bodies began winding down, he lowered his gaze to hers and held it. She wasn't sure what passed between them at that moment but knew something had. Before she could dwell on that thought, he leaned in and whispered "Brycie" again before capturing her mouth in his.

CHAPTER TWENTY-SIX

Kaegan stared at the woman who'd slept beside him in his bed all night as she began waking up. She'd warned him what to expect the day after their lovemaking, and he was hoping after a night like last night, she would change her mind. Ten orgasms had her sleeping like a baby. As far as he was concerned, multiple orgasms couldn't get as sweet as the ones they'd shared. She was still the most passionate woman he knew.

The letter *K* was still tattooed on her backside. He doubted she knew how he'd felt when he'd seen it. To this day he could remember her showing it to him when she'd gotten it and telling him she would always wear it with pride. She'd wanted to get the G, as well, but hadn't been able to handle the pain of both letters. He had appreciated her doing the one.

She slowly opened her eyes and stared at him, blinked and then stared again. He knew she was remembering last night. Every single detail. When a smile spread across her lips, he released the breath he'd been holding. At least she was in a pleasant mood. Should he take that as a good sign? When it came to Bryce, he would take whatever he could get.

"Good morning, Bryce."

"Good morning. What time is it?" she asked, yawning.

"Close to ten."

"Ten?"

"Yes. Were you supposed to help out at the café this morning?" He knew her parents usually opened the café for the early morning church-service crowd.

"No, usually I don't on the weekends."

He nodded. "You're hungry?"

"Why? Are you going to feed me?"

"Of course. How does Cajun fish and cheese grits sound?"

"Like heaven. But first, I need to ask you something."

He lifted an eyebrow. "What?"

"Why is my picture in your bedroom? I told myself I wasn't going to ask you about it, but I have to know."

Kaegan glanced over at the photograph. "Do you remember when you gave it to me?"

"Yes. I was in my senior year at Grambling and figured it was time for you to have an updated photo of me."

He shifted to flip on his back and stare up at his ceiling. "After we broke up I packed all your stuff up that I had, but for some reason I couldn't get rid of anything, so I put it all in storage. It was only when the house was finished here that I arranged for all my stuff in storage to be shipped to me. This house is so large, I figured I had space for it all now."

He paused a minute and then said, "It took me around eight months to go through all those boxes. Then I came across the one with your name on it and again for some reason I couldn't get rid of it, but I wanted everything out of my sight...except for that picture. I figured waking up and seeing it every day would be a constant reminder why I could never trust or love another woman."

She was quiet for a long while, and then she said, "Okay,

I can get that, but now that we're friends again, why is it still there?"

He met her gaze. "Now it's a reminder of what I lost because of my stupidity."

She released a deep sigh and he had a feeling he wouldn't like what she was about to say. "I meant what I said last night, Kaegan. Us sharing a bed wasn't the beginning of anything. We're still nothing more than friends."

Kaegan wondered if she really believed that. He couldn't say he didn't know of friends who slept together, because he did. They thought of themselves as friends with benefits. Kaegan had decided not to indulge in any relationship like that, mainly because there wasn't a woman he wanted as both his friend and his lover. And he sure as hell didn't want that kind of relationship for him and Bryce.

"Kaegan?"

"Yes?"

"We still have that understanding that last night was one-and-done, right?"

If she truly believed that, he wouldn't argue with her about it. She would discover soon enough that when it came to them, there was no such thing. "Yes, there's still that understanding."

"Good."

Easing out of bed, he said, "I think I better get up now and fix your breakfast. I have extra toiletries in the guest bathrooms."

"Okay, thanks. And, Kaegan?"

He turned before entering the bathroom. "Yes?" He noticed she seemed preoccupied with his naked body. Namely, his huge hard-on that made it quite obvious he wanted her again.

A smile touched her lips when her gaze traveled back to his face. "You were absolutely amazing. I never would have thought that…" She trailed off for a moment and then said, "Ten times."

He couldn't help but return her smile at seeing her face in total awe. "Yes, ten times." He turned and continued to the bathroom before being tempted to say there were a lot more where those came from.

A few hours later, after they enjoyed breakfast out on his patio, he was walking Bryce to her car. Sharing breakfast with her had been supernice. He'd done all the cooking and she'd made coffee and set the table. He tried not to think about how she looked like she belonged in his home. Neither of them brought up what had happened the last time she'd been in his kitchen.

They walked side by side and he glanced over at her. A part of him regretted her leaving and he'd thought about asking her to stay, but knew doing such a thing wasn't a good idea after what she'd reiterated that morning. He had Thursday to look forward to, when she would be accompanying him to Boston. "I talked to Sawyer yesterday morning," he said, breaking into the silence. "He mentioned that he and Vashti have decided to find out the sex of their baby."

"Yes, Vashti told me and Ashley that, as well, when Ashley invited us to lunch the other day. At least I thought it was lunch. It turned into a surprise party that Vashti and Ashley planned for me for passing my exam."

"That was nice of them."

"I thought so, too."

When they reached her car, Kaegan opened the door for her. When she slid onto the seat and snapped the seat belt in place, he closed it before leaning down and placing a kiss on her cheek. Considering what she'd said last night and again this morning, he knew not to do anything but make it a friendly peck, although more than anything, he would have loved giving her a long, deep and drugging kiss. One she would remember for a while.

He stepped away from the car to talk to her through the open car window. "Will you be ready for our trip to Boston this coming week?"

"Yes, but it's strictly a business trip. You will remember that, right?"

He didn't say anything as he glanced down at the ground, thinking of just how much he'd enjoyed being with her yesterday and last night. She had wanted him as much as he'd wanted her, and she'd told him so.

"Kaegan?"

He glanced back up at her and gazed into her eyes. Did she think the strong attraction they'd always had for each other could be one-and-done so easily? He had a feeling she would find out just how wrong she was about that. "Yes, I will remember, Bryce. But maybe you should be asking yourself if you'll remember, as well."

He gave her a wink and then turned and walked away.

CHAPTER TWENTY-SEVEN

The next week was a flurry of activities for Bryce as she prepared for her trip to Boston. She'd made her family aware she was leaving town so they could plan accordingly, since she wouldn't be there to help them out at the café. When she'd told them that Kaegan had hired her as his real-estate broker and that she would be traveling to Boston with him, they'd merely nodded and told her that was nice of him to hire her and for her to have a nice trip. Neither her parents nor her brothers seemed concerned that after all this time of disliking each other, she and Kaegan would be taking a trip together.

She was the one who'd begun questioning if taking the job had been the right thing for her to do. Then there was what had happened Saturday. Surprisingly, she had no regrets about that night, mainly because she had needed him in a bad way. Taking care of her physical needs for once had been the best thing she could have done and her body was loving her for it. She felt rejuvenated, invigorated and recharged. Kaegan had been so keen to her needs, and if anyone would have told her she was capable of having multiple climaxes the way she had, she would not have believed them.

At the moment, she recalled his parting words when she'd left his place. Did he think after Saturday night she would develop an appetite for him? If so, he would be disappointed. She'd gone four years without being sexually active with a man and could go another four.

If anyone wondered why she was in such a good mood and smiling a lot, they hadn't inquired about it. When Kaegan had walked into the café Monday morning with Ray and Sawyer, her heart had begun thumping like crazy in her chest the moment their eyes met. She had read that we-share-a-secret look and knowing they did share one had made every cell in her body sizzle. They might be one-and-done, but they'd made enough sexual memories Saturday night to last a lifetime.

He had called Tuesday night to give her flight information and to say he would be flying to Boston a day early for a business meeting. Someone would be picking her up from the airport to deliver her to the hotel. He would like her to tour several vacant facilities and then have dinner with him and Eric Tolbert, the man who would give them insight as to places of interest on the harbor. She was excited about the prospect of meeting Mr. Tolbert and appreciated Kaegan believing in her abilities to handle this aspect of his business.

In a way she was glad he would be leaving the cove a day earlier than she would. Ever since that day they'd returned to the dock late after making that side trip to Eagle Bend Inlet, rumors had begun flying around town about them finally getting back together. She found that odd, since they hadn't been seen around town together. And whenever he came into the café, she didn't talk to him any more now than she had before. Nor had he visited her at her home, and she hadn't been back to his. Because Kaegan lived in the bayou and not in town, she doubted anyone knew she'd spent the night at his place Saturday night. Still, she knew there were those watching her with romantic minds, including her own parents, although they hadn't said a word.

She was busy packing Wednesday night when Vashti called to wish her a safe flight. They hadn't talked much this week since Vashti had been busy helping Gloria plan her wedding. Since it was a second marriage for both Reid and Gloria, they decided the wedding would be small, but the reception would be large. Bryce hadn't told Vashti that she'd spent the night with Kaegan and wasn't ready to share that information with anyone yet. Not even her best friend.

"Thanks, Vash. I'm looking forward to this trip. I've never been to Boston and hope to have some free time to tour the city."

"You're going to love it. I've been there a few times and loved it. And you're okay with Kaegan?"

Bryce lifted an eyebrow. "Okay with Kaegan how?"

"Are you okay being there with him? I know you've accepted his friendship but were still trying to keep distance."

If Vashti only knew how close they'd been that weekend. "I'm representing him now, so, yes, I'll be fine with being around him."

"And you never did say how your meeting with him Saturday went."

"It went fine." Knowing she needed to end the call before she told Vashti information she wasn't quite ready to share, she said, "I need to finish packing, Vash."

"Take some heavy clothing. It's cold in Boston this time of the year."

"Okay, I will. I'll text you tomorrow to let you know when I get there. Love you."

An hour later she had finished packing. Duke's wife had a meeting in New Orleans in the morning and had offered to drop her off at the airport. She was about to strip and shower when her cell phone rang. She glanced at the clock and saw it was nearly nine, so it wasn't too late to get a call. She saw it was not a number she immediately recognized. "Hello?"

"Hello, Bryce, this is Jeremy. I hope I'm not calling too late."

"No, it's fine. How are you, Jeremy?"

"I'm doing okay. I was calling to let you know that I'm going to be in New Orleans this week and was hoping for that rain check on dinner. I'd love to see you."

Undoubtedly, she hadn't been clear in that message she'd left for him that day. Now would be a good time to reiterate what she'd said. "Oh, Jeremy, I'm extremely busy now. In fact, I got my first client as a broker and will be leaving town for the rest of the week."

"That's awesome, Bryce. Congratulations."

"Thanks. Well, it was good talking to you."

"Same here and have a safe trip."

"Thanks."

Bryce ended the call. Jeremy was a nice guy but she wasn't ready to get seriously involved with anyone. But then all she had to do was to remember what she and Kaegan had shared Saturday night. As far as she was concerned, she'd needed physical satisfaction, and now she could move on. Like she'd told Kaegan, it wouldn't happen again.

Kaegan stopped pacing around his hotel room when his phone rang. He picked it up immediately. "Yes?"

"Mr. Chambray, this is Cornelius Duggar. Ms. Wither-spoon has been picked up from the airport and delivered to the hotel."

A smile touched Kaegan's lips. "Thanks for letting me know."

He clicked off the call. That meant Bryce would be coming up to her room any minute—a room that he'd made sure was connected to his. He intended to make sure the door on his side was not only unlocked, but also wide open in case she ever got a mind to visit. It was wishful thinking on his part, but there was nothing wrong with hoping.

Making love to her Saturday night had made him realize more than ever how much he wanted to be the only man in her life. He loved her and knew he had to earn back her love and would do whatever it took to do so. His cell phone indicated a text message had come through. Clicking it on, he saw it was from Bryce, letting him know she'd arrived at the hotel.

Kaegan texted her back and said he would give her time to get settled before their dinner meeting. After placing his phone back on the table, he shoved his hands into his pockets, knowing he couldn't wait to see her, although he'd seen her Tuesday morning at the café. More than once before going to bed, he'd been tempted to call her, but was determined to play by her rules. He had to believe that they were meant to be together and eventually they would.

He glanced out the window and looked at the beautiful view of the harbor, and knew Bryce had the same view. In fact, their balconies were connected. At that moment his cell phone rang. He picked it up only to see it was from a number he didn't recognize. It was the same number that had called him a couple of times this week and each time he answered the person never said anything. He decided to remedy it now by blocking any future calls. He didn't have time for such nonsense.

"Have you heard from Kaegan?" Faith asked Willa as they took their place at the table. They'd decided to come to Spencer's for lunch today.

"Yes. I talked to him this morning and he's scheduled to return on Saturday. But I doubt that he will."

"Why wouldn't he?" Faith asked.

A smile touched Willa's lips. "Because he's not alone. Bryce is with him."

Faith raised an eyebrow. "Bryce Witherspoon is with Kaegan on a business trip?"

Willa nodded with a big smile. "Yes. Last week he hired Bryce to handle all his real-estate business since she passed that exam. Once his business in Boston is over, I can see him extending his time in Boston and not hurrying back here before Monday. He honestly has no reason to do so."

"I think it will be great if they get back together. It's time for him to settle down and they have such a long history. I hope things work out with them."

"Yes, I do, too."

Unknown to Willa and Faith, a man sitting at the table beside theirs had overheard their conversation. Jeremy's jaw tightened in anger. It sounded like Bryce was getting back with her old boyfriend. Had she merely been taking up his time while on the rebound? When he had called her, she'd made it seem as if she would be too busy for him. Obviously, she wasn't too busy for her ex. He'd honestly thought she was someone he could begin spending time with and now he saw she was no different from the others.

The woman had referred to the man as Kaegan. It shouldn't be hard to find out all he needed to know about the guy. He then recalled something else one of the women had said. Bryce and this Kaegan had no reason to hurry back home before Monday.

A smile touched Jeremy's lips. Maybe he needed to give them a reason.

CHAPTER TWENTY-EIGHT

"I think the meeting went well. Don't you?"

Bryce glanced across the dinner table and met Kaegan's gaze. "Yes, it did, and was certainly informative."

He nodded. "What about Eric Tolbert?"

She shrugged. "I'm sure you noticed that he and I butted heads a few times."

Kaegan chuckled. "Yes, I noticed. I guess he had no idea who he was messing with."

"I tried maintaining my professionalism," she said.

"And you did but he was being an ass. You won't have to be concerned with him after today. I intend to inform him that we won't need his services any longer."

"You don't have to do that on my account. I could have handled him."

"Yes, but there was no reason for you to have to. I know your worth. It was up to him to prove his and he didn't. End of story. Besides, it appears you were just as knowledgeable as he was. I don't think he liked that too much."

Bryce honestly didn't know what the man's problem was, but was glad Kaegan had picked up on the fact he had one.

She'd gone toe-to-toe with her brothers often enough while growing up, and like she'd told Kaegan, she could have handled the man. He'd acted like he felt threatened by the fact she was a woman. She had detected how things would probably go down when he kept saying he'd assumed she was a man. After that, he hadn't hid his disappointment in finding out that she wasn't.

She had gotten through the meeting concentrating less on Eric and more on Kaegan. He'd snagged her attention the moment he'd taken off his jacket. She'd seen his massive shoulders flex beneath his white dress shirt and how good his tapered lean thighs looked in a pair of dress slacks. She was used to seeing him in jeans, so seeing Kaegan in something other than that had captured her interest. The same thing had happened the night of the charity dance.

It didn't take much to recall those same shoulders and thighs, naked and pressed against the length of her body last week. More than once, she had to stifle a groan at the memory of how he'd given her those orgasms. Even with all those thoughts running through her mind, she'd stayed alert and was able to answer any questions asked and was able to provide in-depth information about any location upon request. Tomorrow they would be visiting the three properties that she had recommended.

"Would you like any dessert?" Kaegan asked her.

"No, thank you."

What she wanted to do was go to the hotel and up to her room. The more she was in Kaegan's presence, the more her body was beginning to ache with remembered passion, causing a shameful magnetism that was liable to get out of control if she wasn't careful. It had helped somewhat when Eric had been with them. Now it was just the two of them and it was causing spikes of heat to invade several parts of her body...

especially the nipples of her breasts. It didn't take much to remember his mouth on them.

"Are you ready to leave?"

She glanced over at him. He'd asked her a question and was looking at her, expecting an answer. However, the moment she looked into his eyes, it was as if she was incapable of speech. Instead her mind latched on to the darkness of his eyes—eyes belonging to a hot-blooded male. A man with the ability to give her pleasure like none other. A man who could work up a sexual hunger inside of her without much effort.

When she didn't say anything, he asked, "Bryce? Are you okay?"

She snapped back to reality and said, "I'm fine. Sorry, my mind was elsewhere." She was glad he merely nodded and didn't inquire just where that elsewhere was. "And, yes, I'm ready to go."

By the time they'd reached the hotel, she was a heated mess. Riding with him in the car had provided an intimate setting as the driver whisked them through the Boston streets. It wasn't far, yet the ride seemed to take forever. She wasn't sure what was more intoxicating—the scent of his cologne or his hair, unbound and hanging wildly around his shoulders.

When they reached the hotel lobby, she knew she had to part ways with him and quickly. Once she got to her room, she would soak in a bathtub of bubbles before going to bed. They wouldn't be leaving the hotel until noon to tour those other locations. That would give her time to sleep late. If he called to invite her to breakfast, she would decline.

When they headed toward the elevator, she figured now was the time to spare him that call. "I plan to sleep late tomorrow and will probably grab a late breakfast."

He nodded as he walked beside her. She tried ignoring just how in sync their movements were. "Those are my plans, as well," he replied smoothly as they stepped on the elevator.

She noticed he'd pushed the button for her floor, but not his own. She then wondered how he'd known where her hotel room was located when she hadn't told him. But then, his company had made all the reservations, so him knowing shouldn't surprise her.

She figured he was being a gentleman and was walking her to her room. That wasn't necessary but she thought it was nice of him to do so regardless. Moments later they stepped out of the elevator onto the thirtieth floor and he walked silently beside her. More than once, his thigh brushed against hers and caused a heated rush to flow through her. She needed to get to her room and fast.

She stopped in front of her room and then said, "This is my room. Good night, Kaegan."

"Good night and I'm right next door if you need anything."

She blinked. "You're right next door?" she asked, making sure she'd heard him correctly.

"Yes. Good night, Bryce. There are several calls I need to make before turning in." He leaned in and placed a chaste kiss on her cheek.

"Oh. Sure. Good night." She used her passkey to get inside and quickly closed the door behind her.

A couple of hours later Kaegan had made the last of his phone calls, including one to Eric Tolbert, relieving him of his duties. The man had issues with empowered women, something that wouldn't be tolerated.

According to Willa, things were going great in the office. Another large order had come in from the Chappell Group, which had gotten passed on to his shipping manager.

He glanced toward the connecting door, thinking he'd heard a sound, but was certain it was wishful thinking on his part. He intended to keep this trip strictly business like Bryce asked him to do. That didn't mean he wouldn't place temptation in her path every chance he got, but in the end any physical contact between them would have to be initiated by her.

Standing, he stretched his body and glanced at his watch. Both he and Bryce would be sleeping late. Too bad it wouldn't be with each other. Their first appointment was at one and they had three warehouses to check out tomorrow. Then they would be on the plane back to Catalina Cove early Saturday morning.

He would see if she wanted to extend their trip an additional day since this was her first time in Boston. There were so many historical sites he knew she would want to see. He would merely make the suggestion. No pressure. If she wasn't inclined to do so then that would be that.

CHAPTER TWENTY-NINE

"Did you sleep well last night?"

Bryce looked at Kaegan as they left the hotel. She could tell him the truth—that last night had been difficult knowing he was in a bed on the other side of that wall. Her body had known and had wanted him. However, she had fought the urge to walk over to the connecting door when doing so had been so tempting she could barely stand it.

"I wasn't as tired as I thought and got some reading in." She decided to admit that much in case he'd heard her moving around. "What about you?"

"I made my calls and then got in bed but didn't go right to sleep. I wasn't as tired as I thought, either."

She nodded, not wanting to think how two relatively rested people could have spent their time last night. She had to remember the decision not to indulge had been hers, not his. There was no doubt in her mind that had she knocked on the connecting door, Kaegan would have welcomed her into his suite with open arms.

Open arms...

The thought of walking right into his had her heart pounding. Too bad the chance to do so had been a missed opportunity. He didn't seem bothered by anything. No doubt when he had fallen asleep, he had slept the entire night through.

The private car pulled up the moment they walked through the revolving door. The man opened the door and she slid onto the rich leather seat, with Kaegan following behind her. Their thighs touched and it was the first physical contact they'd shared that day. They looked at each other, holding one another's gaze. She wished she could look away but couldn't. Something inside of her was sizzling and she had a feeling he'd felt it, too.

Kaegan turned to Bryce. "Well, what do you think?"

She looked at him and beamed a smile so bright it could have lit the entire warehouse. "I think this might be it, Kaegan."

He glanced around. "I think so, too. And just think, we found it together. You and I."

This particular warehouse had been one of those they'd had on the list Saturday morning at his place. Now she would need to work out a deal to ensure he got it, and he had every bit of confidence that she would.

"I will arrange a meeting with the property manager as soon as we get in the car. Have you decided if you want to buy or lease?" she asked him.

On the ride over, she'd given him the pros and cons of both. "I think I'll lease."

She nodded. "Considering all the tax advantages, that might be your best option. Besides, although the warehouse will accommodate your business needs now, you'd want to consider the possibility of future expansion."

"True."

A few hours later they had returned to the hotel after meeting with the property manager and completing the necessary paperwork. Kaegan was now an entrepreneur in Boston and couldn't wait to get back to Catalina Cove to make an official announcement. As his administrative assistant, Willa, already knew, but others would be surprised to discover, not only had he been thinking about expanding his business to other regions, but now he'd also taken the first step in doing so.

He glanced over at Bryce. Today she was wearing a pant-suit that fit her body well and the mauve coloring accented her coloring and gave her both a feminine and professional look. She was good at that—wearing clothing that brought out elements of her character. Elements he definitely liked.

They had grabbed something to eat at another restaurant near the harbor. It had been sort of a celebratory dinner with champagne to hail this new milestone in his life, and he was glad she was here to share it with him. "I have an idea," he said, as they walked toward the bank of elevators."

"What?"

"Let's spend another day here in Boston. It would be easy enough to change our tickets."

She raised an eyebrow. "Why would you want to remain here an additional day when all your business has been taken care of?"

He smiled over at her. "For you. I recall you saying you've never been to Boston, and because you've been busy with me, you've yet to see any sights. I'd like to share them with you tomorrow."

She began nibbling on her bottom lip and he knew she was considering his suggestion. Both the pros and cons. What she probably saw as the cons, he would see as the pros.

"Are you sure you want to remain in Boston another day?"

He held back telling her that he would remain here another week, month, year, as long as they were together. Instead he said, "Yes. Another day won't matter. I hadn't planned to go into the office until Monday anyway."

"Neither had I planned to go into mine before then, as well," she said, holding his gaze. "Pia has been doing a good job in my absence."

He nodded. "So, will you consider staying in Boston with me another day?" Kaegan knew what he was asking of her and was aware she knew, too. With business out the way, this would become a pleasure trip, and pleasure covered a large range of things. Hell, he was getting excited by the prospect of them spending personal time together for any period of time.

"Yes, I'll stay."

He couldn't help the smile that curved his lips. "That's great! I'll change the tickets for us to leave Sunday." There was no need to tell her he intended for it to be late on Sunday.

"What do you plan to do the rest of the night?" he asked her as they stepped onto the elevator that would carry them up to their rooms. It was close to eight already.

"Shower and relax. I brought a Rock Mason adventure thriller novel to read. I started it on the plane and have been reading a chapter or two whenever I have the time."

He nodded again. "I think I'll call a tour company to arrange our day tomorrow. That way you won't miss seeing anything. There is so much to do and see here."

"And I can't wait."

They stepped off the elevator and walked side by side down the long corridor. Moments later they stopped in front of her room. "Text me what time you want me ready for the tour tomorrow," she told him.

"I will, and enjoy the rest of your evening, Bryce." Like the night before, he leaned in and placed a chaste kiss on her cheek.

She quickly turned and used her passkey to go inside her room.

Bryce leaned against the closed hotel-room door, trying to get her breathing under control. Kaegan's scent alone could drive her wild. And when he'd kissed her cheek, a portion of his long flowing hair had brushed against the side of her face, sending erotic sensations spiraling through her. She had to get a grip or she would be liable to jump his bones at a moment's notice and she couldn't do that.

Why can't you? a voice within her head asked. Then before she could come up with a reason, that same voice stated, *You are the one who put the rules in place. Ditch them or suffer another night.*

Lordy help her, but she didn't want to endure another sleepless night. She was surprised she was as alert as she had been today after last night. But she had to remind herself that she'd implemented the rule for a reason. She had to keep distance between them. Bedroom distance. Since she worked for him, some closeness had to be allowed.

She shook her head, deciding to stick to her rules, although technically the business side of the trip was over. Moving from the door, she placed her purse on the desk in the room and went straight to the bathroom for her shower. At least she had a good book to read by one of her favorite authors. She ended up taking a leisurely soak in the huge Jacuzzi tub instead of a shower. Now she felt clean and refreshed, but still aroused. Slipping into a short nightie, she began pacing the floor, wondering why she couldn't just park her backside into that recliner and begin reading.

She wished she could claim she'd never felt this deep in need before but knew that would not be true. The same depth had gripped her last Saturday night. With every step she took, she actually felt a pounding in the area between her legs.

She stopped pacing and stared at the connecting door, remembering Vashti teasing her about one. If she opened hers and knocked on his, would he answer? Was he even awake? He hadn't texted her yet regarding the time they would start tomorrow's tour. Should she text him? At least doing so would let her know if he was still awake.

She began pacing again, trying to decide what she would do. The more she paced, the more aroused she got. Then her fantasies began getting the best of her. She felt a need to run her fingers through the length of his hair, tangle her tongue with his in a real naughty kiss, and heaven help her, she wanted him to suck on her breasts. Just the thought of him sliding one of her nipples into his mouth and sucking hard only added to her ache. Almost made her come.

She stopped pacing again and slowly walked toward the connecting door.

When she reached the door she drew in a deep breath, wanting to back away, but she couldn't. She stood right there, not wanting to yield to temptation one minute and then wanting to yield the next. Tired of the tussle going on within her, she decided to give in to temptation. Reaching out, she unlocked the door and nearly jumped at the sound of the loud click. Had he heard it?

Extracting courage, she slowly pulled the door open and went still. The connecting door in his suite was wide open and he stood there, across the room by the window, shirtless and in the same trousers he'd had on earlier. His hair flowed around his shoulders, his legs were braced apart and he held a glass of wine in his hand. Lordy, he was one hot male in one hell of a sexy pose.

Their gazes held for the longest time, and the force of his gaze seemed to lick every part of her body. Then she recalled what she was wearing. A thin gown that shielded very little. The heat she saw in his gaze had frissons of fire racing up her spine. Suddenly, she felt hotter than before and desire was clawing at her, making the breath in her lungs tremble.

"Would you like to share a glass of wine with me, Bryce?"

He'd asked like it was a common occurrence for a half-dressed woman to appear in his hotel room. Maybe it was. That made her wonder if he had intentionally gotten them a connecting room for that reason. Had Kaegan expected her to come through that door?

As if he read her thoughts, he said, "I was wishing you would come to me, Bryce. I was wishing real hard."

He'd gotten his wish. And speaking of *hard*...

His erection was a testament to just how hard his wishes might have gotten. Seeing it made sexual need curl in her stomach. Before she could talk herself out of it, she undid the ties at her shoulders, which caused the nightie to slide down her legs and pool at her feet. He watched her every movement and she saw fire light his eyes. Then she heard the throaty growl all the way across the room.

Nervously, she swallowed and then began moving toward him. It seemed every pore and cell in her body urged her forward, closer to him. Closer and closer. And then she was there, standing directly in front of him. "Yes, I'd share a glass of wine with you."

It was as if the sight of her standing in front of him completely naked had him glued to the spot. Instead of walking away from her to pour her a glass, he offered her his glass. She took it and drained the half-filled glass in one gulp. She didn't have time to waste sipping. Ignoring the lifting of his brow, she placed the empty glass on the table next to him.

A part of her knew she should be acting sensibly. At least she should be mentally going over any pros and cons about what she was doing. However, like the wine, she didn't have time. She'd made her decision when she'd walked through that connecting door and removed her gown. Bottom line was that she wanted him, and from the size of his erection pressing hard against his zipper, he wanted her, too.

Dark lashes half lowered over his eyes and the look in his features was intense. Then while she watched, he unzipped his pants and stepped out of them along with his briefs. Her gaze immediately went to his middle. Was he thinking about how things had been for them last weekend? She wanted to know how he radiated such masculine prowess. And why was she allowing it to get to her like this?

Knowing there were no ready answers, she decided to use her time doing something else. She reached out and glided her hands up his sculpted abdomen, loving the feel of his hard and muscular body. Then she lowered her hand to cup Kaegan. The feel of her fingers wrapped around his engorged penis did something to her. Made a rush of desire spike within her. Kaegan Chambray aroused her in ways no other man could. She knew that for a fact. She had tried fighting the attraction but couldn't deny it. Nor did she want to any longer. So much for one-and-done. Her being here in his hotel room now only affirmed another fact. He was more than just in her system. He was in her blood. With that realization, she had to whisper his name. The same name she'd whispered the first time they made love and all the times after that.

"K-Gee..."

Saying his name heightened the beat of her pulse. Before she could draw in her next breath, he lifted her up and she automatically wrapped her legs around his waist.

CHAPTER THIRTY

Kaegan doubted that he could make it to the bedroom, so he decided to not even try. Instead he backed her up against the nearest wall. Leaning in close, he captured her lips, loving the way his tongue slid inside her mouth, and then kissed her the way he'd dreamed about last night.

The feel of her hardened nipples pressing against his bare chest fueled his sexual hunger. At that moment, he wanted to mate with her with a ferocity that overrode his senses. He deepened the kiss and ravaged her mouth with all the passion he possessed and then some. Her taste had the ability to rile him to new heights, fill him with a need that only she could extinguish. She could create a greed in him that only she could feed. Bryce was his pleasure food.

In reality, she was his everything, and tonight he intended to show her how much. When they returned to Catalina Cove, there would be no talk of one-and-done, or two-and-through. Tonight would start the beginning of something that ten years of heartache or heartbreak couldn't destroy. They had done things her way and now they would do things his.

He had no choice. His shaft was throbbing to get inside of

her, connect with her flesh. Unlike before, he wanted to be skin-to-skin. He pulled back, dislodging their mouths. His tongue seemed to jerk in protest to the point where he bit back a growl. The eyes that locked with his were now a turbulent brown, annoyed that he'd ended the kiss. But there was something he had to know before he showed her the action between them was just beginning.

"Are you still on the pill?" he asked, fitting his fully aroused shaft in the cradle of her thighs.

"No," she said in a breathless moan. But before his heart could plummet in disappointment, she said, "I started taking injections six years ago. Remembering to take a pill every day became a nuisance."

His entire body reacted in elation. His hips automatically rocked against hers and he dragged the tip of his tongue across her mouth. In response, she raked a fingernail across his shoulder before leaning in to graze her teeth across his chin. Her retaliation was totally unexpected yet welcomed. He wanted her to do both again.

"I've never gone skin-to-skin with any woman but you. I'm safe, Bryce." He could feel her heart pounding against his after that proclamation.

"It was the same with me. I never wanted another man that way. I'm safe, Kaegan."

Her words did something to him. She had ruined him for any other woman and in turn he had ruined her for any other man. "Now that we've gotten that cleared up…" he said.

He reached up and eased his hand between her legs, then began stroking her there while holding her gaze captive. He fingered all around her curls and in the wet juices he was stroking into existence. Her aroma was filling his nostrils with such a delicious scent. He was tempted to ease her to the floor and bury his head between her legs.

He decided that would have to come later. He needed to

be connected to her in a way he could never connect with another woman. He could tell by the sounds she was making and the heat in the depths of her eyes that his fingers inside her were about to make her come. He wanted to be planted deep inside her when she did. Removing his fingers, he hoisted her body up a little so that her womanly core was right there, near the tip of his shaft. She automatically widened her legs to make the journey easier—they were ready to be skin-to-skin with each other.

Holding firmly to her hips, he began easing inside of her. It was tight, she felt snug, but her wet heat tempted him to keep going and going. He leaned in close, and using the tip of his tongue, he licked the perspiration off her jaw, then groaned out loud as he continued sliding to the hilt. Satisfied there was no way he could go any deeper, he cupped her bottom, tilted her hips slightly and began a slow rhythm, while still locked in her gaze.

He watched her as he began thrusting inside of her and appreciated how the full naked length of him felt inside of her. He could feel her clit quivering on his shaft. He then felt the way her womanly muscles bore down and tightened, his huge erection caught in their grip. They began a mating dance, old as time and more powerful than he'd shared in a long time. Since her.

It seemed every cell in his body erupted with a need that had him thrusting harder and deeper. He then threw back his head when he felt her muscles milking his shaft, trying to pull everything out of him. In time, she would discover that he had a lot to give. It was as if he'd been saving it all for her.

Suddenly, she screamed his name and the sound drove him to thrust even harder. It was as if he couldn't get enough of her. Then something inside of him seemed to snap and his body arched deeper inside of her. He groaned out her name as she continuously moaned out his.

"Brycie!"

"K-Gee!"

It seemed neither had control and he was glad he'd had the mind to place her against a wall that connected to her room. Otherwise, management would have gotten a call about them by now because they were working this particular wall for all it was worth. Her lithe body had no problem responding to his urgent demands. He knew the minute she came again, then a third and fourth time.

Kaegan was still coming from the first, and a continuous flow was shooting from his body aimed right into hers. He loved how it felt filling her up and the sensations of doing so made him shiver all over. Waves and waves of pleasure flowed through him, and he knew at that moment, when she screamed his name yet again, that his woman was pure sexual energy in his arms. And she was his woman and he would do whatever it took to make her realize that point.

Hours later, the ringing of the phone brought Kaegan instantly awake. He reached for his cell phone before it could disturb Bryce. He loved the way her body was pressed close to his and their limbs were entwined. They had made it from the wall in the sitting room to the bedroom, where after making love a few more times, they'd finally drifted off to sleep.

The ringtone indicated it was Sawyer. It was close to two in the morning. "Sawyer?"

"Yeah. Calling with bad news."

Kaegan pulled himself up in bed and the movement brought Bryce awake. Unfortunately, that couldn't be helped. "What happened?"

"There was a fire."

"A fire? Where?" Bryce had pulled up in bed beside him.

"On one of your ships docked at the marina. There was minor damage near the galley."

"What caused it?"

"Not sure. Possibly electrical or equipment malfunction. However, Brody credits Elton for taking quick action. Luckily, he was on board and managed to contain it until the fire department arrived. Like I said, the damage is minor. No need for you to rush back."

Brody Dorsett was the fire marshal in Catalina Cove. "You sure?"

"Positive. According to Brody, an investigation won't be done before Monday. Elton has everything under control." Sawyer chuckled. "I've never seen him so energized. That old-timer stepped right into action tonight. You would be proud of him."

Kaegan smiled in spite of the bad news he'd received. "I'm always proud of him. And if you're sure there's no need for me to rush back, then I'll see you Sunday, as planned." He had spoken with Sawyer earlier to let him know of his change in plans to remain in Boston another day.

"Good. I'm glad you and Bryce decided to take an extra day."

"What makes you think…?" He trailed off his words and glanced at Bryce. She was looking at him with keen interest.

"I know your question and the answer is because Bryce called Vashti earlier tonight to let her know of her change in plans, too. Although she didn't mention your name, just like you didn't mention hers when we talked earlier. Imagine that."

"Yes, imagine that." Wanting to get Sawyer off the phone, he said, "Call me back if anything else develops."

"I will."

The minute he clicked off the phone, a wide-eyed Bryce began asking questions. "There was a fire? Where? Is anyone hurt? Do you need to leave?"

He reached out to run his fingers through her hair before pulling her into his arms. "Yes, there was a fire on one of my ships. No one was hurt. And, no, I won't be leaving to return back to Catalina Cove any sooner than planned."

"How did the fire start?"

"Not sure. There will be an investigation. Sawyer thinks it was possibly electrical or equipment malfunction, but I don't see how. All four ships docked at the marina were just inspected last month."

"Why aren't you leaving to go back?"

"There's nothing I can do before Monday and Sawyer says the damage is minor." He buried his face in the side of her neck and inhaled deeply. He loved her scent. He began pressing kisses to the side of her face. He used the tip of his tongue to lick her skin, loving her taste. "Besides, I refuse to give up my extra day in Boston with you."

She pulled back to stare at him but said nothing. He had an idea just what she was thinking. She, of all people, knew he'd never wanted to follow in his father's footsteps and become a man of the sea. But he had. Now he honestly appreciated Reid for convincing him to stay and take over the shipping company. It didn't take him long to discover being a shipper was in his blood, whether he wanted it or not. The plus side was that there had been good older men, like Elton and others, who'd worked for his father for years, that were willing to stay on and help Kaegan along the way. He'd been determined to make the Chambray Seafood Shipping Company bigger and better than before.

"Who will handle things pertaining to the fire in your absence?" she asked him.

"Elton. According to Sawyer, he was on board the ship asleep when the fire started and is the one who spotted it."

It wasn't strange that Elton was sleeping on one of his ships. The old man's wife had passed over twenty years ago. They never had any children. Kaegan had always considered him part of his family. When he'd built his house he'd even included a guest room just for him. But Elton was a man of the sea and it wasn't uncommon for him to leave his small house on the bayou and drive to the docks and get aboard one of Kaegan's ships and sleep under the stars.

"Elton acted quickly," Kaegan continued. "Well, as quick as you can expect from an eighty-five-year-old man, but what he did is the reason there's only minor damage."

She smiled. "He still has your back."

Kaegan chuckled. "Yes, he still has my back. According to Sawyer, Elton has taken charge and is handling things, so I'm going to let him. There is no doubt in my mind he'll do whatever needs to be done until I return."

"There is no doubt in mine, either. He's always been fiercely loyal to you."

Bryce, of all people, would know. "Yes, he has."

She didn't say anything for a minute. Then she asked, "Are you sure?"

He lifted an eyebrow. "About what?"

"Staying here another day. I will definitely understand if we need to go back, considering what has happened."

He reached out and tilted her chin to lift her face up to him. What they had shared over the past few hours still had him in awe. It had been like an awakening and a revelation to so many things. He hadn't known just how much he missed her, had missed this, until they'd made love last Saturday night at his house. In his bed. And then tonight, here, in Boston, had been totally surreal. Pleasure was rushing through him just thinking about it.

Kaegan held her gaze. "Like I said, I refuse to give up my day with you."

Leaning toward him, she slipped her arms around his back and placed her face on his chest. She tilted her head up to stare at him. He wondered if she knew that particular position gave him total access to her mouth.

Kaegan had a feeling that wasn't her intent. He could tell by the way she was looking at him that something was bothering her. He had an idea what it was and decided they needed to get things out now so they could enjoy tomorrow. He wanted that for him and for her.

"We made love again," she finally said softly.

He nodded. At least she hadn't referred to it as having sex. "And?" he prompted.

He knew she was hesitating, trying to decide what to say and how to say it. Funny, how he could still read her after all this time. "Bryce?"

"I enjoyed it immensely, but I'm not sure sleeping with you again was the right thing to do, Kaegan. Especially when I said I wouldn't."

"You have the right to change your mind." There was no way she hadn't felt the sexual pull that was there whenever they were together. She had to be as affected by it as he'd been.

"Yes. But I shouldn't."

He gathered her into his arms. "I know I hurt you and I'm fully aware that it's not going to be easy for you to trust me with your heart again, but I'm not sure I can give you up, Bryce."

"I have misgivings about anything developing between us."

He wondered if she didn't realize that they were beyond the developing stage. "And it's up to me to remove those misgivings, Bryce."

She shook her head. "I'm not sure if you can."

He drew in a deep breath, refusing to believe that. "Will you let me at least try? You believe we could never have what we once had. I think you're wrong. In fact, I think we can have something bigger and better. We aren't the same people. We've grown. We've changed. Matured. But the one thing for me that has remained constant is my love for you, Bryce. Even when I wanted to hate you. I tried but couldn't."

She gave an unladylike snort. "You could have fooled me."

He heard the hurt in her voice. Little did she know the only person he'd been actually fooling was himself. "And I'll regret doing so for the rest of my life."

She licked her bottom lip, and as he watched her he couldn't help but think that she was the only woman who had ever claimed his heart, and ever would.

"Why do we have to be so serious about anything? Why can't we have a—"

"Casual affair?" He knew how her mind was working.

"Yes."

He reached out and pressed the palm of his hand against her cheek. "I don't think we can do casual. We could never be friends with benefits."

She gave him a pointed look. "How do you know?"

"Trust me, I know. So will you let me try to win back your heart, Bryce?"

Bryce nibbled on her bottom lip again. Could she risk it? No one, not even Vashti, knew the pain she'd gone through, and it was pain she had survived only because she had made a promise to herself never to put herself in that position again. But when she thought about the time they'd spent together last weekend, and now in Boston, she felt sensuously giddy inside.

Kaegan had shown her that he had respect for her profession and had even allowed her to handle things in that meeting. And then a few hours ago, when her body had all but demanded its desire for him, she had conceded with no regrets. What she hadn't counted on either time was her body's need for him and only him. It was a deep, vicious physical thing that she wasn't able to control.

Could they try again to regain what they'd lost? Did she

want to even try? He had made a mistake but should she hold it against him forever when she claimed she had forgiven him? Forgiving didn't necessarily mean reconciliation. Should she change her way of thinking for him? For them?

She studied his features—grown-up features that were more mature and intense, but as handsome as ever. The same features that she had gazed at while they'd made love. He'd always been able to take foreplay to a whole other level, but now he was so skilled at it. Just thinking about some of the ways he'd gotten her prepared filled her with immense heat.

And nothing they did was brief. The kisses or the lovemaking. He had a way of prolonging things and getting the most out of them. He gave multiple orgasms like there was nothing to them.

"Bryce?"

Hearing him say her name made her realize she hadn't answered his question. "Are you sure you want to win back my heart, Kaegan?"

He brushed his lips across her chin. "My life won't be complete until I do."

She bit her lower lip again while thinking about just what winning her back could entail. Catalina Cove was a small town, where some people made it their business to know everything. "If we get back together people are going to talk."

He pulled back and lifted her chin so she could look into his eyes. "Will that bother you?"

Seeing the intense look in his eyes, she understood why he was asking. "No. Being your girl didn't bother me and it wouldn't bother me now, Kaegan. It's not the talk I'm worried about, but my heart. Your father took joy in spreading the word that you'd dumped me, although he'd kept them guessing as to why."

"Now those same people will see me busting my ass off to get you back. They'll realize whatever the reason that tore us apart was me and not you and I'm trying hard to get my act together."

She didn't say anything for a minute, knowing more than anything she would like things between them to be like they used to be. No issues with trust. "Okay, Kaegan."

"Does that mean you understand that I want more from you than spending time in my bed? That I want you back in my life? That in winning you back I intend to make sure you know, that you will always know, that you're the only woman I want? The only woman I need?"

More than anything, she wanted to believe all that he'd just said. "I want to believe you, Kaegan," she said, fighting to keep her voice from breaking when emotions tried to consume her.

"Neither of us can change the past, Bryce, although more than anything I wish that I could. I wish there was a rewind button where we could return to that night when I'd come home unexpectedly to surprise you. But we can't rewind. We can't go back. All we can do is move forward. Will you let me work hard to earn your love and trust again? Will you give me that chance?"

Bryce drew in a deep breath, no longer able to deny his request. She was taking a chance with him, this man who'd been her best friend, lover, confidant and protector. However, more important, she was taking a chance with her heart. "Yes, I'll give that to you."

CHAPTER THIRTY-ONE

Kaegan glanced up at the man who walked into his office. Brody Dorsett had graduated from Catalina Cove High School the same year he had. Brody, who was parts French, African and Spanish, had also been born and raised in the bayou. His ancestors had been known as Bayou Creoles. Like others, Brody had left the cove to go to college and had taken a job elsewhere. He'd lived in Memphis, where he'd been a fire captain for a number of years.

Brody had returned to the cove last year to take over as fire chief investigator when Brody's father and Catalina Cove's longtime fire chief investigator retired early due to illness. Brody's father had passed away nine months ago. Kaegan always liked Brody and knew he was well respected in the cove and many were glad he'd returned.

"You got something for me, Brody?" he asked, offering him a chair. He'd known that Brody and his team arrived early that morning to check out the damage on the ship.

"Yes, Kaegan. It was arson."

Kaegan went still for a minute. "Arson?"

"Yes. I suspected it Saturday night but wanted to wait until I did a thorough inspection to be sure."

Kaegan was dumbfounded. "Who would want to deliberately start a fire on my ship?"

Brody shrugged. "I don't know. The perpetrator was sloppy, or he didn't care if it was discovered the fire was caused by arson. He was quick and tossed one of those lighter-fluid containers in a ball filled with heat with the intent for it to catch fire. It did. I guess they hadn't counted on Elton being on board that night. It's a good thing he was, otherwise there would have been more damage."

Kaegan nodded, still perplexed. He had arrived back in Catalina Cove yesterday evening after having shared a wonderful time in Boston with Bryce. "What happens next?"

Brody stood. "Now I work with Sawyer to bring the person to justice. A copy of my report will be filed with your insurance carrier and a copy will be given to Sawyer. More than likely the two of us will be meeting with you sometime this week. When will be a good time?"

"Whenever it's best for you guys. I'll make time."

After Brody left, Kaegan went to the window and looked out at the impaired ship. Sawyer had been right about the damage being minor. However, knowing the fire had been deliberately set was a game changer. Who would do such a thing? Why?

Kaegan knew there'd been a rash of arson-related fires in several parishes in Louisiana over the past year, but none in Catalina Cove. Churches, vacant homes and warehouses had been torched, but this was the first time he'd heard of a fire deliberately being set on a boat or ship.

He needed to call his office staff together and let them know. With small-town gossip the way it was, it wouldn't be long before news spread. He would rather they hear it from him. Moving to his desk, he pushed a button on the intercom.

"Yes, Kaegan?"

"Willa, please get everyone together for a meeting in my office."

"Okay."

Ten minutes later his office was filled with the members of his office staff—Willa, Faith and Toby. He rarely called these types of gatherings in his office unless it was to announce big news. Just that morning he'd gotten them together to announce the expansion and they'd been all excited about it. Now this.

"Brody just left here with the findings of the fire that happened Saturday night. It was the result of arson."

Willa sucked in a shocked breath. "Arson?"

"Yes, so there will be a full investigation by both Brody and Sawyer. I have confidence in their abilities and believe the person or persons responsible will be caught. More than likely during their investigation all of us will be questioned."

"Why would we be questioned when the fire happened when the office was closed?" Toby asked.

"Just standard investigation procedures to see if perhaps you noticed anything during the hours the office was opened. They will probably want to know if any of you recall seeing some strange person hanging near the boats or anything. And, Willa, knowing Sawyer, he's going to want a complete list of everyone who volunteered for that oyster netting two weeks ago."

"Okay."

He then glanced around at everyone and said, "Thanks and that will be all."

Kaegan pulled into the parking lot of Bryce's real-estate office. He'd gone to the café, hoping to see her there, only to be told by Duke she hadn't come in today because she needed to catch up with some things at her office. So here he was, with the food her mother had asked him to deliver. Ms. Debbie figured Bryce had probably gotten busy and missed both lunch and dinner.

Getting out of his truck, he looked around, liking how well lit the area where Bryce's office was. Although the other businesses around here had closed for the day, there were still a number of cars in several parking lots, which meant Bryce wasn't the only person working late.

Holding tight to the bags, he walked up to the door and rang the bell. She opened it, saw him and smiled, and then stepped aside. "Mom called to let me know you were coming over with food."

He entered, remembering the one and only other time he'd been here. That had been when he'd come to apologize to her again. "She sent enough for two," he said, grinning.

Bryce chuckled. "Of course she did. You can come this way. I need a break." She led him down a hall to where he knew her office was located. They also passed a room with a long table and several chairs that he figured was used as a conference room.

They entered a huge area that appeared to double as a kitchen and break room. "We can sit there and eat," she said, pointing to a large round table. "I heard Cajun pork chops are in that bag."

"I hadn't checked." He tried not to stare at her too much. She was wearing a pullover sweater and a pair of dark slacks. Both looked good on her. "How did your day go?" he asked her.

She'd been pulling the containers out of the bag and now paused. "I should be asking you that question. Mom said Brody suspects the fire on your ship was due to arson."

"Yes, although I find it hard to believe someone would do such a thing."

"People are crazy, Kaegan, and it's probably nobody from around here. Chances are it was a drifter passing through. Either way, I believe with Brody and Sawyer working together the person will get caught."

He knew she was right. Sawyer was ex-FBI, and when it came to investigations of any sort, he put 100 percent into it. Kaegan knew Sawyer still had contacts at the Bureau when an investigation went out of his scope. "Although what you said is true, I can't help but feel angry about it."

"And you should."

"The damage wasn't too bad, but dealing with the insurance company is a nightmare. They are sending their own people out this week, as well. I've taken precautions by asking Isaac if he would install the same type of high-tech security devices he did for me on Eagle Bend Inlet to where my ships are docked. That way I will be alerted if it happens again, which I'm hoping it won't. I've also hired a security guard to make periodic rounds."

Wanting to change the subject, he asked if she'd talked to Vashti.

She chuckled. "Are you kidding me? My phone was ringing the moment I walked into my house last night. She and Sawyer figured there was a reason we extended our time in Boston. I told her that you'd been kind enough to enjoy the city with me since it had been my first visit there."

He looked at her. "Did that satisfy her?"

"Of course it didn't, so I ended up telling her that you and I are trying to work things out. She was glad about it, Kaegan." She paused a minute and then said, "Mom and Dad asked me about us, as well. I told them the same thing."

Kaegan nodded as he held her gaze. He loved her and knew it would take time and was glad she was giving them a chance to rebuild what they'd had before. In the meantime, he would continue to prove to her that he was worthy of her love and that he wanted forever with her.

They talked about other things while they ate, and when

they finished, he helped clear the table. "How much longer do you plan to be here tonight?" he asked after placing the garbage in the trash.

"Probably another hour. Why?"

"Mind if I hang around? I want to escort you home."

She quirked an eyebrow. "Escort me home?"

"Yes. I'll follow behind you in my truck. You're my girl again and I want to be there for you." When she didn't say anything, he crossed the room to stand in front of her. "Do you have a problem with me doing that?"

She released a deep sigh. "Yes and no. I haven't been anyone's girl for a long time, Kaegan. I've gotten used to my space. Having anyone inside it will take some getting used to."

"I understand." And he did. Bryce was now fiercely independent. He could appreciate that, but when it came to her, he'd always been just as fiercely protective. "What about a compromise?"

"What sort of a compromise?"

"It's been a while since we've been together and in the same town. At least not since high school. You were away at college and I was in the military. Having a steady girl living in the same town is something I have to get used to, as well. That means I'm going to need for you to let me know when you think I'm invading too much of your space. Then I'll back up. Agreed?"

She nodded, and he saw relief on her face. "Agreed. I guess this time around will be both different and challenging for us."

He reached out and wrapped his arms around her waist. "Yes, but I'm determined to win back your heart, Bryce. For me there has never been another woman. You're it." He leaned in and kissed her.

Jeremy was upset as he paced his hotel room in New Orleans. That fire hadn't gotten Bryce and her boyfriend back to town any sooner and the thought of that annoyed the hell out of him. He'd honestly liked her, but like the others, she needed to be taught a lesson. He wouldn't allow her to play another man for a fool.

He'd read the news article about the fire and the fire department's ruling of arson. However, he wasn't worried about getting connected to the fire in any way. He'd checked out the place the day before and hadn't spotted any video cameras, which was a foolish and costly mistake on Kaegan Chambray's part.

Jeremy's only regret was that more damage hadn't been done due to some old man who'd been on the boat at the time. He hadn't seen the old man, and according to the newspaper article, the old man claimed not to have seen anything.

Now all Jeremy had to do was figure out a plan to take care of Bryce. He would teach her a lesson she wouldn't forget.

CHAPTER THIRTY-TWO

Wednesday morning, Kaegan walked into the Witherspoon Café and joined Sawyer and Ray. As he slid into his seat he saw Bryce serving a customer. "Good morning, fellas."

"Morning," both Ray and Sawyer replied simultaneously.

"So what's going on?" he asked them.

Ray took a sip of his coffee and then said, "First for the good news. Bryce might have found someone interested in leasing out my house."

Kaegan smiled. "That is good news. What's the bad news?"

"I guess it's not really bad news," Ray said solemnly. "I got a call last night that the authorities finally ID'd the guy they thought was me in the car that went off the bridge. You know, the hitchhiker I picked up that day that pistol-whipped me and left me for dead before hijacking my car."

Kaegan lifted an eyebrow. "How were they able to identify him?"

"By traffic cameras along the interstate. Since I was able to recall the exact location where I picked him up, they reviewed footage from that day taken along there. They sent photos of several hitchhikers caught on the traffic cam and I was able to pick out the guy. It took them only a few weeks to discover his identity."

"Who was he?" Kaegan asked. He figured the reason Sawyer wasn't asking any questions was because he already had all the details.

"He was a man by the name of Freddie Monroe. According to the FBI, he was also wanted for murder in another state. That of a woman in Gary, Indiana."

"Well, I'm glad that mystery is solved," Kaegan said, hoping that would give closure to Ray.

"Thank God for video cameras," Sawyer said. "I know some people think of them as an invasion of their privacy, but you wouldn't believe the number of crimes that are solved after we've gone back and pulled video footage for businesses. Too bad there weren't any on the docks," he said to Kaegan. "Had there been, we would have possibly gotten an image of the person who started that fire on your ship."

"Well, I'm not waiting for the city zoning board to approve video cameras along the pier. I've already hired Isaac to install my own. I hate pulling him out of retirement again, but he agreed to set up the same kind of security system around my ships that I have on Eagle Bend Inlet."

"That's a good idea," Ray said.

"Good morning, Kaegan. Would you like the usual?"

Kaegan glanced up at Bryce. She was smiling and he smiled back. "Yes, the usual is fine." She nodded and walked off, and his gaze followed her until she was no longer in sight.

"This is going to take some getting used to," Ray said, grinning.

Kaegan lifted an eyebrow. "What?"

"You and Bryce being nice to each other."

Kaegan smiled. "Yes, but you might as well get used to it because that's how things will be from here on out." He switched his gaze to Sawyer. "Any leads on the fire?"

Sawyer shook his head. "So far, none."

"I understand you and Brody talked to the people in my office yesterday."

"We did."

Bryce reappeared with a cup of coffee and a basket of blueberry muffins. "Thanks, Bryce."

"You're welcome, Kaegan." She smiled at him before turning to walk off.

Ray chuckled. "That's too much sweetness this time of morning."

Kaegan rolled his eyes. "Whatever." He saw Bryce remove her apron as if she was about to leave. "Excuse me for a second. I need to talk to Bryce before she leaves."

"Fine. Just so you know, you're next on our list to interview, Kaegan. Will you be available around ten this morning?"

"Yes. Ten is fine."

Bryce smiled at the woman who was her first appointment for today. Although they'd never met officially, the woman, Victoria Madaris, was coanchor for the morning talk show *Hello, New Orleans*. Because there were no television stations in the cove, all their programming came from New Orleans, which meant Victoria Madaris's face was seen by many living here. She'd always thought the woman was gorgeous on television and she seemed even prettier in person. She looked to be in her midtwenties and Bryce found her to be friendly and down-to-earth.

"I'm glad you're thinking about moving to the cove," Bryce said.

Victoria smiled. "I fell in love with the town when we did a segment on your Shrimp Festival last year. I was smitten. I grew up in a large city, and I found Catalina Cove so appealing. The town seems so quiet, quaint and peaceful."

Bryce nodded. "What about the hour drive to and from New Orleans five days a week?" she asked.

The woman waved off her concern. "That won't be a problem for me. Since my show starts at seven each morning, I'll be on the road by five, when most people will still be sleeping. Besides, I'm used to Houston's traffic. At least it will be a straight shot from here to New Orleans."

That was true, Bryce thought. "You want to lease and not buy, right?"

"Yes. And I'd like a two-year lease if possible. That's the length of time I have left with my contract at the television station, so that timing would be great. The lease I'm in now in New Orleans won't end for another month."

Bryce's smile widened. "I might have just the place you need. It's the size you want and everything. Currently, it's occupied. The couple is having a new house built that should be ready for them to move into in another month. After that the house will be ready for occupancy. I think you're going to like it. It backs up to an apple grove."

Victoria's smile widened. "An apple grove? That's nice. Do you think I'll be able to see it today?"

"Yes. The owners are friends of mine and they have no problem with me showing it today."

"That's great!"

A few hours later Bryce was back in her office. Victoria Madaris had loved Ray and Ashley's home and had immediately signed a two-year lease. Now Ashley and Ray were glad their house wouldn't have to sit vacant while she found someone to move in. The timing was perfect. They would move out, and in a month, Victoria would be moving in.

So far today had gotten off to a great start. She'd seen Kaegan first thing this morning. It felt strange getting back into a steady relationship with a guy. Especially one who was not just any guy, but the same guy she'd fallen in love with once

but was terrified of loving again. She knew few people understood why she'd put such an impenetrable barrier around
her heart. Unless they'd gone through the hurt and pain that
she had, she didn't expect them to understand. She honestly
wasn't sure Kaegan even understood. He wanted what they
had before, but she wasn't sure she was capable of giving him
that. She'd stopped believing in forever-after years ago, and
for her the burden of trying to believe in it again was something she wasn't sure she wanted to take on.

How she could go from feeling she meant nothing to him
to begin feeling she was his everything again was just something that was hard for her to believe right now. Like she'd
tried explaining to him, it had taken her years to move on
and rebuild her life, restore her self-esteem after his actions
had torn it down. But she had. He wanted to regain her love
and trust. At least he'd been duly forewarned that he had a
difficult task ahead of him.

She would admit she'd liked how he'd been there this
morning to walk her to her car when she'd left the café. It
had reminded her of past years, when they were teens and
he'd been there whenever she left the café to either walk her
to school or home. And she'd liked the kiss he'd given her
when she'd gotten behind the wheel of her car.

He had invited her out to dinner Friday night. To the
Lighthouse. The cove's lighthouse-turned-restaurant was a
luxurious place to dine. Usually, you had to make reservations weeks, sometimes months, in advance. Kaegan must have
used some mighty strong connections to get them a table for
Friday night. She was feeling a little bubbly with excitement.
This wasn't the first time he'd taken her out to dinner. However, she knew it was the first time they'd dined together in
public in Catalina Cove. This dinner would officially announce them as a couple. A part of her couldn't help but feel
a little nervous about it since most people living in the cove

knew their history. But at the same time, she felt thrilled that Kaegan didn't mind announcing to the cove that she was the one he wanted.

She almost jumped when the intercom on her desk buzzed. "Yes, Pia?"

"There's a Mrs. Corsuti on the line. She wants to ask you about available warehouse property in town."

Bryce smiled. Usually Wednesdays were her slow days, but so far things were hopping today. She couldn't help but be overjoyed. "Please put her through."

Kaegan stared across his desk at the two men. "Okay, what questions do you have for me?"

"All right, then. Let's get started," Brody said, taking out a writing pad. "Any enemies, Kaegan?"

Kaegan knew the question was a routine one to ask under the circumstances, but it still gave him pause. "Not that I know of."

"Any unusual occurrences lately? Anything you noticed odd? Either here or at home?" Brody asked.

Kaegan rubbed a hand down his face. "Nothing I can think of." Then he remembered something. "A few weeks ago someone slashed my tire, but I mentioned that to you, Sawyer."

Sawyer nodded. "You thought it was bored teens with nothing to do on a Friday night."

Brody lifted a brow. "Bored teens with nothing to do on a Friday night?" he asked, chuckling. "When the Livewire is feeding them free pizza? That's one of the first things I was told about when I returned to town. My team have to make sure the place is never over capacity."

Brody shifted in his chair and then asked, "What did you do with the tire after you changed it?"

Kaegan worked his shoulders to get out the kinks. He had

to remember that in Brody's profession as an investigator, he thought like a cop, too. "Since it couldn't be repaired, I bought a new one from Lester's Auto Repair Shop. Lester kept the old one."

Sawyer nodded. "I'll swing by there to see if Lester still has it."

"Why?"

"You have an SUV. Slashing a tire for that vehicle isn't easy. I want to see the tire to determine what type of instrument was used—knife, blade, box cutter or whatever."

"I see."

"What about jealous girlfriends, or the boyfriends of ex-girlfriends?" Brody asked.

"None."

Brody raised his brow. "None?"

"None."

"Are you saying you haven't dated women?" Brody inquired.

"Not your typical definition of dating."

Sawyer chuckled. "In other words, Brody, Kaegan and the women had an understanding of just how deep their commitment level went."

"I'll still need their names."

"Only one woman living in Lafayette named Jodie Metcalf, but we haven't been together for a while now," Kaegan said. "More than over a year."

"And since then?" Brody asked.

"No one, although I would admit a woman named Sasha Johnson was making a nuisance of herself by calling me. I blocked her number and then told her brother about how she got my number since it's private."

"Her brother?"

"Yes. Farley Johnson. He works for me as team lead on one of my boats. It seems Sasha got my number off his phone. He raked her over the coals about it, and I understand she got mad and left."

"Left?"

"Yes. She moved back to where she came from."

"Which was?"

"Some place in Texas."

"Are you seeing anybody now, Kaegan?"

He nodded. "Yes. Bryce Witherspoon. She and I started seeing each other again on a serious level a week or so ago," Kaegan said, making sure Brody understood the relationship he had with Bryce was different from the one he'd shared with Jodie. Bryce was different. In his mind she was his forever girl. He thought about the engagement ring he'd intended to give her ten years ago. A ring he still had.

"What about jealous ex-boyfriends of Bryce's?"

"I wouldn't know."

"We'll find out when we talk to Bryce," Sawyer said.

Kaegan didn't particularly like the sound of that. "Is that necessary?"

"Yes," Sawyer said. "I don't plan to leave any stone un-turned."

"Anything else you can think of that might have happened recently?" Brody asked.

Kaegan rubbed his chin and said, "No. There is nothing that I can think of."

CHAPTER THIRTY-THREE

Bryce looked at the man walking by her side up the steps to her home. "I really enjoyed tonight, Kaegan. Everything was wonderful. Dinner, the music, the service—now I see why people come from miles around to the Lighthouse. It was truly a great experience."

They reached her door. "I'm glad you enjoyed it."

She didn't say anything while she pulled her door key from her purse. She looked back up at him and asked, "Would you like to come in for coffee? Mom made blueberry pies and sent me one. I don't mind sharing a slice or two with you."

He chuckled. "Or maybe three? You know how much I love your mom's blueberry anything."

"Yes, I know," she said, chuckling while opening the door to her home.

He followed her inside, and the minute the door closed behind them, he pulled her into his arms and his mouth swooped down on hers. The thought of pushing him away never entered her mind. She'd been anticipating this kiss all night.

Although she didn't fully understand it, she needed this. She hadn't seen him since Wednesday morning, when he'd walked her to her car. He hadn't come to the café yesterday morning or today. He had called Wednesday night to let her know he needed to go out on one of his ships to do inspections with his insurance company for two days. Although the fire inspector had ruled the fire was caused by arson, the insurance company had wanted to make sure for themselves that all his ships were in tip-top condition.

They had talked each night. He'd asked her how her day had gone and she'd asked about his. However, he would end the call telling her he loved her and how much he wanted her in his life. And he would tell her what he intended to do the next time he saw her and at that moment he was making good on his words.

His kisses were always long, deep and totally enriching. They had the ability to send a maddening amount of lust through her and his masculinity drew her to him like a magnet. Kaegan had always had an air of charisma that fascinated her. Made her desire him even when she didn't want to.

He was one of those men that women would pause and then drool over whenever he walked into a room. She had been so comfortable and confident in their relationship that she hadn't been prepared for how it had ended. Pushing thoughts of the past from her mind, she concentrated on this long, deep, drugging kiss and how he was making her feel. How it was making her keenly aware just how skilled he was in using his mouth and his hands.

And how at that moment she was powerless to resist him.

He suddenly broke off the kiss and he stared down at her with his dark, penetrating gaze. The one that could easily make her panties wet. Then he was lowering his mouth and kissing her again. Her purse dropped to the floor and she wrapped her arms around his neck. He was using his tongue and lips in ways that had her moaning, and then she began shattering in his arms as her body sprinted into one powerful climax. Only Kaegan had the ability to do this to her. Make her come from a kiss.

And then he was kissing her even deeper than before and she was absorbing all the satisfaction she felt in every part of her body. She felt the way his hands were cupping her backside as if it belonged to him and she clung to him, fearful if she let go she would slide to the floor.

Her hands moved from around his neck to stroke a pair of powerful shoulders. There was so much masculinity in this man. When she was able to get her breathing back under control, she looked up at him. "You could have waited until I invited you to my bedroom."

"And were you going to invite me to your bed, Bryce?"

She knew the answer to that. "Yes." Her body had begun throbbing for him the moment he'd shown up to take her to dinner. She figured the only reason he hadn't kissed her then was because Duke had been there replacing the knob on her dishwasher.

"Then do it, Bryce. Invite me to your bed."

She had a feeling for her to issue an invitation was important to him. What if he wanted to stay overnight? His truck was parked in her driveway for all to see. Should she care? Inwardly, she knew that she wouldn't care. She was thirty-two, a few months shy of thirty-three, and was too old to care what people thought and what they would say.

"Would you join me in my bed, Kaegan?"

He smiled down before sweeping her into his arms and then heading toward her bedroom.

"Your mom does wonders with blueberries," Kaegan said, as he and Bryce sat at her kitchen table sharing a slice of blueberry pie with cups of coffee.

It was crazy. They'd made love so many times during the past four hours, yet his body was hard, ready for a repeat performance. She was sitting across from him wearing his shirt. Unbuttoned and nothing else. Did she not know what a sexy image she presented? How hard it was to resist her?

"I'll give Mom the compliment," she said, intruding into his thoughts. "By the way, Sawyer came to see me today on official police business. He questioned me about any jealous ex-boyfriends."

He looked over at her. "Do you have any jealous ex-boy-friends?"

She chuckled. "None that I know of, but he still wanted names of anyone I've dated in the past year."

"Well, I happen to know one jealous boyfriend of yours."

She raised an eyebrow. "Who?"

"Me."

She looked shocked. "You?"

"Yes. Even when I was supposed to dislike you, I was jealous of any guy who paid any attention to you. I remember seeing you out on a date a few times and it took everything I had not to break some man's jaw."

She frowned. "That doesn't make sense. You didn't even like me then."

"I'm thinking that maybe I did, but was refusing to admit it to myself. Even when I wanted to believe the worst about you, I still couldn't let you go. I used to drive Ray and Saw-yer crazy."

And because somebody said that confession was good for the soul, he added, "I even warned Isaac, Vaughn and Brody to stay away from you when they moved back to town, in case they got any ideas."

She stared at him and he wondered how long it would take for her anger to boil over. He figured she wouldn't like what he'd said, mainly because he'd had no right to do that. But he preferred telling her now than letting her find out later and use it as a wedge between them.

When she didn't say anything, but just sat there staring at him, he asked, "You don't have anything to say about it?"

She just finished off the slice of her pie while sipping her coffee. Then she finally said, "I thought I was the only one who felt that way. The only one bothered by the thought of someone else in your bed. I would tell myself you weren't worth the pain you had caused me, yet when I heard you were messing around with Jodie, although not publicly, it bothered me nonetheless."

Maybe confession time was a good thing, he thought. If nothing else, this discussion would get her to think about a few things. They had the bedroom thing down pat, but needed more work on the Kaegan-and-Bryce thing. They had issues, he knew that, but he was willing to work beyond them and wanted her to be willing to do so, as well.

"Why do you think it bothered you?" he asked her.

She shrugged her beautiful shoulders before pushing aside her plate and coffee and then lifting that pretty yet stubborn chin. "Because in my mind, you were mine and had always been mine. I believed that we had fit perfectly, and no other woman would fit to you as I did."

She leaned in closer and added, "I believed every part of you belonged to me. And the thought of another woman touching you, and you touching her, caused me so much pain. It hurt me something awful and made me mad. So, I guess you weren't the only jealous one, Kaegan."

He knew it must have taken a lot for her to admit that to him. Causing her pain would always be something he promised never to do again. Now all he wanted to do was be the cause of her happiness, if she gave him a chance. If only she would trust him with her heart again.

"Don't you find it rather strange, Bryce, that even when we weren't supposed to like each other, we still felt possessive toward one another? Why was that?"

From the way she tilted her head, he knew his question had stumped her. It was giving her something to think about. Kaegan was glad he'd planted that little seed of thought into her mind. She believed she didn't love him and couldn't ever love him again. Hopefully, she would accept that wasn't true for all the reasons she'd just told him.

He stood, went around the table and swooped her up into his arms. He loved this woman with every part of his body, and she was right. He did belong to her.

Sheriff Sawyer Grisham was a suspicious bastard by nature. It couldn't be helped. He'd been a part of the US Marine Corps Military Police and when he'd left the service he'd become an FBI agent. Now he was sheriff of Catalina Cove. He viewed his career in law enforcement and his move to the cove as his two best decisions in life. Had he not moved here, he would not have met his wife and claimed another daughter.

Life was good. But the one thing he despised was someone breaking the law. Especially in the town he was duty-bound to protect, and specifically, when the victim was a close friend. He saw solving a crime like working a puzzle. You might have a lot of little pieces, but eventually they would all get put together.

He reread all the interviews done this week regarding the fire on Kaegan's ship. He had a feeling there was something he was missing and wasn't sure what. There was a gut feeling that something wasn't right. And for some reason his mind kept returning to Kaegan's slashed tire. He refused to believe it was the work of bored teens.

He stood and stretched a minute before sitting back down. He then pressed the intercom on his desk to summon Trudy Caldwell, his office manager. Trudy was the best office manager a sheriff could have. He appreciated that, and although she claimed she would be retiring soon, she hadn't yet. Having worked for the previous sheriff, she'd become someone Sawyer had come to depend on over the years.

He heard the knock on the door. "Come in."

Trudy walked in smiling. No matter what, she always smiled. Often said life was too short not to. "What do you need, Sheriff?"

"I want several video cams pulled." He then gave her the locations and the dates. Knowing just how efficient she was, he would have the requested videos on his desk within hours.

"What are you doing? Making this movie night here?"

He chuckled. "Yes, something like that." He was covering for one of his deputies, whose wife was celebrating her birthday.

"In that case, I'll start pulling these." Trudy left, closing the door behind her. Sawyer wasn't sure what he would find on those videos, but he was just certain he would find something.

CHAPTER THIRTY-FOUR

"So you had an overnight guest on more than one occasion, I hear."

Bryce made a face at Vashti before bursting out laughing. They were sitting outside on the gazebo that faced the ocean at Shelby by the Sea. It had become their favorite place whenever they spent girl time together.

"I guess it's good to know Catalina Cove's gossip pipeline is still in working order. Next time I'll stay over at Kaegan's place since very few people will travel out to the bayou to see whether or not I'm sharing his bed."

Vashti smiled. "Next time? Does that mean the two of you plan to keep it up?"

Bryce shrugged her shoulders. "I don't see why not. The man is walking testosterone. He has the stamina of a bull."

Vashti lifted an eyebrow. "And you?"

At that moment, Bryce couldn't help the gloating look on her face. "The woman benefiting from it."

Vashti laughed and Bryce joined in. It felt good to talk about Kaegan without any negativity for a change. "Well, keep benefiting from it because it definitely has you in a good mood, Bryce."

Now she shot her friend a smirk. "That's what multiple orgasms can do for you, girl."

They burst out laughing again and it was a while before they could contain themselves. Bryce picked up her glass of apple cider and took a sip. "I'm enjoying my time with him, Vash. Both in and out of bed. We went out on his boat after church on Sunday. We packed a lunch and everything. It was nice."

Vashti took a sip of her apple cider. "So where do you think all this will lead? I know he's trying to earn back your love and trust. He's told Sawyer as much."

Bryce thought about that and then said, "There are days when I think I need to have my head examined for being back with him. Then there are days that I thank my lucky stars that I am, and to do otherwise is fighting the inevitable."

"And what do you see as the inevitable?"

Bryce swallowed hard. "Falling back in love with him."

Vashti nodded and then asked softly, "Would that be so bad, Bryce?"

A ton of memories flooded Bryce's mind. Memories of just what they'd done for the past week, what they'd done on his boat Sunday and what she looked forward to doing tonight, this time in his bed. Just thinking about all the pleasure she would be getting made her shiver.

She drew in a deep breath. "We're older now, Vashti. He owned up to what he did and I accepted his apology, but it seems the one thing I can't do when it comes to Kaegan Chambray is release the hold that fear has on my heart."

An hour or so later, when she left Vashti's place and was heading for home, Bryce thought about their conversation. What she'd told Vashti was the truth. She wasn't sure she could give her heart to Kaegan. But yet whenever she thought of joining him later at his place for dinner she felt giddy inside. She truly enjoyed the time they were spending together and not just in the bedroom. And she couldn't help but miss him whenever she didn't see him. She was used to seeing him in the mornings at the café and hadn't realized just how much until those mornings she didn't see him.

Then there were those times they talked each night at bedtime. She looked forward to his nightly calls. Those were the times she wished he was there with her, holding her in his arms. Sleeping beside her.

He had invited her to dinner tonight but she would have an overnight bag packed just in case he wanted to make it into something more. She had a feeling that he would, and when he did, she would be ready to accept. At that moment she realized what else she was ready to accept, something she now knew. She had fallen back in love with Kaegan. Had she truly ever fallen out of love with him, or had she been ardently protecting her heart and had built this unbreakable shield around it? A shield he had broken, anyway? Did it matter?

Deep down she knew that it didn't matter. The important thing was that she was ready to share her heart with him again, and tonight at his home, over dinner, she would tell him so. Her parents had been right. Kaegan had been right. Vashti had been right. There would always be a Kaegan and Bryce.

A call came through Bryce's car's speaker. "Hello, this is Bryce Witherspoon."

"Ms. Witherspoon, this is Mrs. Corsuti. I'd like to see that vacant warehouse you told me about."

The woman had called previously, inquiring about warehouse property in the west end of town. Mary Corsuti planned to start an online fabric shop and needed space to store her materials. The warehouse she was inquiring about was at the far end of town before heading toward the bayou.

"Yes, Mrs. Corsuti. I would be glad to show it to you to-morrow. When would be a—"

"I'm sorry, but tomorrow won't work for me. I'm only in the cove for today. I'm leaving for a two-week cruise out of New Orleans tomorrow. I am here at the address you gave me, and I would like to see inside the building now."

Now? Bryce glanced at her watch. It was close to five and it would take her at least twenty minutes to reach the area. Kaegan was expecting her to arrive at his place around seven. She would give the woman a quick tour since there wasn't much to see in an abandoned warehouse.

"All right, Mrs. Corsuti. I can meet you there in twenty minutes."

Twenty minutes later Bryce pulled into the empty lot and saw the parked car. It had gotten dark and the area looked deserted. Bryce honestly didn't like being here at night. The smart thing to have done would have been to tell the woman she could not meet with her tonight, regardless of how eager she was to see the place. But she was here now, so she might as well get it over with so she could go home and get ready for dinner with Kaegan.

She got out of her car and began walking toward the parked car, and when she got within five feet of it, suddenly, the front passenger door flung open and a big hulk of a man jumped out. From the fierce look on his face, she immediately knew something was wrong and quickly turned to run back to her car. She wasn't fast enough, though, and he caught her from behind.

She fought him and then she felt something prick her skin, but she kept fighting, trying to get away, but began feeling sluggish. The will to fight, to resist, was slowly leaving her and she then lost consciousness.

Kaegan smiled when he heard the sound of his doorbell. Bryce had arrived. He had looked forward to her coming to dinner all day. Had it been just a week ago when he'd taken her to dinner at the Lighthouse? A lot had happened since then, and deep down he believed although it had only been a week, a lot of progress had been made. He enjoyed the time they were spending together and honestly believed she did, too.

He opened the door and tried to keep the disappointment out of his features when he saw it wasn't Bryce, but Sawyer. "Oh, it's you."

Sawyer quirked an eyebrow. "You don't have to sound so disappointed."

"Yes, but I am," Kaegan said, moving aside to let Sawyer into his home. "I thought you were Bryce. She's coming for dinner at seven and she's thirty minutes late. That's so unlike her."

Sawyer frowned. "I went by her house to talk to her and when she wasn't there I remembered she was visiting Vashti at the inn. When I called Vashti she said Bryce had left hours ago for home to change and come here."

"Well, she must have stopped somewhere because she hasn't arrived yet." Kaegan took in Sawyer's expression and got a bad feeling. "Is something going on I need to know about, Sawyer? Why were you trying to find Bryce?"

Sawyer rubbed a hand down his face. "This isn't a personal visit, Kaegan. I'm here on official police business, and when I heard Bryce would be here, I figured I could talk to you both together."

"About what?" Kaegan asked, crossing his arms over his chest.

Sawyer released a deep sigh. "We believe we have the identity of the person responsible for setting that fire on your boat."

"Who?"

"Let's go sit down and I'll tell you everything."

Kaegan nodded, and when they got to the living room, Sawyer sat down on the sofa and Kaegan slid into the chair across from Sawyer. "Okay, man, who set the fire and what does it have to do with Bryce?"

Sawyer met his gaze. "I have reason to believe for the past month or so Bryce was being stalked."

Kaegan flinched. "Stalked? Bryce?"

Sawyer nodded. "Yes. All last night and most of today I've been watching footage from various traffic video cams. Something was bothering me ever since you mentioned your tire had been slashed. I pulled the video cam from the traffic light on the corner where Bryce lives for that Friday night and for other nights."

Kaegan got to his feet with a worried expression on his face. "And?"

"And I noticed a vehicle making random drive-bys down Bryce's street. Not too often but often enough to get my attention."

"The same vehicle?"

"No, but the license plate identified them as rentals."

Kaegen felt the hairs on the back of his neck stand up. "Go on, Sawyer," he said, when his friend got quiet.

"Although there are no video cameras at the end of the pier that branches off to the docks where you keep your boat, there are cameras at various merchants along the pier, as well as one in the parking lot and a video cam at the intersection leaving the parking lot."

"And you saw something?"

"Yes—another rental vehicle. I was able to get the make and model as well as the tag number. I noticed the same rental vehicle car parked in the lot during the time your boat would have been set on fire."

Sawyer paused, then said, "I've spent most of the day working with several car-rental agencies at the New Orleans airport before I was finally able to get a name of the person who rented those vehicles. He's a man by the name of Jeremy Skinner, an attorney in Shreveport who travels a lot to try cases in other areas."

"An attorney?"

"Yes. Has Bryce ever mentioned him to you?"

"No."

"Well, she mentioned him to me. When I interviewed her, she gave me his name. Not as someone she thought was a jealous boyfriend, but as someone she'd seen a few times over the past few months. They met when he stopped to fix her flat tire one day and met for coffee a couple of times in New Orleans before the start of her classes.

"I was able to get a picture of the guy and I recognized him as the same guy who'd come into the café that morning. The same one you were getting all hot behind the collar about when he and Bryce seemed too friendly."

Kaegan immediately remembered the guy. He glanced at his watch, really getting worried. He glanced over at Sawyer. "Bryce is now an hour late. I'm worried about her, man."

Sawyer nodded. "So am I. The reason I went straight to Bryce's house first is because Jeremy Skinner is somewhere in the area. He's been here since Wednesday."

At that moment Sawyer's phone went off and he pulled it off his belt and clicked it on immediately. "Sheriff Grisham."

Kaegan knew from the look on Sawyer's face that he wasn't going to like what he was about to be told when Sawyer ended the call. "What is it, Sawyer?"

"That was one of my deputies. They've found Bryce's car at an old abandoned warehouse, but she is nowhere to be found."

CHAPTER THIRTY-FIVE

Bryce heard voices as she slowly regained consciousness, but she refused to open her eyes. The first thing she noticed was that she was lying on her side on a wooden floor. Her mouth was gagged and her hands were tied. Who would do such a thing? And was that the scent of the ocean she smelled?

She forced herself not to panic. Where was she and who was the man who'd taken her? Had he taken Mary Corsuti, as well? Fear swept through her when she recalled hearing about women missing, presumably connected to human trafficking. She fought back the feel of more fear. Nobody knew where she was. She did not have a scheduled meeting with Mrs. Corsuti, and when she'd left Shelby by the Sea, she had told Vashti she would be going straight home to get dressed for dinner with Kaegan at his place.

Would he panic when she didn't show up? Even if he did, he wouldn't know where to look for her. She didn't even know where she was. She was too afraid to open her eyes. Were there other women here, too? The thought of not getting away from her captors made her feel sick. What if she never saw Kaegan again? What if she never got the chance to be held by him again? What if she never was able to tell him that she knew that she loved him, that she'd always loved him and wanted to move ahead? She wanted all the things she'd wanted with him years ago. A life with him. Marriage. Children.

Suddenly, she cleared her mind of all thoughts when she heard footsteps. And the voices were coming closer...

"And you're sure she isn't dead?" a male voice asked someone.

Bryce tried to remain deadly still but was certain she recognized that voice.

"I'm sure. I just shot her up with a small dose. She should have awakened by now...unless she has heart problems or something," another deep male voice said. It sounded like it belonged to a much younger man. Bryce had a feeling the voice belonged to the man who'd grabbed her.

"Heart problems?" the older male voice said in a panicky tone. "I don't want her to die before I tell her why I'm getting rid of her."

That man wanted to get rid of her? Why?

"I don't care what you do with her, Jeremy, just pay me and my wife for my troubles."

Jeremy? Bryce fought hard not to scream in shock. Why would Jeremy Skinner be doing this to her?

Bryce heard the sound of the shuffling of papers, which sounded like money being counted out and exchanged. Jeremy had paid this man and his wife to capture her and bring her here, wherever here was? That meant there was never a Mary Corsuti?

Then footsteps moved away and the place got quiet. Bryce knew she was alone again and squinted her eyes open just a little, in case someone had stayed behind. She drew in a deep breath as she tried to understand what was going on here.

Bryce saw she was on the floor of a boat. She had to tilt

her head in a painful way to read the sign. Blackmon Boat Rentals. Jeremy had rented a boat from Jack Blackmon and she was on it. She worked her mouth back and forth. It felt sore from having the cloth tied so tight around it.

Suddenly, she heard footsteps returning and then a pail of water was dumped in her face, and she jerked forward and opened her eyes. She stared up into Jeremy's grinning face.

"I thought that would bring you around. I couldn't wait to tell you why you're here."

Because of the gag covering her mouth, Bryce couldn't say anything, but that didn't mean she didn't try. Her efforts only made Jeremy laugh. "I don't want to hear anything you have to say. I know all about you dumping me for your old boyfriend."

Bryce watched as Jeremy began pacing and then he stopped to come stand over her again. "When I met you, I thought you were different. I knew you were interested in me, but then you tried breaking things off. You never told me the man you were going out of town with was your ex-boyfriend."

At what had to be a surprised look on her face, he said, "Yes, I know about him. I heard a couple of ladies talking in Spencer's about how they hoped the two of you get back together. Then I knew I'd been played."

Played? Bryce was trying to follow what Jeremy was saying but it made no sense. Where had he gotten the assumption that there was more between them than friendship? Hell, they'd never held hands or even kissed.

"You aren't the first woman who tried taking advantage of my kindness and they got the same fate that you're going to get. That will teach you a lesson."

Bryce moaned against the gag in her mouth. The man was an attorney, for Pete's sake… At least that was what he'd told her. Had he lied about that, too?

"It won't do you any good to try to get away, Bryce. There's nowhere for you to go off the ship unless you want to be eaten by gators. We're in the swamp."

Her head jerked up. *The swamp?* Surely he wasn't going to throw her overboard. The thought of such a thing made her tremble all over.

As if he read her mind, he said, "I haven't decided what I'm going to do with you yet. You used me," he sneered. "At first I retaliated by going after your guy. You should not have called and canceled our meetings. I found out where you lived and checked out your place. Imagine how I felt when I saw that guy spending time with you. That made me mad enough to slash his tire one night. Then I wanted to rough you up a bit and tried breaking into your place one night when I knew you were there. I accidentally bumped into your garbage can, and then I figured it was best to get the hell out of there when I saw your neighbor, some old man, wandering about looking for some damn cat."

Bryce heard what Jeremy was saying and remembered hearing a sound outside on her patio that night. That was the same night Vashti had sent Sawyer over to investigate.

"And, of course, there was the fire."

His words reclaimed her attention and she stared at him. He smiled. "Yes, I'm the one who set the fire on your boyfriend's boat when I found out the two of you were out of town together. You couldn't spend time with me, yet you were spending time with him."

She stared at him, unable to say anything because of the gag still in her mouth. As if he was tired of talking to her, Jeremy turned and left, locking the door behind him.

"Calm down, Kaegan."

Kaegan stopped pacing and glared over at Sawyer. "The woman I love is missing and you want me to calm down? How would you feel if it was Vashti?"

"He's right, son," Chester said, coming to place a hand on Kaegan's shoulder. "You need to calm down. Why don't you come and sit with me, Debbie and the family."

Kaegan shook his head. He didn't want to sit down. He wanted to lash out, beat the hell out of someone. He glanced around the café, which was now closed. Everyone close to Bryce was there. Her parents, her brothers and their wives, Ray and Ashley, Vashti and Sawyer. And him.

According to Sawyer, they were checking more video cameras in the area to see if Skinner's car had been spotted anywhere, but so far it hadn't. News had spread quickly that Bryce was missing. One of the café's regular customers who owned a printing shop had put Jeremy Skinner's picture on flyers that were being passed around town in case anyone recalled seeing him in the area.

So far no one remembered anything. Sawyer had alerted the FBI and an agent had come and gone, talking more to Sawyer than to anyone. Sawyer hadn't shared what the man had told him. But Kaegan had a feeling it hadn't been good.

"This is my fault," Kaegan said, brokenly.

"How?" Chester asked.

"We should never have broken up ten years ago. We could have been married now and then she wouldn't have had a reason to meet up with a bastard like Skinner. She would have called me that day when she'd gotten a flat tire and she sure as hell wouldn't have met him for coffee at any time. Hell, some boyfriend I am. I couldn't even protect her."

"There was no way for you to have known, Kaegan," Vashti said, coming up to him to give him a hug. "I knew more about the guy and I didn't suspect a thing. Neither did Bryce. Don't give up. None of us can give up. We have to believe Bryce is safe and will return to us."

More than anything, Sawyer wanted to believe that. He

honestly needed some kind of reassurance that the woman he loved was all right, but nobody could give him that.

He looked over at Sawyer. "What do you know about Skinner?" He knew Sawyer knew something. Why wasn't he saying whatever that FBI agent had told him?

"I can't tell you anything about him right now, Kaegan."

"Like hell," Kaegan said angrily.

Suddenly Ray appeared at Kaegan's side. "Come on, man. Let's take a walk outside and get some air. I think you need to cool off a minute."

He was about to tell Ray he didn't want to take a walk outside when he figured maybe doing so would be for the best. He was headed out the door when the beeper on his watch went off. Knowing someone had trespassed on his property was the last thing he gave a damn about now. He had more important things to deal with.

"I know it's going to be hard to do, Kaegan, but you need to pull yourself together, man," Ray said when they were outside. "Sawyer and his guys are doing all they can do."

"I know that, but the FBI guy told him something and I want to know what."

"If he could have told you then he would have, Kaegan. You have to respect the fact that in addition to being our friend, he's still the law."

"I'm leaving. We got a possible lead."

Kaegan and Ray turned when Sawyer quickly walked out of the café. Kaegan's heart jumped. "Where?"

"Over to Blackmon Boat Rentals. Jack Blackmon recognized the man on the flyer being passed about as a man who rented a boat from him earlier today. I'll call and let you know what I—"

"I'm going with you, Sawyer."

Sawyer suddenly stopped, and with a fierce frown on his

face, he turned and stared at Kaegan. "You need to stay here with the others. This is police business."

"Then deputize me, dammit," Kaegan snapped. "You've done it before—that time when several of your men came down with the flu."

Sawyer seemed to consider his words and then said, "Fine, but do what you're told, Kaegan, and if you try and take matters into your own hands, I will arrest you myself."

He then raced toward the police cruiser with Kaegan right on his heels.

CHAPTER THIRTY-SIX

There was only a quarter moon in the sky. The night was drenched in total darkness and Bryce had no idea where she was. Jeremy had returned to the cabin, pulled her up and practically dragged her off the boat.

"I discovered this place a couple of months ago when I came here to go fishing. It's a private island off the swamp and I'm told people are afraid to even come here," he said, finally removing the gag from her mouth.

Bryce's heart began pounding as she began working the soreness from her mouth. Had he brought her to Eagle Bend Inlet? Would she lose her life here? Jeremy hadn't said what he intended to do with her, and she was too afraid to ask him.

"Please let me go, Jeremy," she said, backing up away from him. "It's not in you to hurt anyone." She wanted to believe that.

He laughed. "If you think that then you really don't know me, Bryce. And had you truly known me you would know I'm a man who doesn't like being ignored. Two others found out the hard way."

Fear settled in her stomach when he slowly began walking toward her. Was he saying he'd hurt two other women before her? How could she have thought he was someone she wanted to be interested in? Someone who could help her move on from Kaegan?

"Please don't do this." Even with the low light she saw another rope he held in his hand. It was similar to the one her hands were tied up with. Did he intend to strangle her, squeeze the life out of her here? She backed up. "No, Jeremy, please don't. Just leave me here to die."

"Why should I make things easy for you?" he asked her, grinning.

"You won't be making it easy," she insisted. "There's no way I'll survive the swamp," she said quickly, hoping she could convince him to let her live. If this was Eagle Bend Inlet, Kaegan would have gotten an alert that someone had trespassed on his property. At least she hoped he would.

Jeremy stopped walking, as if to consider her words. "Hmm, you just gave me an idea," he said, as a huge smile touched his lips.

He pulled his phone from his pocket and clicked on the flashlight. "I'll give you a five-minute head start, Bryce. Then I'm coming after you. You better hope I don't find you."

Bryce still couldn't believe he was doing this. It was dark and she could barely see her way around. She could just imagine herself falling into quicksand or wandering back into the swamp. And what about those animals that came out at night? But five minutes were five minutes and she would take it. It would be a run for her life. With her hands still tied behind her back, she turned and took off running.

"Yes, that's him," Jack Blackmon said, pointing to the likeness of the man on the flyer. "I would never have rented him a boat had I known he intended to hurt someone, especially Bryce."

"Did he say where he intended to go?" Sawyer asked the man.

Jack shook his head. "No. He said he was going fishing, and that was all he said. He's supposed to have my boat back to me by morning. Claimed he would be doing night fishing."

At that moment, a black car pulled up and two men got out. Kaegan recognized one of the men as the FBI agent he'd seen earlier. Sawyer walked off toward the men and Kaegan strained his ears to hear. One of the men said, "We picked up a couple a half hour ago who were trying to charge something with Bryce Witherspoon's credit card. They claim Jeremy Skinner planned to take Ms. Witherspoon to some island he saw one day in the swamp and bury her alive."

Goose bumps began forming on Kaegan's arms at the same time the beeper on his watch went off. That was the second time tonight it had done that. "Damn!"

Everyone glanced over at him. "I know where they've taken her," he said, rushing over to Sawyer. "The alert has gone off twice tonight on my watch. I got a feeling the bastard has taken her to Eagle Bend Inlet."

Sawyer turned to Jack Blackmon and quickly said, "We need to use one of your boats."

CHAPTER THIRTY-SEVEN

Bryce ran until she couldn't run any more. She ran so much at one point she was convinced she was running around in circles and that eventually she would run right back into Jeremy. She still didn't know where she was and hadn't seen anything familiar. But then it was blue-black dark and she could barely see her own hands. Hands that were still tied. She was at a disadvantage and he knew it.

Then there were the sounds of the night. Eerie sounds, and she didn't want to think about what animals were making them or the possibility she could step on a snake or alligator at any moment. The thought that she was being hunted down like an animal made her want to scream, but screaming would alert Jeremy to where she was, and she had to keep moving. She couldn't let him find her. How long would he look for her? Would he stop then start up in the morning when he had more light? She had to believe people were looking for her. Kaegan would know something was wrong when she hadn't shown up for dinner.

Needing to catch her breath, she leaned against a tree. She was tempted to cry but refused to do so. She had to keep running. She turned and saw that, because of the angle of the moon, light shone on the tree she'd rested against. Was she imagining things or did this tree have markings on the side? Markings of *K & B* that seemed to glow in the dark?

It was her and Kaegan's tree. A semblance of hope filled her and had her glancing around. She *was* on Eagle Bend Inlet. Bryce wanted to jump for joy.

Suddenly, she heard a noise and quickly looked over her shoulder and could see a light moving back and forth. Jeremy! Fear raced through her again and she quickly moved, headed toward the right. She stopped quickly and deliberately moved to the left. If Jeremy was using the flashlight to check her footprints, then she needed to confuse him. The last thing she wanted was to lead him straight to the bunker. After making sure he would assume she'd gone in another direction, she backtracked to her right and found the tall trees that were covered in grassy moss and thick vines.

Walking behind the trees, she managed to push back a lot of the mossy vines with her tied hands and find what she was looking for. The door opened and she quickly slid inside. The sound of footsteps crunching on the grass meant Jeremy was not far away. When the door closed shut behind her, she let out a relieved breath and prayed he would not figure out where she'd gone.

When her feet touched the stairs, security lights came on. Moving quickly, she went down the stairs and headed straight for the kitchen. The first thing she needed to do was find something to cut the ropes from her hands. She managed to maneuver the bottle opener in a way that after so many tries, the rope began shredding apart. When her hands were free, she rubbed them together, seeing the marks the tightened rope had left behind. But she didn't care. She was safe. She raced up the stairs and locked the door from the inside in case Jeremy figured out where she was and how to get in.

She needed time for Kaegan to get here and she had to believe he would come. She had to believe that.

Satisfied that she was safe at the moment, she walked back down the stairs and moved over to the love seat, and she sat and waited. Kaegan was coming. She had to believe in her heart that he would be coming for her.

"Remember, you're not a police officer, Kaegan," Sawyer said once they reached the inlet. "Don't let me regret allowing you to come with us. Let my men do their job. Understood?"

Yes, he understood, although he didn't like it. He would have loved to beat the crap out of Jeremy Skinner. He just hoped Bryce was safe. It was pitch-dark. What if she hadn't managed to get away from Skinner? What if she got away from him, but hadn't managed to find the bunker in the dark? He had to believe Bryce was safe. He had to believe that.

"Kaegan?"

It was then that he realized that he hadn't answered Sawyer. "Yes, I understand."

It seemed as if it took them forever to reach Eagle Bend Inlet, and when they rounded the bend, they saw the small cabin cruiser. The moment they were close enough to shore, Sawyer and his four deputies were off the boat in a flash. "I'll call for you when you can come ashore."

"Yeah, right," Kaegan said, knowing he had no intention of staying put. He just wouldn't get in anyone's way.

One of the men erected a huge beacon, and when it was turned on, it seemed to light up the entire island. Sawyer had a bullhorn that he spoke through and said, "Jeremy Skinner, you are under arrest. Come out with your hands up."

With the island well lit it was only a matter of time before the man surrendered, walking toward them with his hands in the air. "Where is Bryce Witherspoon?" Sawyer asked him.

He shrugged and then said, "I don't know. I gave her a head start and then I couldn't find her."

Kaegan heard what the man said. He'd given her a head start? Before what? Before he tried hunting her down like an animal? Fury raged inside of Kaegan and he moved toward the man only to find his path blocked deliberately by one of Sawyer's men. As soon as Skinner was handcuffed and led away, Sawyer looked over at Kaegan and said, "Now go find your woman."

Kaegan jumped off the boat and raced to the area where he knew the bunker was. When he saw it was locked from the inside hope sprang inside of him. He used his handprint, and in no time the door was sliding open. He stood at the top of the stairs and glanced down. Bryce was sitting there, flipping through one of his shipping magazines. Even from where he stood, he saw the tears brimming in her eyes when she said, "It's about time you got here for me, Kaegan Chambray."

He quickly raced down the stairs and she moved toward him. He pulled her into his arms, needing the feel of her there. He needed something else, as well, and lowered his mouth to hers. The kiss seemed to go on forever, and when he released her, he looked into her eyes and said, "You okay?"

She swiped at her tears. "Yes, I'm okay."

He pulled her into his arms. Needing to feel her there, close to his heart. "I love you, Bryce."

She tilted her head to look up at him and wiped more tears from her eyes, then said, "And I love you, too, Kaegan. So much."

He raised his brow in surprise, and before he could tell her to repeat what she'd said, she leaned up and captured his mouth in hers.

It was barely daybreak when Kaegan and Bryce eased between the sheets in his bed after taking a shower together.

He knew that for as long as he lived he wouldn't let her out of his sight. In fact, he'd told her so several times tonight. He'd told her and a number of people, including her parents, her brothers, Vashti and Sawyer, Ray and Ashley, several of the deputies, those two FBI agents and anyone who'd cared to listen. Hell, he'd even told Jack Blackmon when they'd returned the man's boat. The man thought that was a good idea. Bryce was his and he would never let anyone try to take her away from him again.

"Tell me again," he whispered to her.

She smiled as she slid closer toward him to wrap her arms around his neck and entwine their legs together. They'd made love in the shower and he looked forward to making love again in his bed. "I love you, Kaegan. I had planned to tell you over dinner last night, but then Jeremy interfered with those plans."

Sawyer had finally told him what the FBI agent had confided to him earlier. When federal agents in Shreveport had gotten a warrant to search Skinner's home, there was evidence that two women who'd been missing for two years had been there. The authorities had discovered some of their personal belongings. Bryce had corroborated the findings by telling the FBI agents what Jeremy had told her about the two women.

"I'm glad it's all over and you came for me," she told him.

"You found your way home, Bryce," he said, referring to their private place on the inlet that he would always think of as their first home together. "And I found my way home, too. My home will always be in your heart."

"Oh, Kaegan…"

"I have something for you." He eased out of bed and went to the safe behind the framed picture on the wall. After pulling out the small box, he returned to the bed. "The reason I'd come home that night ten years ago was to surprise you with this," he said, handing her the box.

She took it with shaking hands, then opened it and looked up at him. Tears suddenly sprang into her eyes. "An engagement ring?"

"Yes. I had planned to ask you to marry me that night. I kept it all these years. Since I know it's never too late for us, will you marry me, Bryce?"

He saw happiness on her face when she smiled through her tears and said, "Yes! Yes! I will marry you!"

Smiling brightly, he pulled her into his arms for a long and deep kiss, knowing they'd both found their way home again.

EPILOGUE

"Wasn't Gloria a beautiful bride?" Bryce whispered to Kaegan as they walked around the grounds of Reid's estate, where the wedding had taken place. Her son, Percelli, had given her away, while her granddaughters, Jade and Kia, had been her flower girls. Her daughter-in-law, Alma, and Vashti were her maids of honor. Reid hadn't spared any expenses in making this a beautiful day for a wedding.

"Yes, she was, and I could tell from the look on Reid's face that he's happy, and I'm happy for him. They make a beautiful couple. But then, so do we."

She beamed over at him. "Yes, we do."

Kaegan and Bryce had decided on a June wedding under the gazebo at Shelby by the Sea. The wedding was seven months away, but they had plenty to keep them busy in the meantime. There was the expansion of Kaegan's company to Boston and the increase in her business since she was now a multistate real-estate broker.

They would make their home on the bayou and Bryce was looking forward to moving in. In fact, she'd sort of moved in already since she spent most of her weekends at his place anyway.

Ray and Ashley hadn't attended the wedding since Ashley had given birth to twins two weeks ago. A boy and a girl. Despite Ashley's mother's objections, they had named the boy Devon and the girl Ryan. Kaegan and Bryce had seen the babies and thought they were mini Rays. Kaegan said he couldn't wait to have babies with Bryce. They had talked about it and they wanted at least four. She wondered if, like Ashley, she could return from her honeymoon pregnant.

"I can't believe how grown up the girls look," she said of Reid and Gloria's granddaughters, and Sawyer and Vashti's daughters, Jade and Kia.

"Girls? I think you mean young ladies of eighteen. I noticed how Sawyer is keeping his eyes on any of the young men vying for their attention tonight."

Bryce laughed. "I noticed, too."

"Would you care to dance with me, the future Mrs. Chambray?" Kaegan asked her.

She smiled up at him. "I'd love to."

As he took her into his arms, she knew it might be ten years in the making, but they had finally found home again with each other. This time it would last forever.

★ ★ ★ ★ ★

Don't miss *Follow Your Heart* the next Catalina Cove story
from *New York Times* bestselling author Brenda Jackson
and Mills & Boon

Read on for sneak peak

PROLOGUE

"KAEGAN AND BRYCE, I now pronounce you husband and wife. Kaegan, you may kiss your bride."

Victoria Madaris swiped at the tears in her eyes as she watched the couple at the front of the church seal their marriage vows with a kiss.

Kaegan Chambray and Bryce Witherspoon—now Bryce Witherspoon-Chambray—made a beautiful couple. You could see the love in their eyes when they'd recited the vows they'd written. When Kaegan, a member of the Pointe-au-Chien Tribe, had spoken to Bryce in his Native American tongue and she responded in that tongue in kind, it had been the most touching thing. Although Victoria was certain she wasn't the only one who hadn't understood what they'd said, the important thing was that *they* had understood.

A handkerchief was suddenly shoved in her hand. "Here. I can't believe you're carrying on like this at a wedding, considering your fate."

Victoria fought the urge to glare at her brother Corbin. Today was Kaegan and Bryce's day. It had been such a beautiful ceremony. Everything had been perfect and romantic. Even the weather had cooperated. Although the forecasters had predicted rain, there wasn't a cloud in the sky. Today had been a totally awesome February day in Catalina Cove, Louisiana.

"Honestly, Corbin, do you have to be so negative?

There's nothing wrong with falling in love and getting married," she said as people began exiting the church. When she'd received a wedding invitation for the same weekend he'd planned to visit, she'd invited him to be her plus-one.

"So says the woman whose single days are numbered," her brother grumbled. "Glad it's you and not me."

Victoria decided not to point out that he better be glad it was her, otherwise it would indeed be him. "I'm going to tell you the same thing I told Nolan. I have no problem with our great-grandmother finding me a husband if she's inclined to do so. Mama Laverne has an astounding track record as a matchmaker, and whomever she chooses will be well vetted. It will certainly save me the time of trying to figure out if the man is worth my time and attention."

"You honestly want a husband?" Corbin asked, as if appalled at the very thought.

"No, but if Mama Laverne has chosen one for me, I'll take him. I trust her judgment. She's the best."

It was a well-known fact that at ninetysomething, the matriarch of the Madaris family was determined to marry off her great-grands before she left to go with the Lord. It bothered Victoria whenever Mama Laverne would say such a thing because Victoria couldn't imagine a world without her great-grandmother in it.

Over the years, Victoria had seen her work her magic on some of the staunchest bachelors in the family. They had fought her all the way. But then the next thing she knew, they had fallen in love with the women Mama Laverne had chosen for them.

The last match had been Victoria's brother Nolan, and everybody knew that Nolan had had no intention of ever getting married. He was singing a different tune these days with Ivy. The two would be celebrating their second wedding anniversary soon, and people suspected a baby was on the way. Victoria hoped so. She was looking forward to the day that she became an auntie.

"This is a pretty nice town, Victoria."

She glanced around when they reached her brother's car. "Yes, it is. I love it here. It's so peaceful and the people are friendly. Mom and Dad came to visit last month and said the fishing here was great."

"So I heard, but don't get too attached to the place. You're a Texan. Remember that."

Victoria rolled her eyes. Like there was any way she could. The Madaris family had settled in Texas seven generations ago, back in the 1800s, after acquiring a ten-thousand-acre Mexican land grant. At a time when most newly freed Blacks were still waiting for their forty acres and a mule from the United States government, Carlos Antonio Madaris, half Mexican and half African American, along with his wife, Christina Marie, were shaping their legacy on land they used to raise cattle. A parcel of land they named Whispering Pines. Today Whispering Pines was a huge cattle ranch run by her uncle Jake.

"Now tell me why you're living here and not in New Orleans when that's where your job is," Corbin said as he pulled out of the church's parking lot.

Victoria knew he'd heard the reason from their parents, but if he thought there was another version that he hadn't gotten wind of, she had no problem bursting his bubble. "I came to Catalina Cove to cover a story about the shrimp festival they hold each year. It took me less than an hour to get here. I loved the place immediately and decided although I worked in New Orleans, I didn't have to live there when I liked this place better."

Corbin nodded. "You've only been here a couple of

months and already you've made friends who invited you to their wedding?"

She smiled. "Bryce was one of the first people I met. She's the Realtor I contacted to find me a place to lease in the cove. And you have to admit my place is nice."

"It's small."

She figured he would say that, since his condo in Houston was bigger than most houses. "It's big enough for me, Corbin. And I love that apple grove in the back. There's nothing like waking up to the smell of apples every morning."

"How's your job going?"

Victoria glanced over at him. She knew that her brothers hadn't particularly liked the idea of her taking a job as a news reporter in New Orleans when a similar job had been offered to her in Houston. She tried to get them to understand it was time for her to spread her wings. Besides, the Madaris name was well-known not only in Houston, but also in the entire state of Texas. She didn't want to worry about taking a job and being treated differently because her last name was Madaris.

"My job is going great, although I miss being out on the beat." Six months ago, she'd been promoted from a beat reporter to coanchor one of the morning shows.

"I'm glad the political season is over. I couldn't take interviewing one more politician," she said. There was no reason to explain to her brother why she felt such deep animosity toward politicians. Most of the family already knew why. To change the subject, she asked, "So what's going on with your love life, Corbin?"

She laughed when he let out an expletive. She knew one sure way to get her brother riled was to ask about his love life. Like most single Madaris men, he intended to stay a bachelor forever.

"Don't worry about my love life. You need to be concerned with your own. I'm not the next person on Mama Laverne's list."

"Not for long. I've been summoned. I got a call from Mama Laverne. She wants to see me, so I'm going to Whispering Pines next weekend."

Stopping at a traffic light, Corbin glanced over at her with an arched eyebrow. "Do you think she's going to tell you who she's chosen as your husband?"

"Probably, since I can't think of any other reason for her to want to meet with me, especially when I spent time with her over the holidays. It has been almost two years since she told Nolan I was next in line. You know what that means, right?"

Corbin shook his head. "No, what does that mean?"

Victoria smiled. "It means since I don't plan to give Mama Laverne grief about anything, I'll probably have a June wedding and then she can turn her attention to you, since you're next on the list."

Corbin frowned. "Like hell."

Victoria laughed at her brother's reaction. "I suggest you start enjoying your final days as a bachelor, Corbin."

The following weekend

"Uncle Jake and Aunt Diamond, how are you?" Victoria asked as she entered their home on Whispering Pines and gave both huge hugs. She adored her grand-uncle and grand-aunt. She also loved Whispering Pines, the place everyone in the family considered the Madaris homestead.

Whispering Pines was an hour drive from Houston and

encompassed hundreds and hundreds of acres of land for grazing cattle. The ranch was renowned for raising only the highest quality grass-fed Texas longhorn cattle. Victoria thought the ranch house, a massive hacienda-style villa where Jake and his family lived, was a real piece of art. It had always been beautiful, and since marrying former actress Diamond Swain, who'd put her special touch here and there, it was even more so.

Jake, a distinguished rancher, had once made the cover of *Time* magazine when they'd applauded his efforts in aiding the British government with England's cattle industry's mad cow epidemic. Not only was her uncle a great rancher, but he was also highly intelligent when it came to investments. Thanks to him, all the members of the Madaris family had a hefty amount of stock in the family business. He managed the portfolios for all his nieces and nephews, and they all had lucrative trust funds. Jake was well-respected in numerous circles and his name carried a lot of weight in Texas. As far as Victoria was concerned, he was the best grand-uncle in the whole wide world.

"I hope I didn't arrive during the time Mama Laverne is napping," she said.

"No. She's expecting you and delayed her nap until later," Diamond said.

Jake studied his grand-niece. "I guess you have an idea why you're here."

Victoria nodded. "Yes, I have an idea."

"You're not bothered by the fact Mom is about to interfere in your life?" he asked.

Victoria saw the concern in her grand-uncle's eyes and decided to tell him the same thing she'd been telling her brothers and cousins. "I'm fine with everything, Uncle Jake.

Even you have to admit Mama Laverne's track record for hooking people up successfully is astounding."

"Well, just as long as you're okay with it."

Victoria touched her grand-uncle's arm to reassure him. "I'm okay with it, and I'm really anxious to know what man she's chosen for me."

A few moments later, Victoria was knocking on the door to her great-grandmother's suite.

"Come in."

Opening the door, Victoria found her sitting in her favorite chair, knitting. Felicia Laverne Madaris had taught Victoria to knit when she'd been eight, and for her great-grandmother to still be able to use her hands to knit the way she did, and as often as she did, was amazing.

"Hello, Mama Laverne," she said, leaning down to place a kiss on the older woman's cheek.

"And hello to you, Victoria."

Her great-grandmother was wearing a pretty floral button-front dress with her signature pearls around her neck. Perched on her nose was a pair of reading glasses. While growing up, Victoria thought her great-grandmother was one of the most stylish women she knew. She still thought so.

"You look pretty today, Mama Laverne."

"Thank you and so do you. Would you like some of the Madaris tea?" Mama Laverne asked as she placed her knitting aside and removed her reading glasses.

Victoria loved the Madaris tea. The recipe was known only to certain Madaris family members. "Yes. You want me to pour?" Victoria asked.

"That will be fine, dear."

After pouring them both cups of tea, Victoria noticed Mama Laverne studying her intently. She knew there was a reason for her doing so and figured if she was patient, her great-grandmother would tell her what was on her mind.

After taking a couple of sips of tea, Mama Laverne said, "I'm sure you know why I wanted to meet with you."

Victoria nodded. "Yes, I do have a good idea."

Mama Laverne took another sip of tea. "I know some of you merely see me as a meddling old woman, intent on destroying your lives. But as you can see, I haven't steered anyone wrong yet."

Victoria chuckled. "No, you haven't. Nolan is happy with Ivy, Lee is happy with Carly, Reese is happy with Kenna, Luke is happy with Mac...need I go on?" All the cousins she had mentioned—Lee, Reese and Luke—had their marriages prearranged by the woman sitting before her.

"Heavens no. You don't have to," Mama Laverne answered. "I just want you to believe that you will be happy with the person I've chosen for you, as well."

Goose bumps formed on Victoria's arms and butterflies began floating around in her stomach. "Who is he, Mama Laverne?" she asked excitedly.

Felicia Laverne Madaris placed her teacup down to give her great-granddaughter her undivided attention. "Now *that* I can't tell you."

Victoria lifted an eyebrow. "You can't?"

"No. Nor can I tell you when he will make the first approach to you. He's a very busy man and falling in love is the last thing on his agenda. At least so he thinks."

Victoria's forehead bunched in confusion. "I don't understand. Why can't you reveal his identity? It's not like I'll have a problem with whoever you've chosen because I know you will look out for my best interests."

Mama Laverne reached out and took Victoria's hand firmly in hers. "Yes, I will, and I appreciate your faith and confidence in me. It's refreshing to have a willing participant instead of an unwilling one like your brother and male cousins have been."

She paused a moment and then said, "The reason I am withholding his identity for now is because although you might be ready to accept him as your mate, the man I've chosen for you might not feel the same. If he knew what I had planned, he would fight it all the way and become extremely difficult."

Victoria shrugged. "But don't they always fight it, anyway?"

"Yes, but he needs to feel that he's fallen in love with you on his own and not because he's being manipulated. For that reason, keeping his identity from you is the only way. You're going to have to trust me on this."

Victoria did trust her great-grandmother, although she wasn't sure this was the best approach. "Is it someone I already know?"

Releasing Victoria's hand, Mama Laverne picked up her teacup and took a sip, then said, "I can't tell you that, either."

Victoria released a deep sigh. "But how will I know it's him?"

Mama Laverne smiled. "Trust me, dear, you will know."

PART 1

Your heart knows things that your mind can't explain.
—Anonymous

CHAPTER ONE

Six months later

VICTORIA MADARIS ENTERED Susan's Bakery and immediately inhaled the aroma of beignets. They smelled divine, which wasn't a surprise, since this was a favorite shop for so many New Orleans locals—the line at the counter was long. She glanced at her watch to make sure she had time before heading over to the television station to prepare for her show and saw that she didn't. The line was moving at a slow pace and waiting wasn't an option today.

She had been elated when her boss, Mr. Richards, had called her into his office last month to let her know that due to her hard work and dedication, as well as her popularity with the television audience, she was getting promoted and would be switching from the morning slot to the noonday hour. She would be joining two other women in a very popular talk show called *Talk It Up*.

Guest slots had already been filled for the next six months and she was very impressed with the lineup. She knew the other two women, Debra Morris and Icelyn Crews, had been doing the show for a while. Debra was a veteran with the network and Victoria was eager to learn from her.

Victoria was about to turn around to leave when she hit what felt like a solid wall. It was only when a hand reached out to steady her and keep her from falling that she realized it hadn't been a wall, but a man.

"Hey, you're 'Little Nolan,' aren't you?"

Victoria cringed. She hated when people who knew her oldest brother referred to her as if she didn't have her own name or identity. She looked up into the smiling and handsome face of Tanner Jamison. Tanner was good friends with her brothers and male cousins. She was surprised he recognized her since it had been years since she'd last seen him.

She figured most women would have felt honored to have been recognized by one of the most eligible bachelors in Houston, and he was certainly that. Tanner was extremely good-looking. She remembered that he was best friends with her cousin Blade Madaris. In fact, she recalled that Blade, Tanner and another one of their close friends, Wyatt Bannister, had been known as notorious bachelors. Years ago, in her late teens, she'd eavesdropped on a conversation between one of her brothers and male cousins to learn just how notorious Blade, Tanner and Wyatt were.

Blade had since settled down and married Samari, and they had a beautiful little girl. However, last she heard, Tanner and Wyatt were still out there on the prowl and sowing their wild oats. "Yes, I'm Nolan's sister, *Victoria*."

His smile widened. "Victoria, that's right. Now I recall Ms. Felicia Laverne mentioning that you were here in New Orleans."

Victoria lifted an eyebrow when a red flag suddenly went up. When had he talked to her great-grandmother and why would her name come up in their conversation? "You talked to Mama Laverne?"

"I sure did. I dropped by Blade's house earlier this year and she was there visiting. She'd made her delicious bread pudding and invited me to talk to her while we ate some and drank coffee. At least I drank coffee—Ms. Felicia Laverne had tea. We had a nice chat."

"You did?"

"Yes."

Victoria wanted to ask what their chat had been about, but knew that wouldn't be the proper thing to do. However, she did want to know when their conversation took place. "And when exactly was this? I know you said earlier this year, but do you remember the exact month?"

If he found her inquiry odd, he didn't say so. "It was in January," he said. "I specifically remember the month because I dropped by to watch the NFL playoffs with Blade."

Victoria nodded. Her grandmother had summoned her to Whispering Pines in February...the month after her chat with Tanner. Interesting.

"Ms. Felicia Laverne even gave me a couple of gift cards to this bakery," he said, and nodded. "She said the owner was the granddaughter of an old friend who'd sent her a few gift cards as a Christmas gift. Since she knew I was headed this way, she passed those gift cards on to me."

Umm...interesting. Her great-grandmother had given some of the same gift cards to her, as well. Had she done so hoping that she and Tanner would run in to each other here? "That was nice of Mama Laverne."

"I thought so, too. She knows how much I like sweets and was looking out for me."

Victoria shook her head. The man was being played and didn't even know it. She was about to ask him more about his meeting with her great-grandmother and the gift cards when he asked her a question.

"How do you like New Orleans, Victoria?"

She couldn't help but notice all the female attention Tanner was getting. Because of her brothers and older male cousins, she was used to seeing women's reactions to them. Some things never changed when it came to a good-looking man and she had to hand it to him. Tanner was definitely good-looking.

"I like it. I've been working at a television station here for almost two years now, but I live in Catalina Cove. That's an hour drive from here."

"I'm familiar with the place. It's a beautiful little town."

"Yes, it is," she agreed. "Are you in town visiting or sightseeing?" she asked him.

"No. I'm opening a new club in town."

"You are?"

"Yes, it's the third Gentlemen's Club to open and the first one outside of Texas."

Victoria had heard all about the Gentlemen's Clubs that he co-owned with Blade and Wyatt. From overhearing her brothers talk, the members of the all-male club were far from being gentlemen of any kind. She'd heard what went on in their clubs, especially about the strippers who were hired to entertain the men. All legal, but definitely pushed to the extreme. Women who went to the club had to be invited by the members. "Congratulations on the opening of your new club. I'm sure it will do well. Now if you will excuse—"

"How about dinner?"

She tilted her head. "You're asking me out to dinner?"

He chuckled. "Yes. Nothing wrong with that, is there? You're the sister and cousin to several of my close friends. That's the least I can do since it's like I'm practically a member of your family, anyway. And I did tell your great-grandmother while I was here that I would check on you." He chuckled again. "In fact, she all but insisted I did."

Oh, she did, did she? From the sound of it, Mama Laverne was making sure that their paths crossed here in New Orleans. Was Tanner the man Mama Laverne had chosen for her? A man who wore bachelorhood like a badge of honor? A man who'd been just like her brother Nolan and several male cousins that Mama Laverne had successfully married off? Did Mama Laverne actually believe Tanner Jamison would give up his man-whore ways for her?

"Victoria?"

She looked up at him. "Yes?"

"Will you have dinner with me? I just flew in today and haven't had a chance to go grocery shopping yet."

She blinked. "You're moving to New Orleans?"

His smile widened and she noticed several women in the bakery who weren't hiding the fact they were listening to their conversation, and seemed to be holding their breath waiting for his answer.

"Yes. We bought an old nightclub that needs renovations. It's easier for me to move here temporarily while the work is being done than to fly in two to three times a week."

She nodded. How convenient for Mama Laverne. "And how long do you think the renovations are going to take?"

"Our plans are to have the club open and ready to jam with a New Year's Eve party."

There was no doubt in her mind it would be one wild party. "Then I'm sure it will be ready."

He glanced at his watch. "So are you free for dinner tonight?"

Honestly, she wasn't. However, if he was the man Mama Laverne had chosen for her, then the opportunity would present itself for them to run in to each other again. Tonight she already had plans. Her cousin Christy was flying into town to attend a conference, and Victoria promised she'd pick up Christy from the airport and have dinner with her.

"I'm sorry, Tanner, but I have a prior dinner engagement. Maybe some other time." If he was disappointed, he didn't show it. In fact, his smile widened even more.

"How about a rain check?" he asked.

"A rain check will be fine."

"What's your phone number?" he asked her, pulling out his cell phone.

Victoria told him her phone number and he punched it into his phone. When she heard her phone ring in her purse, he said, "And now you have mine, as well. If you ever need anything, just call." He slid his phone back inside his jacket. "You take care, 'Little Nolan.'"

She was about to remind him that her name was Victoria and not "Little Nolan," but decided not to waste her time. "You take care, too."

She then quickly left the bakery to get to work on time.

A SHORT WHILE later Tanner Jamison walked out of the bakery smiling. Women. He just had to love them, and he did. While standing in line, he'd gotten numbers from four different women. All nice-looking, single ladies with bodies he couldn't wait to try out. He had a feeling he wouldn't regret the six months he would be living in New Orleans.

His phone rang when he reached his car and he quickly clicked on, recognizing the ring tone. "What's going on, Blade?"

"Just checking to see if the renovations are on schedule."

Blade Madaris and Wyatt Bannister were his partners in several financial ventures, including the nightclubs they owned. They had purchased their first club years ago, when all three had been single men on the prowl. They'd figured if women could have a place like Sisters, a nightclub in Houston that catered to females, then there was nothing wrong with them establishing a club that catered to men. Blade was the only one of the three who'd since gotten married. Although he didn't frequent the club like he used to, he was still a partner.

"I met with your construction manager earlier. I went straight there from the airport," Tanner said, opening his car door to get in. "I think we might be ready by New Year's Eve." Since Blade and his twin brother, Slade, owned a construction business, they would be using Blade's company for the renovations.

"Let's hope so. The construction manager I've assigned for the job, Hank Brighton, is good. He's going to make sure we dot every *i* and cross every *t* to open on time. By the way, have you checked in to your condo yet?"

"Not yet, but already I've checked out quite a few beauties here in New Orleans. My black book is filling up. I definitely won't get bored while I'm here."

Blade chuckled. "I'm sure you won't. I don't know who's worse, you or Wyatt."

Tanner grinned. "You mean since you got married and removed yourself from the picture? Wyatt has always been worse than the two of us put together, because he takes after his old man in his younger days."

"Yes, you're right about that," Blade agreed.

"Oh, and by the way, guess who I ran in to at the bakery a short while ago?" Tanner then said.

"Who?"

"Your cousin. 'Little Nolan.' It's been quite a while since I've seen her. She looks good, man. Definitely not a kid anymore. I asked her to dinner, but she had other plans."

"You asked Victoria to dinner? Are you crazy? You know better than to hit on any of my female relatives, Tanner. They're off-limits."

"Relax, Blade, my invitation was nothing more than a friendly gesture. I wasn't coming on to her. I had told Ms. Felicia Laverne that I would look her up when I moved to New Orleans."

"Damn, man, I hope you haven't fallen into my great-grandmother's trap."

"Trap? What are you talking about?"

"After taking Nolan off the singles market, Mama Laverne has made Victoria next on her 'to marry off' list. So unless you want to be the man Mama Laverne marks as Victoria's future husband, I suggest you keep your distance."

Shit, Tanner thought. Everyone knew about Blade's great-grandmother's matchmaking track record, even when marriage was the last thing on their minds. Blade was a prime example of the older woman's shenanigans.

"Come to think of it, I noticed that you and Mama Laverne talked for a long time that Sunday when you dropped by and she was here."

Tanner swallowed. "Yes, but we were talking about a lot of stuff, mainly about some cruise she plans to take this fall and how good she was at playing bingo."

"Are you saying Victoria's name didn't come up, not once?"

Tanner swallowed again. "When I mentioned my plans to move to New Orleans to oversee the club renovations, she mentioned Victoria worked here. That's when she suggested that, being a family friend, I should look her up."

Tanner then recalled something else. "Oh, and that bakery that I just left after running in to Victoria…"

"Yeah, what about it?"

"Your grandmother is the one who told me about it.

Suggested I try out some of their baked goods. She even gave me a few gift cards for free coffee and Danish rolls."

"Umm, did you not wonder how a little old lady in Texas would know anything about a bakery in New Orleans?"

Tanner shrugged. "Yes, when I asked, she said the owner was the daughter of a friend of hers."

"That's how it always starts," Blade sighed. "She connives with the old cronies in her church group who want to marry off their grands or great-grands, as well. That's how she arranged for Lee to marry Carly."

Tanner didn't like the sound of that.

"I bet you anything that she gave Victoria some of those same gift cards with the intention of the two of you running into each other. It appears her plan worked. She's set you up real nice like."

Tanner resented the amusement he heard in Blade's voice. "Ms. Felicia Laverne might manipulate her family members into marriage, but she can count me out of it."

"Nice try, Tanner, but you and Wyatt have been my best friends for years, so don't think she doesn't consider you as part of the family. So the way I see it, it's too late to count you out."

Tanner disagreed. Sex was sex and a serious relationship with a woman was something altogether different. They were mutually exclusive in his book. He only had time for sex and nothing more. Engaging in a relationship for a specific purpose—like marriage—was way out of the league he intended to keep playing in.

"It's not too late, and since now that I'm on to what she's trying to do, I will keep my distance from Victoria."

"Not sure you can at this point," Blade said.

Tanner frowned. "Watch me."

Follow Your Heart coming May 2023